Vienna

Vienna

A Novel

by

Nick Thomas

RESOURCE *Publications* · Eugene, Oregon

VIENNA
A Novel

Copyright © 2019 Nick Thomas. All rights reserved. Except for brief quotations in critical publications or reviews, no part of this book may be reproduced in any manner without prior written permission from the publisher. Write: Permissions, Wipf and Stock Publishers, 199 W. 8th Ave., Suite 3, Eugene, OR 97401.

Resource Publications
An Imprint of Wipf and Stock Publishers
199 W. 8th Ave., Suite 3
Eugene, OR 97401

www.wipfandstock.com

PAPERBACK ISBN: 978-1-7252-5639-2
HARDCOVER ISBN: 978-1-7252-5640-8
EBOOK ISBN: 978-1-7252-5641-5

Manufactured in the U.S.A. 12/13/19

For my family

In memory of Tim Collard

Part One

April 1984

1

THE JOURNEY TOOK A DAY AND A NIGHT BY RAIL AND FERRY, A WASTE of time unless it were a ritual preparation that could only begin once home had been left behind. Some travellers know this, that the leisure to think through the space makes arrival a beginning, not an end. Others just want to get there, and then get back again.

When the train pulled into Frankfurt at midnight, Frances Christie was less startled by the sudden brightness outside than by her son leaping from his seat again to snap off the light-switch by the door. Then he fell back in his seat, holding the handkerchief in front of his face. Doors banged, haggard travellers lugged their luggage along the platform, and Frances waited. Now he didn't move. She sighed and looked down at her book, but it was too dark to read. The platform glare didn't penetrate, and the blinds on the internal windows had been closed since Ostend. Minutes passed, and he lowered his handkerchief, seeming to relax a little.

"Mickey?"

He stirred, but said nothing.

"Mickey, dear, do you think we might have the light back on now?"

"Quiet, Mother. We don't want people coming in here."

"But what if the train's full?"

"Then we'll have to let them in. But it won't be. Certainly not first class. Just keep quiet until they're settled."

She gave up with another sigh, and let her eyes wander over the long, alien words on the signs outside. The sound of new passengers soon dwindled to nothing, and with it the chance of having someone to talk to.

It was true that there were not many first class passengers. Herbert and Elspeth had gone in search of an empty compartment for their talk, and hadn't come back. Her husband, her daughter-in-law. Her son. The words were hollow, when strangers offered the only hope of company. How she wished they had taken the plane.

"Mickey dear, why do you keep pulling out that handkerchief?"

"It's so that people outside will think I've got something wrong with me."

"Oh how ridiculous."

"Not at all. I do it a lot on the run into Victoria. I need the elbow-room."

"Mickey it's too bad. I do think you might talk to me."

With a smoothness unknown at Victoria the train began to move again, and Mickey backed from the light-switch to his seat, head down, the spiral-bound pages of work already in his hand.

"I'm sorry, Mother. I've got to read this thing, and know what it's all about, before I go back to the office. I'm not going to have the chance once we get to Vienna, am I?"

Frances fidgeted by way of answer, and glanced unhappily at her book.

"We might have met someone interesting," she said. Mickey snorted, a response that had always offended his mother, and didn't look up.

"I doubt that. I've never met anyone interesting on a train. And all you'll get here are a lot of people who don't speak English anyway. People who can't afford to fly. Oh, and dotty old generals sick with nostalgia, of course."

"Your father is not dotty, Mickey, don't say that. Although I must say I don't see why we have to put up with this. Twenty-four hours. It's a long journey at his age. But he would have it, so there we are. I must say I think it's very silly. Positively childish . . ."

She stopped, aware that he was no longer listening. Why couldn't he just talk? The sadness of the question silenced her. She turned again to the window, but Frankfurt was long gone, and she found herself staring at darkness through the ghost of her own weary face.

A few feet away, his eyes fixed on the rows of numbers in his lap, Mickey Christie was also wishing they had taken the plane. In essence he agreed with his mother; this was a daft way to travel. But for him the train journey was a political defeat, and he had to make the best of it. His father could easily have made this trip by himself, might well have wanted to. But then Elspeth, greedy for glossy fame and sensing a story, had invited herself along with that charmless innocence that was so perfectly American. A mysterious legacy awaiting a celebrated Englishman in an old imperial capital would make great copy in New York. So Mickey, faced with a week of unaided domestic management, or of keeping his mother company, or both, had decided to take a holiday in a city of which he knew little and cared nothing. Then his father had announced that they would cross the continent by rail.

Mickey and Frances had objected, but Elspeth had again betrayed them. The ride from Ostend would give her the opportunity to interview a captive subject; for the general himself, much decorated for the forgotten virtue of gallantry, and a Knight Commander of the world's last and greatest empire, was as much a creature of the flagged and turreted European past as the city he was to visit. New York would love it.

Here Mickey had made his stand. Assuming responsibility for the arrangements, he had booked four first class tickets, but no beds. When challenged, he would say that couchettes were uncomfortable and a waste of money, his mother would rebel in disgust, damn the expense, and fly alone. And she would have done just that, had not Elspeth begged her to join them, gushing about the plush, adjustable seats she'd seen in the brochure, and invoking, with genuine respect, the magic phrase 'Army wife'.

Mickey knew this much of his mother's history, that the colonel's daughter had longed only to be an officer's wife, and had achieved a sort of bliss when her husband had exceeded her father's retiring rank. He also knew that regarding her position as some kind of job gave the service wife a special self-respect, and that her comforts and her arrogance could always be justified by tales of mucking in, of muddling through and roughing it. So Frances had stirred up her pride, and determined to muck and muddle and rough it half way across Europe, pioneer and martyr, trouper and English lady, mother and pain in the neck.

Mickey looked at her with sudden, silent fury. But then he remembered that lately—over five years? Ten?—the arrogance had mutated into something more complex and harder to dismiss, a plaintive clinging, a petulant self-pity. Elspeth had struck a chord with the ethic of the officer's wife; but the greater truth was that Frances Christie would cheerfully have walked to Siberia if someone, anyone, had specifically requested her company. Now she stared in silence at the window, helpless, miserable, and yet still obtrusive and crying out to be bullied.

"Mother, do you want to try and get some sleep? It's past midnight."

"Oh, I hardly think I shall be able to sleep like this. Never mind. I can catch up once we're there. You try, if you want to."

"No, I've got a couple of hours of work ahead of me yet. I just thought . . ."

"I'll wait and see what your father wants to do. I suppose they'll be yacking into the small hours."

Mickey winced, but there had been no reproof in his mother's tone. It was funny, the way a woman's grievances seemed to surface automatically in her conversation. Then he smiled, as he reflected how this generalisation, like so many others, excluded his own wife. Elspeth seemed to have no grievances at all. Maybe that in itself would irritate him, in time, and foul the sweet, narcotic taste of her. But for now he was content to relish the freewheeling ease of the ride, and laugh at his luck.

"Mother I'm going to have a stretch and a breath of air. Will you be all right?"

"Yes, Mickey, all right."

He put his papers to one side, got up, checked his pockets for cigarettes, and opened the door.

There was a pleasant breeze in the corridor, and noise, and movement under the floor. Mickey took a few steps away from the compartment, and pulled out the new packet of duty-free cigarettes. There was a flurry of green at the other end of the carriage, a perfectly pressed uniform, a peaked cap. Mickey looked uneasily, wondering if the man were going to tell him not to smoke. Was he police or army, or what? He wore a gun, but he looked about sixteen, marching self-consciously with his eyes on the window-sills. Finally he stopped, and nodded.

Mickey held out his packet and said;

"Cigarette?" The peaked head shook once. "It's OK?" Another nod.

"Are you British? Passport, please."

Mickey handed over his passport and lit up while the youth made a creditable but transparent pretence of understanding its contents. It occurred to him that his first words could easily have passed, in the noise of the corridor, for German, and he said;

"How did you know I was British?"

The officer looked up quickly, a helpless look.

"Please?"

"How," said Mickey, "do you know, that, I, am British?"

The passport was handed back, slowly. Mickey smiled.

"You. . . You look British."

"Ah. Right. Thank you."

"Thank you!" said the boy, and beamed, maybe with pride at the passable "th" he had just produced, took a step back, and saluted. Mickey nearly laughed, but managed just to smile again and give a stupid little wave as the young soldier, or customs official, or policeman marched, more boldly now, into the next carriage.

Mickey turned to the window, and considered his reflection. So, he looked British, did he? How nice. Of course the man had been referring to his clothes, the crew-neck sweater, the cords. The face certainly evoked no bowler hat, no cricketing nonchalance. To him it often looked barely human, let alone British. It was a poor inheritance, worn by his father as a young man, before the straight nose had been smashed twice in different wars, and age had blurred the black sharpness of the brows to feral grey. The face was getting a second chance.

He let his lazy eyes focus deeper into the dark, beyond his own image, and realised he was standing outside the compartment where his father had been giving up his life story, though Elspeth wasn't there. There was just the old man, sitting with his arms folded and his long legs tucked and crossed under the seat, staring, like his wife, like his son, into the void beyond the glass. This was the famous soldier, Lt General Sir Herbert Christie, V.C. and all the rest, slumped in a corner without bearing, looking, as he always had to Mickey, like a retired office-boy who had hoped for nothing better.

He wondered how much Elspeth had so far been bored or disappointed by her subject, and decided to stay put until she came back. She had not known his father very long, had never really had the chance to find out what an unlikely hero he was. Well, she would know by now.

Mickey remembered the questions and the taunts of schoolboys unable to believe that the diffident Old Boy presenting the prizes was really what the headmaster had claimed. He remembered, also, turning into the drive at the start of one summer holiday, the two serving officers walking away from the house, and the words he caught as they passed;

"Bloody strange. Of course the record commands the highest respect."

What he could not remember was the last time he had asked his father to tell him a story, a real war story, a tale of his own daring career. Simple reticence, common to men who have lived through combat, Mickey could have respected, even as a child. But there was none of that. There were campaigns and bombardments and solo missions, and wounds inflicted and sustained, and blood, and burning flesh, and death. There was everything except excitement. The great events of the mid-century were presented without emotion, a history crib of dates and battles. The child quickly lost interest in the story, and sank instead into unhappy acceptance of a narrative in which listener and narrator alike seemed superfluous. His father was talking about his own life, and yet talking, as though he had also lived, merely to pass the time. The record commanded respect, true, but precious little pride or admiration, the building blocks from which a small boy creates love for his father. Respect alone was a dry thing. There were many men still living, many Germans and Chinese, who respected Herbert Christie. For this was a great man, this crumpled figure in a corner, staring through the watery, twice-reflected shade of his own son. He hadn't moved. He was still sitting and living just to pass the time, waiting without impatience for the next thing to happen.

"Hey, what are you doing out here?"

"Just getting a breath of air." Mickey turned and looked down at the glistening peaks and dimples of make-up that he recognised as his wife, and thought *Why does she always look so happy?* "Mother was getting a bit much, as well. How's the interview?"

"Oh, Mickey, it's just amazing. I just had no idea. I mean, what a life! And you know the really strange thing?"

"No, Pet, tell me the really strange thing."

"Your father is so humble?"

"Ah."

"He is amazingly humble. And he's just such a big man, you know what I'm saying?"

"Humility. I see. I'd often wondered. Have you got much out of him, then?"

"Have I ever! My note pad's nearly used up. And he's said some like really important things. Mickey, I'm looking at a series here. Maybe a book. I guess I'll call Henry from the hotel."

"You're going to call New York? From Vienna? Bloody hell."

"Well, I could just call his office and have him call me right back. Is that OK?"

"I think that would be a good idea."

"There was something your father said a while back. . . I know I have it here. . . I really wanted to show you. . ."

She pulled the silly designer notebook out of her handbag, and started flipping through the pages, while Mickey waited, without interest. He was annoyed at having been caught unawares by Elspeth, at having missed her approach. He most enjoyed looking at her from a distance, with her pent-up bobbing gait, and the blood of a dozen races playing glorious merry hell with her face and figure and hair. At close range her beauty was lost in the detail of its parts, like the face of the moon. Still, at least she always looked happy.

"It doesn't matter, Pet. I've probably heard it before."

"Oh, here it is, right here." Mickey sighed, and looked back at his father. No change. "Mickey? You want to hear this?"

"Sorry Pet. Go on, I'm listening."

"OK. So I was asking him about war, right? And I said, you know, did it ever bother him, to be all the time mixed up in killing people and all that real destruction . . ."

"Good grief."

"What? You think I shouldn't have asked?"

"Well. . . Oh I don't know. Why not? You're a journalist, after all."

"Right. And I'm family. I think it's OK. Anyhow, he said it was a really good question. Then he sort of looked up at the ceiling, and said it reminded him of something his uncle had said, like fifty years ago, in Vienna. He said, 'If men have to die, they might as well die believing there's a reason.' Don't you think that's really beautiful?"

"Whatever is he thinking about in there? He's just staring out of the window. He hasn't moved."

"I don't know. I guess I've been stirring up a lot of memories. But don't you think that's a really beautiful thing to say?"

"Is it? I don't know that it's beautiful, exactly. I mean it seems to imply that there actually isn't a reason. That doesn't strike me as a particularly happy thought."

"Oh sure. But I've asked that question before, you know? This friend of my dad who's a general, a couple of guys who were out in 'Nam. . . I got a lot of stuff about doing your job, just being a pawn in the game, stuff like that. Your father's really something else. He's like a philosopher."

"He's unusual, I'll give you that."

Mickey turned again to look at his father, and she joined him with a reverent contemplation of her own. For her the mystery still lacked the power to distress. Then she grabbed his arm suddenly, alive with a new topic.

"Hey, you want to hear something funny?"

"Please."

“When I went out, just a little while back, I met this young guy in uniform, I mean really young, he looked like he should still be in school. Maybe he’s a guard or something.”

“Probably a policeman, if it’s the same one who checked my passport. I don’t think railway staff carry guns, even in Germany.”

“I meant maybe a border guard.”

“Oh. Sorry.”

“Anyhow, he looked so young and shy and everything, and I asked him to tell me the way to the bathroom, and he just looked so embarrassed. He didn’t say a word. And he turned really red. Don’t you think that’s cute? Just because I asked for the john?”

“I don’t think that was the reason, Pet. He speaks hardly any English. He wouldn’t know where to begin with you.”

“Oh really? Oh, well. I guess I’ll go back in now. We ought to get some sleep, some time. It’s too bad you didn’t reserve some beds.”

“No point, honey. They only do singles.”

Mickey kissed his wife on the mouth, and left her to daydream about the double bed to come. At the door of the other compartment, with the other woman in his life still hidden by the blinds, he turned to catch a long-range view of Elspeth. She was leaning against the wall, still holding her notebook, with an absent smile on her face and one ankle gently stroking the other, up, and down. Mickey smiled. He was looking forward to that room as well, and he didn’t give a damn about the view.

2

THE TRAIN WAS MOVING FASTER NOW, HITTING ITS STRIDE AT TOP speed, and grabbing a few seconds' lead on the timetable. The speed in the darkness seemed reckless, then unreal, as though the rails must arc wildly into the sky to take up the time, with Vienna still nine hours away. It couldn't take that long to cross little Europe at such a rate.

It had been thirty-nine years since Herbert Christie had seen Vienna, although it seemed longer, for he had never quite been able to believe in the defeated, starving capital with its four foreign masters in the aftermath of war. The place had looked not so much damaged as incomplete, as though a rough copy of the city he had known in 1934 had been hastily and haphazardly erected for his personal deception. He had not seen Vienna, in a Europe still technically at peace, debauched by swastikas, neither had he known the Vienna that sent its men to the war, only to watch them bring it home with them. Destruction, invasion, these were things he had seen elsewhere, while the streets and cafés of his memory remained intact. They shared the private immortality of people whose deaths he had not witnessed, his parents, grandparents and many friends, who lived forever on the list of those he would visit again, one day, when he had the time. Thus the dozens of the living who waited for a visit or a letter from Herbert shared their status in the mind of their friend with others whose loss was too painful to acknowledge.

Now Herbert was going to make one of those visits. The Viennese, he knew, had repaired their city, with much foreign help. He had been told that the place felt now very much as it had before the war, that he could look forward to finding again, in all its bright complexity, something he had lost when he was nineteen, if only he could dare to believe in it.

But belief was the problem, accepting that desire and reality could be one. The present so quickly became the past, and memory, romanticised and stripped of detail, became more precious than the truth itself. Accepting reality was the real leap of faith.

She was back. Herbert remained still, listening to the door open and close, the two footsteps, the body settling itself on the seat opposite him, a waking prisoner counting off the sounds and the seconds before he must face the lights again. The pages of the notebook turned, the pen clicked ready. This was it.

"Ah! Elspeth. I'm sorry, my dear, I. . . I was miles away. Where were we?"

She showed no sign of fatigue, this girl. She was bright and eager for more. She had even adjusted her make-up.

"Well, ah. . . I think we've covered everything outside of the central theme. . ."

"The central theme?"

"I mean of the book. I'm sure I'm looking at a book here. But the guts of it will be you, you know, coming back to Vienna after all these years, and climaxing with your uncle's will, and how it ties in with what happened back then. The rest of your career will be kind of a build-up for that. So let's talk about Vienna."

"Well, we can, of course. . . but there's lots more, you know, that I haven't told you, much more about Burma, and Berlin, Malaya, Korea. . ."

"I really want to get into Vienna now. We can always go back, later on. I just want to know, like, where I am, when we get there. Is that OK?"

"Of course, of course."

"OK. . ."

She referred again to her notebook, to the pages at the back where she kept the questions. Herbert braced himself. This was going to be the hardest part, the part he didn't want to disturb. He wanted to see the place again before he brought its memory into the light. Memories were gossamer to the touch, no matter how powerful.

"OK. So, you were, what, twenty?"

"It was February of 1934. I was nineteen, nearly twenty, yes."

"And why did you go there?"

"Oh. . . my parents thought it would be good for me. I didn't really know what I wanted to do. I was thinking about the Church, but I wasn't really sure. It would have meant Oxford, probably, and my mother wasn't keen. I don't know. Anyway, it was arranged that I should go and stay with Uncle Wolf. He lived in Vienna, an uncle by marriage, the aunt died before

I was born . . . that's neither here nor there . . . Wolf was considered to be, I suppose, the family intellectual."

"Uh-huh."

"Yes. So off I went." He reached into the small bag he'd brought with him from the other compartment, and produced a fat brown envelope. "Actually I found something that might interest you. Wolf's letter, inviting me to stay, with a lot of helpful information about the neighbourhood. In fact my father had written to him, but. . . It is in English."

"Oh, wow!"

She took the packet of paper as though it were an orphaned chick, and looked, for a long moment of awe, at the postmark. Herbert sat back and took a break. He had glossed over that, at least. He would not have to return, now, to that dreadful year after school when he questioned everything, the bewilderment and distress of his parents, the rector's irritation. In that year he had been branded both as a religious maniac and an atheist, and had narrowly escaped the charge of lunacy—which meant a torture-cell and family shame, back then.

Wolf would sort him out, they decided. Funny old Wolf, whom no one had seen since the Great War, a shady character, a black sheep by marriage, was nonetheless undoubtedly learned, and lived far away, in a city famed as a centre of ideas. The sickly mind was packed off to a warmer mental climate.

Elspeth looked up, wide-eyed.

"And this was the uncle who died, and left the pile of stuff, and said, what was it. . .?"

"Left instructions that the parcel should be opened fifty years after his death. Yes. It's going to be two months late, but I don't suppose it matters. The lawyers were quite right, I think, to wait for me. I am the only relative, apart from Mickey, of course."

"Two months. . . Oh, were you there when he died?"

"Oh yes."

"Oh my, how awful!"

"Yes. Yes it was, quite. I was very young, you see, and a long way from home. And I couldn't stay, really, with the. . . well, it was almost civil war. It was, really, but it didn't last long, as it happened."

"So did your uncle die in the war?"

"Yes . . . no . . . that is he wasn't shot, or anything. He died of a heart attack. He was well over eighty, he'd had a rough time of it here and there. It could have happened at any moment. But, as it was . . ."

Elspeth stared in silence, humbled by grief. He wished she would say something, now, anything, rather than leave him there, looking down at the rigid face of the old man, with the sobs and the screaming all around. The red wine on his uncle's shirt looked like a splash of blood, but there was real blood on his own hands as the windows shattered in. There was firing outside, and a girl near him screaming at a pitch too high for her voice, a dry, silent scream, with both hands held to one side of her face. She was the pretty one, the one he never got to know because she didn't speak English. Then the blood started running from her arms onto the dead man, dripping from her elbows onto the stiff white shirt, bloody tears shed for the death of beauty.

The door slid open, and Mickey said;

"What's the matter with you two? Somebody died?"

"Oh honey, your father was just telling me about his uncle."

"The mysterious Uncle Wolf? Good Lord, it sounds as if you've only just started."

"We've been kind of filling in the background. Like I told you."

"I see. Well, Mother was wondering when you were planning to turn in. If at all."

"Give us a few more minutes, OK? A half hour, maybe."

"OK. See you later."

The door closed again, and she leaned forward to look at him, solicitous, apologetic.

"You OK?"

"Oh yes, I'm quite all right, thank you. I just couldn't help thinking . . . It's a long time ago, of course, but it made a very profound impression on me, for one reason and another."

"Right, right."

"I was there, you see."

"Right."

"I was with him when he died, as he died."

"Right, OK. You want to talk about something else?"

"No, no, that's all right. I don't mind."

"Because there was something else I wanted to ask you, aside from Vienna and everything."

"Oh?"

"Yeah. . . It's kind of personal?"

Herbert allowed himself a small smile, which he hoped would appear as one of encouragement. How much more personal was she going to get?

"Ask away, Elspeth. I don't mind, I assure you."

"OK. I just wanted to ask you, are you a really committed Christian?"

"Well, yes . . . as I told you, I was thinking of entering the church . . . I have always been a believer, I think, in some way."

"Right. Only, you know, Mickey's name is really Miles? Miles Christie, doesn't that mean Christian soldier?"

"Christian soldier, soldier of Christ. Without the final E it would, yes."

"Right. Was that deliberate? I mean, was that why you named your son Miles?"

"Christened him, you mean. Yes, oh yes. I thought it was . . . appropriate, perhaps, or rather, shall we say, suitable. No different, really, from an ordinary saint's name, like yours, in that way."

"Hey, I didn't mean to embarrass you, I'm sorry. I just think that was a really beautiful thing to do. I want to tell you that."

"Ah . . . yes. Yes, thank you. I don't know if Mickey would agree. I intended it really as a gift of sorts."

"A gift of God. Right."

"Actually, I'm afraid, a gift from me. A gift from the past. Do you understand what I mean?"

"Yeah, I guess."

"I had no title, you see, no coat of arms. Money, of course, but he could make that for himself."

"But you're English. That would be enough."

"Ha! How nice of you to think so."

"I do. Really."

"We used to think so, too, we English. But never mind about that. I wanted to give him something he could carry with him, something, as I say, from the past, a thread of continuity, of something precious."

She was letting him ramble, he realised, while she sat there with her lips parted and her pretty eyes huge and blank. He could run on and on, making a fool of himself, not that it mattered. But making his faith appear foolish, that was something else. That would never do. He added;

"Of course I could have laid down a case of claret, but 1956 was such a terrible year."

She nodded in glum agreement.

"Right. I did a course in college, big years in history. Suez, Hungary... oh sure."

"Ah, actually I was referring to the wine production. But you're right, of course. An interesting theory, that the vines could respond to international events. I wonder what '38 was like. Can't remember."

"You mean '39?"

"No, no, Czechoslovakia, and the Anschluss, that was really the beginning. Yes, the Anschluss. I thought so, anyway."

She hid her eyes in the notebook, clearly confused. Could he really see the words 'wine production' appearing there?

"Well, Elspeth, I think we ought to be settling down for the night. I'm sure we'll have ample opportunity to talk further in Vienna."

"Oh sure. OK. You want to go back?"

"I think we'd better."

"I don't know if I can sleep. I'm too excited! Do you ever have trouble sleeping?"

"From time to time, like everybody else. Some people count sheep. I count soldiers."

He knew she wouldn't understand, but she thought she did and wrote it down anyway.

In the other compartment Frances and Mickey were already stretched out in their seats. Frances was almost wholly concealed by her blanket, although the train was warm. Herbert pulled out the seat next to her, and took her hand. She squeezed his fingers, and smiled briefly with her eyes still closed.

"Mickey dear, would you turn out the light when you're ready?"

"All right, Mother. Sleep well."

"Goodnight, dear."

Soon the compartment was dark and quiet, with the even hum and racket of the train deeper than true silence. It was a neutral sound that could be all the right chords to the simple refrain of a symphony in the mind, or a background of summer birdsong, or the chanting of a crowd, or the blare and clatter of midday traffic in a city long ago.

Herbert knew that he would sleep badly, but the memory that caught him was one he didn't expect. He was tempted to curse his daughter-in-law, poor innocent fool that she was. Oh, how unfair, he thought, how very unfair. She couldn't know, even if she were told. She could never see her husband, barely seven years old, using his turn on the telephone from an English prep school a hundred miles from home . . . Miles, little Miles Christie, Christie, M., sobbing and desperate, demanding to know why his parents had done this terrible thing to him. Suddenly Herbert had understood, had pictured perfectly the classroom in which he, too, had learnt his first words of Latin, the new vocabulary striking his small son like a cane, the bored schoolmaster on the look-out for cheap laughs, and the remorseless ridicule at which small boys excelled. Then Frances had put down the phone, and turned in distress to her husband, with a question made redundant by that far belated rush of intuition;

"Herbert, Herbert, why on earth didn't you tell him?"

Until then he had believed that the name would be a source of pride, and a cherished gift, and now it would bring sorrow, perhaps for a terrible week or two, before the boy came home again. He would learn to cope, of course, but what would he think of his father now? Herbert closed his eyes, and opened them again to darkness. He still didn't know the answer to that question. He had been sure, for a while, that his son was quieter, and talked to him less, but small changes were quickly lost in the rush of growth. He would never know, now, whether his gift had done more harm than good in the end; he would never really have known that. All he had done was to illuminate a difference between father and son, and the times of their growing up. For big, strong Herbert had suffered no bullying at a school still uncritically Christian, while his more bookish son had developed different, more subtle resources at the dismal dawn of a more sceptical age; and, within months of that awful day, everyone was to know him as Mickey Christie. The gift had been buried, perhaps for good.

Herbert turned, and stared unhappily into the darkness of his wife. Sometimes memory was just a random spin on a wheel of failure. And he couldn't even trust the detail; buildings, weeks and conversations conflated in the press of a mind crowded by age. A moment's pain could fill a night, but to relive a month might only take a fraction of a second's dream. Yet he must pursue this mood, work it out, exhaust it. In the solitude of the night his life and his memory were the same. There was nowhere else to go, whether he slept or not.

3

EVEN BEFORE SHE OPENED HER EYES ELSPETH FULLY KNEW THAT SHE was awake, and that the morning had arrived. She stirred and looked about her. She had never before seen Frances asleep, and was struck by the resemblance between mother and son; both slept on their backs, maintaining the same expression of grumpy boredom through the night. Herbert was different, lying half on one side, brow furrowed, mouth open a little, but perfectly still. After a moment she remembered what it was that he evoked; the crusader killed in battle, preserved in stone above his own tomb in the English church where she was married. She must remember to write that down.

As quietly as she could, Elspeth slipped from her overcoat and let herself out of the compartment. No one else seemed to be moving yet, although the day was shockingly bright. The train was moving slowly, easing, perhaps, into its last stop before Vienna. Soon the adventure would begin in earnest. She decided to go to the end of the carriage for some fresh air, and found she wanted to skip along the corridor, giggling with childish excitement. This was nothing to be ashamed of; she laughed affectionately at herself, and walked, trailing her hands along the wall and the window sills, ready to laugh again at anything that happened next.

By the time she reached the plated joint between the carriages the train had almost stopped, and there, standing at the open door, ready to step off, was a figure she would have hoped to see, if she could have imagined him. She gasped, and felt a little thrill of gratitude for this perfect sight to begin the day.

He was tall and dark and young, and wore a moustache. His uniform was topped by a long blue cape, with a braided collar and epaulettes, and a peaked cap. Beneath the cape were two perfectly polished black riding-boots. Soldier? Band-leader? Elspeth didn't care. He stood on the step, looking eagerly toward the station, proud and happy, unconscious of the anachronism of his appearance, though not of its splendour. He smiled at her, with his eyes narrowed against the wind, a flirtatious smile of contentment with his smartness and his health and the freshness of the early morning, and Elspeth smiled back.

In a moment they stopped, and the blue uniform flourished and disappeared, leaving her standing with her heart beating fast, the beat of a little girl with a crush. And she knew that she would never forget that brilliant snapshot, framed so perfectly in the doorway of her first European train.

4

MICKEY LEANED ON THE RAIL OF THE NARROW BALCONY FIVE FLOORS above the street, and felt his mood brightening with the day. The pain at the back of his head was still there, but it was good to be off the train at last, and so far from all the ordinary things. Perhaps unplanned holidays were a good idea after all. In the room behind him the little sounds of unpacking suddenly stopped.

"Mickey? Mickey, honey? Do you think I'm going to need this?"

Without turning he said;

"No, I'd leave it at home if I were you."

"Funny. Funny guy."

"That's me."

It was the best kind of spring day now, clear blue sky and lots of it, with no tower blocks to get in the way. Indeed Vienna seemed to be a bit on the small side, in every dimension, for a capital city. Then again, the scale of the streets was deceptive, row upon row of big square buildings with roofs a size too small, giants' cottages artfully converted to five or six floors for human use. The buildings were not the same height, but they were all of a piece, standing shoulder to shoulder with no gaps to be filled by the nasty little shops and foul alleys of central London. Yet there was nothing austere about this smartness. Most of the blocks sported some hint of baroque around the windows or the guttering, some little touch of wedding cake to brighten the façade. There was also, in the view from Mickey's balcony, a fair sprinkling of Austrian flags, red, white, red, gathered, three at a time, in white mountings on the walls to advertise particular historical interest.

It was a jolly-looking place, dated but full of life, like an old lady who had kept her health and wits and sense of humour, and was generally described as 'wonderful'. Mickey's smile sagged a little then, as he thought of his mother, and then instantly, again, of London.

He turned at the sound of the doors to the balcony on his left being opened, and smiled hello at his father.

"All right in there, Mickey?"

"Yes, fine. I've left the unpacking to the little woman."

"Very wise."

Mickey smiled again and looked away. It was a joke he could have shared with any man.

"Lovely view," he said.

"It's just the city, you know. A view of the streets. Still, yes, it is rather fine in its way, I suppose."

"Can you tell me about any of it?"

"Gosh no. Have a look at your guide book. I'd probably get it all wrong, what I think I can remember. That's St. Stephens over there, of course. That big spire. The official centre of town."

"What period?"

"Oh, all sorts. Quite a lot of the fabric must be new."

"Really?"

"Oh yes. Last time I was here it had a bloody great hole in its roof." He looked away from the cathedral, and slowly across the close network of the streets. "Yes, quite a lot of this must be reconstruction after the war. They've done a good job, I must say. Not like Coventry, eh? Or London for that matter. A spot of common sense, you see. No stupid, knee-jerk rejection of the past and all its works. And they lost the bloody war. I don't know."

"It looks like it did before the war, then?"

"Well. . . Yes and no. It's the same city, put it that way."

A telephone rang through the sound of distant traffic on the breeze, and the old man turned without a word, and went inside.

"Hallo? Ja. . . Yes, speaking."

Mickey felt the edge rub off the holiday mood. They had been there half an hour, and already someone was ringing his father, apparently in English. Business as usual.

He turned back into the room and found that Elspeth had deserted him for some reason. Clearly she would be back very soon, or she would have told him, so he was left with an indeterminate number of minutes to waste. He cast an eye over the helpful advice for visitors in seven languages, then opened the wardrobe. This was good for a laugh. His wife had turned him into an American, hanging up his clothes in the wrong combinations, tweed jacket with blue chinos, golfing jacket with cavalry twills. It wasn't worth making a fuss about. He decided to have a bath, and reorganise the clothes as he dressed. He was just pulling on the chinos when she returned, and as soon he saw her he knew she'd found something exciting, extraordinary, something that had just absolutely made her day and brought her back to him hot and out of breath, full of energy and words.

"You should have taken the lift," he said.

"Sure I did. I'm sorry I was so long, I just went out to get some cold cream—can you believe it? I forgot to pack cold cream—and it took just forever to find somewhere, and then the help didn't speak English, and I had to wait—but then, on the way back here, I saw something—"

Mickey raised a hand.

"Don't tell me. You found an old building."

"Hey, don't make fun of me! This is really exciting."

"OK, OK. Excite me."

"Well there was this poster, OK? And it's for this exhibit that's on until May 1st, all about the civil war that happened here, when your father had to leave, back in 1934! I asked someone, to make sure I had it right. It's the fiftieth anniversary, you know? Mickey we have to see that show. It's really important."

"Yes, fine, fine. Where is it?"

"It's not in the centre of town. I copied down the address, I figured we could take a cab, maybe this afternoon?"

"This afternoon? For heavens' sake, Pet, aren't you tired? I just want to have some lunch and lie down on a bed that doesn't move."

"Hey, I didn't come here to sleep. You know, we only have a week, and there's a lot to see."

With a groan, Mickey flopped back on the bed, and bathed his eyes in the emptiness of the ceiling.

"All right. See how I feel after lunch. Maybe a bucket of very cold gin and tonic would help."

"Aspirin would be better. I'm sure your mother has some."

"Undoubtedly, if she didn't pop them all on the train. OK. Let's look in on the old folks."

When Mickey knocked on the door of his parents' room a moment later, there was no answer. He waited, and was about to knock again, when his father opened the door just enough to let himself out, and then quietly locked it behind him.

"Your mother's asleep. Probably better to let her rest while we have some lunch. What do you think?"

The question was rhetorical, although Mickey had no objection to raise. He would have been quite happy to let his mother sleep for the week.

He decided to adopt the gin option to relieve his headache, and secured a large one before he sat down again. The hotel restaurant seemed disappointingly familiar in its decor and menu; the Austrian influence could have been the work of any enterprising London manager pursuing a novel theme. That wasn't all. He noticed, not for the first time, that he had automatically taken the right-hand seat of a pair, Elspeth the one on his left. Every meal was like getting married all over again, especially these occasional meals with only his father facing them, smiling, expectant and benignly in command, and so much more like an elderly vicar than the soldier he was supposed to be.

"I see they have Chablis. Elspeth I know you're not very keen on wine. Mickey, will you have some, if I order it?"

"I will."

Dimly he remembered learning that marriage was a sacrament. It was not only the Last Supper, then, that could be commemorated in food and drink, though this was probably some sort of heresy. Certainly his father would know.

"Do you two have anything planned for this afternoon?"

"Well. . ."

"Your mother mentioned something about having a general conference over the maps and guide books."

"Actually, Elspeth's found an exhibition she wants to see. It might be a good idea to get it out of the way today, with so much else to do."

Elspeth turned to him, and beamed.

"Oh, you feeling better?"

"Quite restored, thank you."

"Oh that's great. Herbert it would be really good if you could come too. It's the fiftieth anniversary of the time when you were here."

"Yes, I know."

"I mean. . ."

"Oh, the uprising? I'm sorry, I see what you mean now. Really? Well that would be interesting, certainly. It's on for a while, is it?"

She nodded, with her mouth full of bread.

"Until May 1st."

"Ha! Of course, it would be. Well, to tell you the truth, I don't think I'm really up to it today. I must try and get there, though, before we leave. Ah. Have we decided?"

Mickey looked up at the waiter, and flinched. The man's expression of supercilious contempt was probably misleading, but it was enough to cow an enfeebled tourist.

"Dad I'll have whatever you're having. I can't make up my mind."

"I only really want an omelette."

"Fine."

"Very well... Elspeth?"

"Do you have Wiener Schnitzel?"

Mickey closed his eyes, but strangely the waiter didn't whistle up the entire hotel staff to jeer and take photographs, but merely thanked them and went away. Elspeth said;

"Can you tell us some more about it? I mean I know that was when your uncle died..."

"Oh yes, but that was nothing to do with it, really. I don't know, Elspeth, the exhibition will tell you more than I could, I'm sure. Funnily enough, you see, although I was there... here, I didn't have a clue what was going on. It seemed like the end of the world, that's all I know."

"Sure, but just, like, in general terms..."

"Oh... well there was the Left, and the Right, and a lot of paramilitary groups, some of them armed to the teeth. Austria was a real mess in all sorts of ways after the first war. When I was here the government was more or less a dictatorship, and it was having to lean pretty heavily on an outfit called the Heimwehr. Home Army. Austrian Nationalist. They really wore the trousers in the country, although Vienna was pretty solidly socialist. This was four years before the Nazis took over, remember. They wanted to keep Austria independent of Germany, and they hated the Italians like sin because of the pasting they took in the war . . . some of them wanted the Emperor back. Quite hopeless, of course." He paused to smile his thanks at the waiter pouring the bottle of Chablis, then stared at his glass in silence. Eventually Mickey said;

"So what happened?"

"Well... the socialist lot, the Schutzbund, were getting to be too much of a nuisance, and there was some sort of raid in Linz, when they had all their guns taken away. There was a lot of commotion here, as well, demonstrations, people leaving parcel bombs. Anyway, they organised a general strike here, and the government decided to clobber them once and for all. There was some street fighting, artillery fire, bit of house-to-house. It was a foregone conclusion, I'm afraid. A few people were shot, a lot more were jugged, and it was all over. After that it was the Nazis who caused all the trouble. But I was out of it by then."

He started to work on the omelette that had just arrived, then looked up, towards Elspeth, unmistakeably on the point of asking her about her Wiener Schnitzel to change the subject. Quickly Mickey said;

"But Dad, where were you when this was going on?"

"Me? Uh, I was . . . I was here and there, you know. Not now, please, there's a good chap. How's your lunch, Elspeth?"

Mickey sat back with a jolt, shocked dumb. His father had always had a way of making good stories uninteresting, but it wasn't like him to clam up altogether. This was a puzzle. Mickey looked past his wife, out of the wide window at her side, to the grey roofs and the traffic, and the soft outline of distant trees beyond. The same city . . . Could a man who had talked freely of the butchery of war really be silenced by something that had happened in this gentle, tiny place? There would have to be more to it than that.

"Dad? What was that phone call about this morning?"

"Oh. That was the lawyer bloke, Gruber. Apparently we are to have a distinguished guest tomorrow morning. Bit of extra colour for you, Elspeth."

"Oh really? You mean someone else is going to be there, when they open up your uncle's stuff?"

"That's right. Some chap who's fairly high up in the government service, something to do with the U.N., asked if he could come along."

"That's a bit thick, isn't it?" said Mickey.

"Do you think so? Maybe. Actually Gruber was very apologetic. It seems he was talking to this bloke at a party about a week ago, and mentioned that our thing was coming up—quite an event, apparently—and the bloke asked if he could sit in on it. He's pretty senior, and Gruber felt he couldn't just tell him to get lost. I don't mind. It's quite flattering, really. You don't mind, do you Mickey? I should have asked you, really, since you're the only other surviving relative. Not that we're relatives at all, except by marriage, still . . . Poor old Wolf. Do you mind?"

"Oh no, I suppose not. I don't really feel it's much to do with me."

"Nonsense. It's as much your business as mine, in a way. I don't suppose Wolf counted on there being any legatee to receive the stuff. After all, in those days the prospects for a young man reaching my age didn't look too bright, what with all the modern military hardware. Things haven't changed much, have they? I told Gruber to expect us about eleven-thirty. No point in getting up at the crack."

Mickey nodded absently, thinking hard. He had been looking forward to the revelations of his great uncle's estate no more than to the rest of the trip, but now he was suddenly curious. He was almost excited.

As he waited for his wife to dress herself for the afternoon, he brooded about the hidden history of Vienna. There was something here, something that had been here, that made the place far more important to his father than he had been letting on. Now they were here together, and it seemed impossible that Mickey could go home again without finding that something, and knowing what it meant. Maybe he was making too much of it, maybe not. In any event, he realised that he had, as it were, closed the file on the riddle of his father's character long since, and that it had now been reopened. The riddle might actually be solved, through the catalyst of some dusty package giving up its secrets in a lawyer's office. The notion was irresistible.

"Hey, you OK? I'm ready to go now."

"Yes, Pet, I'm ready."

"So what's eating you?"

"Oh. . . Dad. He wouldn't talk about what happened to him here. I thought I'd heard everything, at one time or another, but not this. And he wouldn't talk about it. It's not like him at all. He'll always talk about things. He doesn't make much of them, it's true, but you get the facts. I've never seen him do that."

"He's just tired, honey. He'll tell us later. Tomorrow maybe."

"Maybe. Maybe tomorrow will tell. Come on. Let's find a cab."

5

BEFORE FRANCES WAS FULLY AWAKE, BEFORE SHE HAD ESTABLISHED where she was, either in the world or in the course of her life, she knew that Herbert was not with her. Was he fighting in the Far East? Would she open the door to a strange officer, and hear the news she dreaded? She opened her eyes and forgot her dreams.

It was seldom, these days, that she slept without him, but on the rare occasions when some trivial circumstance separated them, waking always took her back to the early years of their marriage. It had been bad enough during the war against Hitler, but thrilling, too, as the man she had loved as a schoolgirl became a hero not only to her, but to his country as well. Sleeping alone, then, would have been the natural condition of engagement, war or no war. She had been able only to guess at its piquancy. She had thought that their wedding, late in Victory year, would unite them for life; but then Malaya and Korea had brought years of solitary waking, and loneliness in foreign countries. Where was he now?

She looked at her watch, and found that she had been asleep for two hours. Presumably, then, he had gone off to get some lunch and left her to rest. He would be back soon. She picked up the pocket-sized guide book she had bought in London, and turned to the map of the city. The centre of Vienna appeared as a wavy cartwheel with a cathedral at its hub, the sort of place that would be quite easy to walk around without getting lost; but she could not work out where the hotel stood in relation to everything else, so the plan conveyed very little. There was not a great deal of point, in any case, in getting her bearings, for the days when she could comfortably walk all afternoon were long gone.

She turned the pages of the book, and found a picture of an open horse-drawn carriage in which a driver quaintly dressed in an ornamental waistcoat and bowler hat would conduct private guided tours around the sights, albeit for a price. That was for her. It was the sort of excursion, she knew, that would appeal little to the others of her family. She would have it all to herself, a private luxury, riding around the city like a princess with a bag of those famous chocolates in her lap. Bliss.

Frances got up and washed her face, being careful to avoid looking at it in the mirror. She knew that her face grew lazy in sleep, every muscle and wrinkle smeared downward to a bottom-heavy mask. She must smile and yawn and talk a while before she would look fully alive again. She wondered how long Herbert was going to be. It was probable that one day she would have to begin another stretch of years of waking up without him, when it would be a matter not of waiting for him to return, but of waiting for the end of waiting. She never wondered how she would cope with that time. Already so much of the joy in her life was in her memory, the pleasures of the present largely to be found in old, familiar things that didn't change. She would simply go on trouping.

She opened the doors of the balcony, became a little more awake as the fresh air blew gently in, and heard the bells of the city faintly tolling, with the resonance of many centuries, tolling three. She yawned, and felt better. He would be back soon.

6

THEY WERE ALREADY INSIDE THE BUILDING, AND STANDING UNCERtainly behind the rows of chairs arranged in front of a television screen, when Mickey said;

"Oh Pet, we are a couple of fools. It's all in German."

The exhibition was not crowded. A young couple with twin toddlers sat in the third row, arms folded, attending to the video lecture with an air of sullen duty. Isolated twos and threes of people could be heard shuffling through the labyrinth of boards and curtains to the left. The place had the time-marking feel of a Thursday matinee. Elspeth looked up, and gave her husband a sheepish smile.

"I guess we can just look," she said.

"We'd better, now we're here. What do you say we skip the video?"

The first section of exhibits was devoted to reconstructions of pre-war shop-fronts, all dark polished wood and hand-painted gothic lettering. One window contained a less than life-like dummy, dressed in the winter fashion of 1933/4. Was she a model of a Viennese woman, or of a Viennese dummy, of fifty years ago? In any case both she and her setting, of miscellaneous goods and posted advertisements, seemed unremarkable to Mickey, and quite unworthy of the time and wonderment Elspeth was devoting to them.

He felt himself becoming very bored. It was an automatic reaction that had been part of his make-up for many years, for as a boy he had always sensed in this sort of exhibition a history-without-tears subtext that directly threatened his natural academic advantage. It had been a point of honour to learn nothing from such a source. Even to his adult mind there was an oppressive pointlessness to this tacky celebration of what was, after all, rather recent history. There was not yet any shortage of living people who had been part of what was represented here, nor, as his father had said, of streets and shops that had changed less than those people. The exhibition was outside, in a city where reconstruction eclipsed innovation, where there was still very little even of the neon light with which some capitals had been ablaze for more than half a century. It occurred to him that there might, after all, be a novel twist to this dreary display of the unsurprising. For it was not the continuity of human life that was being stressed here, but rather the presentation of the past as a museum piece made it more alien than it really was, a static recreation that marked it firmly as part of an age that was dead. A point was being made, an axe loudly ground.

He moved on, overtaking Elspeth, to a display of magazine covers and handbills, interspersed with posters and over-enlarged photographs. He cursed himself mildly, as he had occasionally before, for choosing Greek instead of German at school, simply because the Classical language was harder and less popular. Then again, there was some entertainment in inferring sense from context. The leaflets bore the stamp of propaganda, with their bold headlines and short paragraphs, the naïve exhortation betrayed by frequent exclamation marks, the whole headed by complex emblems and mirthless cartoons. There was a hint of real history here, in the associations of pre-war dictatorship; yet even in this the impression of age was less enhanced than dominated by that of foreignness, for it was the provenance of the material, not its period, that was remote.

And there was nothing more foreign than a foreign past. No English cartoonist had ever given birth to such blackened grotesques as these symbolic caricatures of Italy, communism and Jewry, with the heavy brushed shadows more substantial than the leaden figures that cast them. Neither had any English magazine ever borne the clean, elongated lettering found here. For some reason a language packed with long words had not generated longer street signs or wider pages. Instead the streamlined type-faces that had replaced the gothic had embraced the false economy of upward growth, like skyscrapers on a booming island.

Mickey wandered on round the corner, glancing only very briefly at the photographs on the way. Scenes of street violence were timeless and universal, and portraits of politicians, whether ancient or modern, held no interest for him. But the next item on the tour, though still tainted with the breathless pride of the school project, was at least surprising.

It was a representation in hardboard of a building whose imposing size and structure were skilfully implied by the exaggerated proportions of its model. The conflict of curves and right angles seemed less to evoke the architecture than the science fiction of its period, involving a gratuitous waste of space. Through the bottom of the façade was cut an enormous low curved arch topped with a decorative keystone, its massive presence emphasized by the little doors and windows placed at noticeable distance from its sides, in response to the structural rectangles within. Another empty curve beyond one of the doorways suggested that the archway was one of a series, above whose tops the windows in groups of three, punctuated by the keystones, formed a straight line, while, rising directly above each keystone, a cubist totem pole, jutting from the wall behind, of double windows flanked by paired balconies added another five floors to the whole. The building was obviously a familiar landmark to the Viennese, and of some historical importance, for its model stood in mute dominance, unexplained. One had simply to walk through the arch.

Now it became clear that the scene-setting was over. The building that had arrested Mickey's attention for a moment became revealed as the symbol for the beginning of open war, the site of a revolt or a siege, the home of a conspiracy. Beyond the archway the style of the exhibition was maintained, but the photographs had greater prominence, the tableaux were more violent, the propaganda bolder and more strident. Between these were glass cases containing uniforms, rifles, pistols, machine guns. Then came more photographs, of damaged houses, of frightened people nursing the wounded, and formal portraits of men in civilian dress; the dead, the captured, the beaten. It was over.

He hurried on, tiring of the blurred black and white and the pages of German print, and found another surprise, essentially a tent, from whose flimsy ceiling hung staggered rows of white flags, most bearing names, some left blank for the nameless. It was a simple affair of curtain draped over scaffolding, yet it managed to assume the presence of a chapel.

Mickey stood still in the gloom, looking up at the receding rows of names that meant nothing to him, and quietly admitted defeat. The people who had designed this place had obviously intended that it should leave a deeper mark on the visitor than the displays that preceded it. They had tried to make this plain memorial more evocative of the sadness of armed struggle than any number of pictures and rusting weapons, and they had succeeded.

"Mickey! Mickey! There you are. Mickey did you see what was back there?"

"What do you mean?"

"You missed it! Mickey you've got to come and look!"

Reluctantly, Mickey followed his wife, back the way he had come. He was fairly sure he knew what the matter was; the possibility of the coincidence had been lurking, almost feared, at the back of his mind all afternoon. Somewhere among all those photographs, in the middle of a crowd, was a striking, black-browed face that might truly be that of his father, and Elspeth had found it.

Lengthening his stride to preserve an appearance of calm, he matched her pace back through the uniforms and guns, and through the symbolic arch to the open space that gave it its dramatic power. On the far side of this Elspeth now stood in heraldic support of a large, board-mounted photograph, beaming as though she had just been called upon to declare it open.

Mickey remembered having passed the picture. It showed a small confrontation between uniformed men and civilians, one of whom was in the act of throwing a stone, while the others yelled and shook their fists. In the centre was a parked white military vehicle, its lines broken only by an observation slit at the front, and a mounted gun. Elspeth touched his arm, and pointed with her other hand to the background of the picture, empty save for the indistinct façade of a public building, a sweep of pavement white with snow, a lamp-post, and a single tall figure.

"There!"

It was his father all right, no question, but it was not the unremarkable record of his presence in the city that Mickey had expected. It was quite plainly something more than that, in the young but distinctive face almost behind the lamp post, in the arm across the chest, the hand pressed to the metal pillar streaked with snow, most of all in the attitude of the legs revealed in the open greatcoat, bent and meeting at the knee. It was a picture of fear.

This, then, was why the old man refused to talk about Vienna. It was, of course, absurd to suppose that never again, in all his bloody career, had he felt the tension and quickening of the heart that came with the likelihood of imminent pain or death. It was in the ability to derive vital energy from these that the courage of the soldier lay. What was pictured here was the hopeless paralysis of the coward, an enfeebling and shameful dread. This might be the first time, and the last, that Herbert Christie had felt that kind of fear, and the force of it was obvious and terrible.

Now Mickey, with a speed and thoroughness that surprised him, found himself revising his knowledge of his father's life, amending every story and every citation with the footnote *'This is why. . .'* For it was now clear that his father was haunted, not by the things that had scared him, but by the sensation itself of stifling impotence. To avoid reliving that moment he had run headlong into danger wherever he had found it, to the astonishment of comrades and enemy alike. Suddenly Mickey became aware of the awful potential of the picture, a tiny detail of the city's history that could assume the power of nemesis.

"Pet, we mustn't tell him about this."

"You think it might upset him?"

"Are you kidding? Look at it! He didn't seem all that keen to come here anyway. We've got to make sure he doesn't. We'll have to say it's no good, or something. It's too horrible."

"OK. Whatever you say. Do you want to go now?"

"Yes. Do you mind?"

"Sure. Let's go."

They walked out the way they had come in, attracting a few raised eyebrows at the entrance for not completing the tour, and headed in silence for the nearer of the two visible stops along the tramline. Elspeth took hold of her husband's hand. She was concerned about him now, for she realised that she had given him a nasty shock by drawing his attention to something whose discovery had been, for her, a source of pride. Nevertheless she made a mental note to get in touch with the organisers, with a view to securing a copy of that photograph.

Herbert had been so helpful and encouraging, he would surely not want her to pass up the chance of so valuable an illustration for her book. Once he was safely home again in England, it would have lost much of its power to distress him; for she was not entirely blind to its significance. At first the picture had conveyed to her only the fact of Herbert's attendance at a small-scale fracas in the snow. But then, as she studied it more closely, she had noticed that there was something unusual, something disturbing, that could only be suggested by the poor definition of grey and black. There was something odd in the face, but she had despaired of pinning it down until she looked away, and found that oddness reproduced point for point, with perfect clarity, in Mickey's own face. Then it had made sense.

As they sat together on the clean, hard seats of the tram that took them back into the centre of the city, Elspeth quietly gave thanks for the keen eye that had brought them to the event, and picked out Herbert's face in all that vagueness of old newsprint. Elspeth honey, you have the eye of a great journalist. Pulitzer here we come. She had enjoyed the afternoon anyway, even though Mickey might be upset for a while. Seeing how people lived all those years ago, the clothes, the hairstyles, all this had been thrilling as well as informative, and a wonderful aid to the imagination; while the legendary Europe of the dictators, with its fancy uniforms and chanting crowds, sang and marched vividly in her mind as never before. It was good that people could make the effort to put on a show like that. It really brought history to life.

7

COFFEE HAD ARRIVED AND WAS BEING POURED BEFORE FRANCES REalised that she had been talking, almost without interruption, all the way through dinner. The children were definitely subdued. It was normal, of course, for Herbert to defer to her conversational powers in any company. There were husbands who dominated their wives, and there were husbands who accepted the duty of the female to entertain, and Herbert was one of the latter. Mickey could be sulky, true, but Elspeth? In the few months for which Elspeth had been part of the family she had only ever paused from being garrulous to be irritatingly reverential. There was certainly something amiss. They had probably had a row. With dampened enthusiasm brought on by the sense that her remarks about the city of Vienna had not, after all, been uppermost in everyone's thoughts, she went on;

"So I thought we might try and get into one of the rehearsals at the Riding School, and then spend the rest of the morning in the Hofburg. In the afternoon I want to take a fiaker round the city. You don't have to come if you don't want to."

Here Mickey, who had been nodding vacantly over the sugar bowl, came to life for a moment.

"Fiaker? The pony and tourist-trap? Mother you can't be serious. I saw it in a leaflet. They charge the earth, for what it is."

"Well I don't care, not this once. You don't have to come with me. I think it will be fun."

Mickey shrugged and looked down at his cup.

"OK," he said.

Frances stared at him, aghast. She had gone some way towards constructing a moving defence of her tastes and rights against the snobbery of her son, and it was not usual for her to be left with a superfluity of words when they disagreed. She sat back, and surveyed the table with a quite thrilling sensation of command.

"Well. I must say, you two are hardly being the life and soul. What did you do this afternoon?"

Herbert looked up and said;

"Ah, you went to that exhibition, didn't you? How was it? Worth seeing?"

"No," they said, and looked at one another. Herbert and Frances, also, exchanged a glance. Mickey said;

"Not really. It was all rather amateur, in fact. All literary ephemera and fancy graphics, not terribly informative. You know the kind of thing. Miles out of the way, as well."

"And it was all in German," said Elspeth.

"Oh, well perhaps I should go back there with you, and take you through it. You might have missed a lot."

"Oh Herbert . . . I mean, that's really sweet of you and everything, but I really don't think it's worth your while. And there's so much else to see, and Frances seems to have the time pretty well planned out. I think your afternoon was more useful than ours," she added, and gave Frances her best smile.

"Well, the offer stands," said Herbert, "just in case you don't want to take the fiaker. Of course I haven't used my German for ages. Probably very rusty. It's odd. When I was here first I was in your position, hardly spoke a word. Then—Have I told you this?—when I started to learn, after I joined the regiment, they found I'd picked up this extraordinary Viennese accent. It had just stuck, somehow. That's why I got dropped into Berlin, you know, in the middle of it all. They thought I could pass myself off as an Austrian. It worked, as well. Of course I could never have pulled it off here."

Elspeth said;

"You must tell me some more about Berlin, when we have the time. It sounded really dangerous."

"Oh, it was. The devil of it was, now I remember, I kept running into real Austrians. Had to pretend I had flu all the time, to cover up the voice. I was faking a bad leg, anyway, because there just weren't any healthy young men wandering around Berlin in civvies, not by then. I must have looked as if I was at death's door all the time I was there."

"Dad, you're going to keep Elspeth in good copy until she retires. I think you're the only reason she married me."

"Well honey, your father has had the most fascinating life. And you know, it brings you so much closer to things? To actually talk to someone who was there, it's just amazing. That exhibit was a real waste of time."

"Oh, yes. A complete waste of time. Definitely."

"Well, I'm sorry it was such a disappointment for you. I'm sure something quite impressive could have been made of that business, with a little imagination. I would have been quite interested. Still. . ."

Herbert smiled again, and let his eyes rest on his son. Frances was right. They did seem rather tense. Clearly, someone had a problem. Could he help? He decided it would do no harm to try. After all, if there was anything he could do, he would be glad of the distraction, just now. "You know you two do seem to be rather down in the dumps this evening. Anything wrong?"

With visible effort, Elspeth dragged up another of those smiles, and said;

"No, Herbert, there's nothing wrong. It's just the journey, I guess. I wish I'd taken a nap, like you. I'm really bushed."

"Oh dear. Well, so much for the weaker sex. Do you think your husband might be capable of coming out to drink some beer?"

As he had hoped, Mickey instantly looked up, smiling and grateful.

"I think I could manage that," he said. "We haven't been out together for a while, have we? Do you mind, Pet?"

"You go right ahead. I'll stay here with Frances. That is. . ."

"Quite right, my dear," said Frances. "I do not enjoy watching men emptying pints of beer down their throats. A most degrading spectacle."

"That's great. We'll have a lot to talk about."

"Yes, I'm sure. And if we haven't we'll order up a bottle of gin. I suppose they do have gin in Austria?"

"They do, Mother. Or they did. I might have drunk it all earlier on."

"Oh, Mickey. And all that wine with dinner. Your father will have to carry you home."

"Well if you two are going to get bombed on gin, it won't matter much, will it?" said Mickey. "They don't call it Mothers' Ruin for nothing."

Frances laughed.

"Ah, Mothers' Ruin, the memsahib's friend. Elspeth, I shall tell you all about India. You'll be fascinated."

"And that's an order," said Mickey. "Right. Shall we go?"

Herbert slowly rose, and pulled back his wife's chair, while the children sauntered, conferring happily enough, towards the door. Frances looked up, and gave him a gentle smile.

"Do you think you can help?" she said.

"Perhaps, if I can get him to talk, if I can just listen. I'm not very good company this evening, not for you. You don't mind being left, with Elspeth?" She squeezed his arm.

"You do what you can. I'll be perfectly all right. Don't drink too much."

"I'll try," he said.

8

HERBERT SET A BRISK PACE OUT OF THE HOTEL, AND ACROSS THE forecourt to the street.

"I think I remember seeing a café over there, on the right-hand side. Yes, there it is. Shall we try it?"

Mickey shrugged and nodded. Anywhere that sold alcohol was fine with him.

The place was unappealing on the outside and unwelcoming within. One customer sat reading a newspaper at the far end of a line of tables, another two leaned on the bar by the door, in gentle conversation with what looked like a team of husband and wife behind it. Apart from these five, and now the two Englishmen, it was empty.

"Nice and quiet," said Herbert. "Well, it's early yet."

They made their way at random to a table half way along the wall, followed at a respectful distance by the female half of the partnership, who contrived to reach them just as they sat down. Herbert ordered two large beers, and smiled at her as she went away. Then he said;

"Funny place."

"Why?"

"Oh . . . Lack of atmosphere. It really shouldn't be empty at this time of day. I think it must have opened recently. Look, everything's new. No wear on the furniture, no stains on the carpet, or the tables. Let me see . . . Prints of old Vienna, piped music. The furniture's not exactly plush, though, is it? I'd say they're trying to catch the locals and the tourists, and they've fallen in between. It doesn't feel very Viennese, somehow. It feels sort of uneasy. Ah, here comes the beer. I think we'll pay as we go, English style. We're not staying."

"You've been away a long time, you know. Things might have changed."

Herbert counted half a dozen coins onto the small tin tray, and waved away the change. Then he said;

"Oh, indeed. I did look in on a couple of places this afternoon, though. The café Eiles on the Ring, and the café Mozart, not the famous one, another one just along the street here. That was very much the old style. No. I'll ask the girl when she comes back. Bet you the next round the place has been open less than a month."

"I was rather under the impression that this was your treat."

"Really? Extraordinary notion."

They laughed together, and Mickey looked past his father, distracted by a flicker in the mirrored wall at the back. Another single customer had come in, and now hesitated by the bar before sitting down, uneasily, near the door.

"You might not be such a great detective," said Mickey. "Looks like the place is filling up."

Without moving his head, Herbert glanced over his son's shoulder, towards the bar.

"Him? He was in the dining room at the hotel. He must have followed us. No don't look round. You'll embarrass him."

"Are you sure?"

"Quite sure."

"But why?"

"Don't look so alarmed, dear boy. He's not a deadly enemy out of my shady past. Too young, for one thing. He's probably on his own, decided to tag along. I expect he'll work up the courage to introduce himself when he's had a couple."

Mickey smiled, and relaxed.

"Your shady past, of course. I should have known better than to take that bet. I keep forgetting you were a spy."

"Only in the war, with the resistance groups. That's not what people mean by spying these days. Perhaps one does have a heightened sense. I don't know."

"Not a lot seems to get past you, anyway."

"That may be true. Well then . . . do you want to tell me what's on your mind?"

"What do you mean?"

"Of course, you might not want to talk, but I thought perhaps you just didn't want to talk, you know, over dinner. Was it something to do with the exhibition?"

Mickey hesitated, torn between gratitude and anger. Should he own up? This could be his chance to fill in the missing piece, and it might not come again, yet he had deliberately avoided it for his father's sake. Part of him said that if the old man wanted to rob his son of the grown-up dignity conferred by compassion, then he could take what was coming to him; but it was no better to surrender than to be beaten. He looked for guidance into his father's face, and found only the fear of rejection.

"All right, Dad, you win. Yes, I did find the exhibition upsetting, and I thought you would as well, so I decided not to tell you about it. How did you work it out?"

"It was pretty obvious, I'm afraid. What really gave you away was . . . Forgive me, this is going to sound rather unkind. While Elspeth was talking about what a waste of effort it had been, it occurred to me that it was the first time I had ever heard her voice a criticism. I take it there was a difference of opinion."

Mickey looked down again. The partial truth on which he had compromised, which he had hoped would satisfy, had proved inadequate. Now he must add disloyalty to the lie. He said;

"She didn't seem to be as sensitive to it as she might have been." Alas, this was also part of the truth.

"Well, don't be too hard on her, Mickey. She's a super girl, you know, but she's very young in some ways."

"Yes."

"Anyway, you don't have to worry about me. I don't want to go and see the thing."

"No? Why not?"

"Hard to explain. As I said, I did a bit of wandering around town this afternoon, trying to ginger up the memory, I suppose. Looking for things I remembered, things I'd forgotten. It didn't work. You see, even if the city were exactly the same, even with the same people in the same places, I would still be forty or fifty years older. I have changed, so the way I see it, sense it, that's changed as well. It's crazy, I know, but the memories I do have are so different. You lose all the detail, for a start, over the years, you only remember the things that mattered, or still matter. But even the smell of the air, the quality of the light, and the sound . . . My senses have changed.

I'm an old man, and there it is. Nothing to be done about it. But somehow I feel that going to that exhibition would be worse, you know? To see a time I lived through stuck in a glass case, like something out of the pyramids."

"Yes, I know what you mean. I thought it was rather strange, in that way. After all, it's not that long ago."

"Long enough. I'm sure most people in Europe think of the time before the war as pre-history. And I don't suppose many of them remember that Austria had an entirely home-grown fascism that was nothing to do with the Nazis. It was all overshadowed by what happened afterwards."

"Oh yes. I wouldn't have known, and neither would Elspeth. Actually there's something I wanted to ask you, about that exhibition."

"Yes?"

"There was this mock-up of a building, whopping great thing with an archway in the middle, and balconies up the front, and no explanation attached. It seemed to be important in some way."

"Oh God yes. The Karl-Marx-Hof. Whopping great thing, as you say. The Karl-Marx-Hof was part of the pride of Viennese socialism, enormous block of workers' flats, put up after the first war. When I was here first there was a popular myth that the place was bursting with weapons, ready for the coming revolution, comrades. In fact it wasn't quite like that, although I believe there were a few guns hidden in the walls, and the cellar. Anyway, when the balloon went up that February, a lot of the Schutzbund people holed up in there, and promptly found themselves under siege. Then the other side brought up the artillery, and shelled the place point blank."

"Bloody hell!"

"Yes, the buggers. Quite unnecessary. The poor sods on the inside were hopelessly outnumbered, under-equipped, cut off, and half of them didn't want to fight anyway, they just lived there. But it was a symbol, you see, for a lot of them in the Heimwehr, and the government. It stood for the red menace. Well, naming it after Karl Marx was a trifle tactless."

"And were you involved in that?"

"Not really. I went down there looking for someone, and got knocked flat by something going off behind me, probably just a squib of a home-made bomb. But I had a couple of friends who knew what they were doing, and they bundled me over the border and out. That was it."

Mickey nodded slowly. The danger had passed, and he decided he had been right to let it go. Although the frustration lingered, he was sure now that he was getting there, bit by bit.

"Well. Another chapter. You've never told me about that."

"Haven't I? Well, it wasn't a terribly glorious episode, from my point of view."

"Still interesting, though, for me."

"Oh, well I'm glad. All rather gloomy, though, isn't it? Rather like this place. Shall we leave these people to their seance, and take a walk to the bright lights? I think we'll find the beer's the same everywhere."

"Why not."

At the door of the café Herbert paused to exchange a few words with the woman who had served them. The man who had followed them there stayed where he was, absorbed in an English language magazine. After a moment, Herbert again joined Mickey in the street, grinning in triumph.

"The next one's on you," he said. "They've been open three weeks."

It was dark now, but not cold, and they walked at an easy pace as Herbert led the way down the hill and left, with apparent purpose, into a side street. There were surprisingly few people abroad, and the eye drifted naturally to the darkened heights of the buildings that faced one other intimately from each side. To Mickey the uniform antiquity of the stone frontage was almost oppressive.

"Is it still different?"

His father looked about him briefly, and said;

"No. It's still the same. And I'm still different."

"Yes, sorry, that's really what I meant. It's not coming back, then."

"No, I don't know what could do that, unless I get roaring drunk, and forget how old I am. You know I remember it was like this, once, when I went back to the school for some sort of old boys' do, maybe, fifteen years after I left. After the war, certainly. Miserable occasion, actually. Half my year seemed to have copped it somewhere along the way. Anyway, I remember standing there in the house room, trying desperately to conjure up, you know, what it had felt like, to be part of the place. I wanted to squeeze into one of those desk and flap-seat combination jobs and pretend I was a boy again. They didn't have those in your time, did they? But it was all wrong, somehow. Couldn't do it. Do you go back much?"

"Never."

"Really? I expect they'll be trying to screw some cash out of you before long. Funny thing was, though, the last time I was there with you, just before you left, what, ten years ago, I did sort of feel something. You know, all the new blocks were up by then, and they'd got rid of the green paint, and brought in those awful white boards with the felt pens . . . Changed out of all recognition, in other words. But somehow, being there with you, watching you and your friends in the Upper Sixth swanning around as if you owned the place—as one does—it brought it all back. Just for a moment, but strong enough to make me feel that it was all still there, deep down. Very reassuring, that."

"I'll have to try it."

"Would you send a boy of yours to the old place, if you had one?"

"Don't see why not. It's still in the first division, academically. And Grandpa's portrait in Big School would be quite a selling point. If it keeps on growing they'll probably name a house after you one day."

"Ah, wouldn't that be grand!"

Mickey winced. He did not consider his school days to have been the happiest of his life, preferring to hope that those were still to come. Certainly belonging to Christie House would not have improved the experience.

"You're very chatty this evening," he said.

"Am I?"

"Yes. Much better than this morning. You seem very relaxed."

"Ha. Hardly. I'm rather on edge, as a matter of fact. Probably why I'm rabbiting on like this. Ah, there. That looks all right."

They had emerged now, from another winding gorge of a street, into a broad three-way junction dominated by the picture windows of a café on a corner. Herbert led the way across the road and through the door, and at once Mickey realised that the first café had indeed been obviously new. It wasn't just that this second stop was full of people, and bore the stamp of haphazard cleaning. It was the smell. The sudden rush of coffee and smoke and old beer gave the place its long-lived-in feel, unassisted by warmth or comfort, but enhanced by the chilly grime. They secured a table with hard benches fixed on either side, and Mickey parroted their order to the waiter, who went away smirking.

"He knows we're English," said Herbert.

"Yes, I can see that must be incredibly amusing."

"Oh, don't take it personally. They're very hospitable people, you know, they like foreigners, especially the English. Waiters get a bit of harmless fun out of spotting the accents, that's all."

"I suppose. So why are you on edge? Anything special?"

"Nothing you can't work out for yourself."

"Wolf's legacy."

"Yes . . . I don't quite know what to expect. I've been trying to remember . . . Ah, more beer. Have you got forty Schillings?"

"Somewhere."

"Don't forget the tip."

"Must I?"

"Oh yes, always."

Mickey paid up with the best grace he could muster, and the waiter bowed from the neck as he filed the money in an excessively subdivided wallet. Mickey took a long pull at his beer. Like everything else in this city, the glass was a mild but disconcerting distortion of its English counterpart. Daily life here could make you sea-sick, like wearing strong lenses for the first time.

"You were saying."

"Was I? Oh, well it's just that I can't remember anything that will give us a clue. I got a few odd things in the post, months after I got back to England. It's certainly not the whole estate, you see, that was all taken care of at the time. Fifty years . . . It must be letters, I suppose. Stuff about people who are all dead, memoirs perhaps. I just don't know."

Mickey took a breath, and said;

"So what do you remember?"

His father sat back suddenly, and stared at the ceiling for what seemed to be a very long time.

"The cold," he said.

"The cold?"

"It was absolutely freezing all the time I was here. It gets like that, you know. Something to do with being in the middle of a continent. I know it was boiling when I was here in '45. I know it was, but I don't remember . . . But I do remember the cold. That stayed with me, for some reason. You know, years afterwards I used to wake up, sometimes, shivering like hell, convinced that I was back here, freezing to death, and start grabbing blankets like a madman. It happened in Malaya, once. Everyone thought I'd got malaria, but I was just cold, chilled to the bone, in the middle of all that. Crazy."

"Amazing what the mind can do, isn't it?"

"Yes, remarkable. Gives me the creeps, actually."

"And you know, even in Malaya, if you hadn't woken up and thawed out in front of the fire or whatever, you might have died of exposure."

"What a happy thought. Well, it certainly wasn't an illusion. I mean all the chaps were sweating like pigs, standing around squeezing my hands as though I was the risen Christ. They couldn't believe there was nothing wrong with me. But I just bolted a mug of boiling tea, and then I was all right again. I really needed that tea. Still, you're right, of course. The mind can do some very peculiar things."

"Elspeth would have sent you to an analyst."

"Don't be too hard on Elspeth . . . Gosh, you know what? I'm not used to this stuff. I think I'm getting a bit squiffy. Disgraceful at my age."

"Do you want to go back?"

"No, I want some more beer. My round. Herr Ober!"

Mickey felt his spirits sink. Two pints, or half-litres of the smooth, gassy beer was feeling like just enough. He wanted to go to bed. The headache had come back, and his legs felt as though they had been standing in cold mud all afternoon. Now, instead of losing himself in sleep and the soft warmth of his wife, he must sit in this unfriendly place and watch his father get drunk, and hope that secrets would emerge from the talk to make it worthwhile.

But there was another option. He sat forward, resolutely drained his glass, and told his body to find second or third wind.

"Do you think they'd have Scotch here?" he said.

"Yes, I expect so. Probably costs the earth. Never mind."

The drinks arrived quickly, and Mickey knocked back the Scotch in one and lit a cigarette. The effect was immediate. Whisky was the magic ingredient in the evening's formula. Gin, Mosel, claret, brandy, beer, now whisky and more beer. The die was cast.

"You know you could have cheated on that bet," he said. "I wouldn't have known the difference."

"Don't you know even that much German?"

Mickey sat back, and considered.

"I'll tell you how much German I know," he said. "I can order beer, and coffee. I can say yes, no, and thank you. That's it."

"Not please?"

"Oh yes. And I can say 'the daughters of the Rhine are lamenting the loss of their gold.' That's pretty useful."

"Oh, vital. I would never have got through the war without that. Gosh, Wagner. There was a bloke who knew a bit about the passage of time."

"He knew a lot about taking up other people's time."

"True, yes. But I mean all those layers of legend and history, ancient figures bound by an even more ancient past. Remarkable. And Parsifal. Eternal life from the sacrament, and Amfortas with that wound that won't heal. What a mind. They're doing Parsifal here, you know, for Easter. We might be able to find some returns somewhere."

"I can't see Elspeth sitting through four hours of Wagner. She's not really a fan. Actually I'm not all that keen myself, just now. Wagner was such a miserable bugger. I want something mindless. Bit of Mozart. . ."

"Oh, blasphemy!"

"You know, one of those things he dashed off between parties, from an idea on the back of a matchbox."

"You're trampling on my soul, horrid boy. Must see something, though. Can't stay in Vienna without going to the opera."

"Like seeing Naples and not dying?"

"Quite. Like going to Gretna Green and not getting married."

"Or going to Mexico and not getting divorced. Or going to Corsica and not getting kidnapped. Or coming back from India without dysentery. Simply not done."

"And you have the nerve to call Wagner a miserable sod. You'd better finish your beer and have another."

"I can't drink it that fast."

"Well have some more whisky, then. I didn't come here to get depressed."

Mickey drank. He did not feel depressed. He realised, of course, that almost everything about life was either ugly or tragic, that went without saying, but the knowledge did nothing to darken his mood. All illusions of power and responsibility were being dissolved, and he could reflect upon life with happy detachment. Besides, he knew this one. The awareness of cosmic gloom, and the contentment that went with it, were part and parcel of the heightened sound and the vivid colours, the faltering balance and power of speech. He didn't care. Soon he would start to sing. Maybe they would be thrown out, and laugh about it painfully the next day.

"Are you going to have some more?" he said. "Beer, and scotch?"

"Absolutely. First one to fall over's a sissy."

"We'll get done for d and d."

"In Vienna? Don't be ridiculous."

They drank together, and then, momentarily unable to think of anything to say, drank again. Herbert grinned at his son, and Mickey grinned back. A grin could last a long time now, fill up a lot of space. Then Herbert looked down at the table, suddenly subdued. Mickey waited for him to say "God, this takes me back," but the old man didn't speak. Mickey took another drink, alone. Then he said;

"What's up?" His father shook his head, and said nothing. "Come on, Dad, cheer up. You're on holiday."

"Yes."

"Well then. What's the matter?"

Herbert shook his head again, and looked anxiously this way and that. Then he said;

"Oh, it's stupid."

"What is?"

"I shouldn't drink. I always forget . . . I always get like this when I drink, and it's very predictable and very boring."

"I don't think I've ever seen you get drunk," said Mickey.

"No, well there you are. It's a long time. No wonder I forgot. It's bloody silly . . ."

"Dad, I'm in no condition to play guessing games. What are you talking about?"

"It's very commonplace, I'm afraid, I know it's foolish . . ."

"Yes, you said that. So what is it?"

"Oh . . . I suppose it's just . . . getting old."

Mickey sat back, in a pantomimic gesture of relief, and said;

"Oh, is that all."

His father gave a miserable little laugh.

"Yes, pathetic, isn't it?" he said.

"Maybe. Happens to everybody, though. If it didn't get you like that when you were twenty-eight you were bloody lucky, that's all I can say."

"Oh it did. It got me like that when I was twenty, and fifteen, and ten . . . I think it started when I was about six, lying there alone in the dark, in the Tudor bit of the old house, crying myself to sleep, thinking about death."

"Christ Almighty. When you were six?"

"About that. I don't suppose I thought of it in those terms. It was the paradox, you see."

Mickey stirred his brain into a painful effort to make sure he had missed nothing, then said;

"What paradox?"

"Birth and death. Beginnings and ends in the midst of infinity. No barriers, always something beyond . . . Infinity scared me to death. If you see what I mean."

"And you were only six? Bloody hell. But look, you weren't drinking when you were six, presumably."

"No, of course not."

"Well then, what happened?"

"Oh, life became fuller, I suppose. I learned how to forget. But there's a way of remembering, you know, that only happens when you're drunk."

"Oh, I know. But does it still frighten you? Or is it just that you remember being afraid?"

Herbert looked up, surprised.

"I don't know," he said. "I don't know. Perhaps there's no difference."

"There ought to be."

"Yes of course. When you're a child you can't see the difference between seventy years and infinity itself. But now, I've lived through far more years than I can have in front of me, I can almost see the end . . . But it feels just the same. That's why old men look back, to take their minds off it. That's why we have memories."

"You've got some marvellous things to remember," said Mickey. It was a desperate ploy, in the circumstances, but if memory existed as a distraction, there was at least a chance that it could be made to work now. "I'm sure there are lots of things you haven't told me," he added.

"Oh yes, marvellous things. Do you know what I was remembering today?"

Mickey shook his head slowly, on his guard. There had been no change of tone in his father's voice.

"It occurred to me, today, I don't think I've ever thought about it before . . . Do you know what I've been called, more often than anything else? Sir. Out of all the ways in which I've been addressed over the years, Sir comes out on top. Clear winner. Christie probably comes second. Then Major, and Colonel, and Dear, and Sweetheart, and Herbert. . ."

"And Dad."

"And Daddy. Yes. And General. Sir. I should have been christened Sir."

"Well, what of it? It doesn't matter, does it?"

"No. It's just a fact. Think of me, and what do you see? A uniform, an officer, someone called Sir. It's what I am, and what I was. It's what Elspeth sees when she looks at me, when she asks me about my life, all she thinks about is the soldier. That's all there is."

"It's not exactly something to be ashamed of, is it?" said Mickey. "It's a fine thing, a thing to be admired. You're not just a soldier to Elspeth, anyway. You're a great man."

"A stuffed shirt of an Englishman with a lot of medals."

"No! You mustn't think like that. Anyway, who cares? You could give yourself any number of labels, and none of them would be the whole truth. It's a stupid thing to get unhappy about. It looks like self-pity. And that's just ludicrous for a man like you."

Mickey paused, unwilling to continue a theme that he sensed was somehow missing the point. His father stared at his glass, turning it slowly on its axis until the handle came round again towards him. Eventually he said;

"You're right. It is self-pity, and it is ludicrous, and not because of what I am or what I've done, but because there's no point. I know what it is, I know why it's different. When you're six years old you can't see to seventy, you don't know what you're going to be. Now I know. I know what I became, and what I am. Seventy years began, and ended. I have become part of the finite. And when you're part of the finite, you're dead. That's what it is."

"But you're not dead."

"No. Oh Mickey, I don't know what I'm talking about. I'm sorry. I just shouldn't drink, that's all."

"I don't know what you're talking about either. You shouldn't worry about these things. It doesn't do any good."

"Quite true."

"And you were never just a soldier, you know. You've never looked like someone who was just a soldier and nothing more. Nobody here would be able to tell what you were, apart from an Englishman, I suppose."

"They can see I'm an old man, weeping into his beer because he's old. Probably rather comical."

"No . . ."

"Oh it is. I find it so. But then tell them I'm a soldier who feels old because he hasn't killed anyone for thirty years, and it isn't quite so funny. Elspeth made me think about that, as well."

"Elspeth's got a lot to answer for."

"Oh, don't be hard on Elspeth . . ."

"Look, Dad, shall we go? It's getting late. It's been a long day."

"Let me finish this."

Mickey sat back, his head hurting and swimming, and watched while his father slowly finished the last glass of beer. Then they got up, and shambled a path between the fat bodies of Viennese drinkers to the door and the cool, quiet street.

"Where are we?" said Mickey.

"It's all right. I know the way."

They crossed the junction, and plunged once more between the massive walls that would lead them back to the hotel. But the evening wasn't over yet. In a side street bordered on one side by a surprising patch of waste ground, they found themselves standing next to a small window, from behind whose plain curtain shone flickering lights of red and blue. The heavy beat of rock music wafted out into the air. Herbert stopped and said;

"Nightcap?"

Mickey thought about it quickly. This was obviously a small bar full of young people and noise. There would be no place for melancholy here. He smiled and nodded. It might be a good idea. It would certainly be different.

Together they squeezed through the door, and into a mass of tightly packed young, all sweating and laughing in the coloured light. Yes, it is different, thought Mickey; it's hell. The rock music was in English, though too loud to be comprehensible even to an Englishman. On four video screens suspended from the ceiling an English comedian marched awkwardly up and down the stairs of a London bus. No one was looking. There were chairs and tables, mostly invisible beneath perching, rocking, sprawling bodies, and many more people than could sit anywhere, all zig-zagging from group to group, while waitresses with tin trays somehow steered their course through a crowd in which there was no room even to smoke. Then there was a glass of beer in Mickey's hand, and his father, smiling and nodding in grim self-parody;

"So this is what it's like to be young these days. Mickey, I had no idea. There must be so much you haven't told me."

Mickey laughed, desperately, too hard and stupidly loud, just to be heard at all, just to hear himself. It was very hot, and the beer was not very cold, and all around him the young Viennese bawled their guttural noise in his ears, shrieking the fake amusement and horror of bourgeois chatter. Mickey and his father seemed to be the oldest people there, yet the old man was the more at ease, smiling at young girls, exchanging politenesses with the thick-set boys who pushed their way past him in the melee. Soon all the sound became one maddening noise, and the videos flickered brightly on shiny faces and fair hair bathed in dark blue light. Everyone wore the same broad smile, everyone except Mickey, as though the smile were a private rule, or a pass that only he had not been given at the door, as a stigma for being foreign. It could only be some sort of punishment to be left standing in a crowd like this. This was hell.

Back in the hotel, Mickey waited a moment outside the door of his parents' room, and heard his father say;

"Hello Fran. I'm afraid your husband has had too much to drink."

"Oh Herbert, you silly old fool. I'll get you a glass of water. No, don't go to sleep until you've had a glass of water . . ."

Elspeth was awake, too, sitting in the armchair, reading a guide book. She gave him her usual smile. He smiled back, and deliberately fell backwards onto the bed.

"How was your evening?" he said. She answered, but he didn't hear her. He awoke, only moments later, to find her in the final stages of undressing at the foot of the bed. There was a studied, tense way she undressed sometimes, in fact most of the time, watching him with a half-smile as she sloughed off the silk she loved. Alarmed, he stirred himself to disrupt the sequence, and found that he was undressed as well, and firmly in bed.

"Pet . . . Look, hold on, darling. I'm completely smashed."

"Baloney."

"But I am. I had a terrible evening."

"So take your mind off it."

"Oh, Pet, for heaven's sake . . ."

He knew it was hopeless, now. Her mind was made up. For the few minutes of that sleep he had been back on the train, wedged into the hurtling corridor with thousands of screaming teenagers, and fighting for the space to drink a dark blue beer that tasted of air, of nothing. Now Elspeth knelt on the end of the bed, ready to crawl towards him, her face beaming sentiment, her body taut. He let his eyes dwell on her breasts and shoulders, the fetish bust of deep curves and shadows, and felt the appeal of her fight through his fatigue and distaste. Then he closed his eyes, and felt a different, stronger trigger, as he noticed the weight of her on his legs through the covers, full of happy promise like the toy-filled pillow-case on the Christmas mornings of his childhood. He smiled then, and relaxed, for he knew that the weight would soon disperse into a multitude of little joys, and the warm glow of belonging.

9

THE LAW FIRM STURMER, WITH WHOSE PARTNERS WOLF HAD ENTRUSTed the management of his estate, had not changed their premises in more than a century. Herbert remembered the street well, and it was only a short walk from the hotel, down the hill and right, past the high, unlighted façade of the Armenian monastery. The family walked at tourist speed, Frances and Elspeth stopping at intervals to take photographs, while their husbands stood and waited. Herbert grimaced at the brightness of the morning, and cursed himself for bringing on the unfamiliar symptoms of hangover, the hovering stomach, the irritant shame of things he remembered saying, things he might have said. His furtive glances at Mickey told him nothing. The boy was wearing mirrored glasses against the sun, and the shape of his mouth revealed only the physical ill-being of the morning after. Perhaps he had forgotten.

It was exactly eleven-thirty when Herbert reported their arrival to the receptionist in the cool gloom of the Sturmer building. Presently a young girl appeared, all smiles and bobbing blonde hair, and led them, past a mess of decorating work, to an office on the second floor. There they stopped abruptly in the doorway, momentarily blinded by sunshine.

"General Christie! Sir Herbert! This is a great pleasure. I am Bernhard Gruber."

Herbert shaded his eyes, and found Gruber's hand.

"How do you do, Herr Gruber. My wife, Frances. My son and daughter-in-law."

"I am delighted to meet you all at last," said Gruber. "May I present Herr Weiss, from the ministry, Mr Thorne, from the British Embassy. Please." He gestured to indicate a number of armchairs around the room, and everyone sat down.

Herbert could now see properly again, and took a good look at his surroundings. There had obviously been alterations made to this building since the war. The east windows that had blinded him were huge and rectangular, and jutted into the street in shiny metal frames. The furniture, too, was boxy, a pseudo-Scandinavian creation in red leather. Comfortable enough, though. Gruber now stood behind a similarly modern desk, talking to his secretary by intercom. He was well groomed, plump, cheerful, healthy. It was impossible to tell whether his bow tie made him look older, or younger, than he really was. Thorne was certainly younger, quietly diffident with a schoolboy short-back-and-sides, a junior diplomat on his first foreign posting. Still, it was nice of them to show the flag. Weiss could have been Herbert's age, though much bigger, almost a giant and a fat one at that, with an air of perfect confidence in himself. He looked at Weiss, and found that Weiss was already looking at him. They smiled at one another, a smile of recognition. Had they met before?

"General, I must thank you for agreeing to my presence here this morning. I realise I must be intruding, but when I heard . . ."

"Not at all, Herr Weiss. I'm sure we're quite honoured. Do you have, ah, any particular interest?"

Weiss snapped his mouth into a wide, closed smile, and said;

"No, except that I, like you, have lived through these fifty years. A lot of history for both of us. And who knows? Maybe I shall be present at the . . . ah, *Auferstehung*?"

"Resurrection?"

"Thank you, the resurrection of a national archive."

"Frankly I doubt it," said Herbert. "We'll soon know, anyway."

Gruber looked up from his machine, and said;

"I thought a glass of Champagne might be appropriate."

"Oh God," said Mickey. Gruber looked quickly from son to father and back, suddenly concerned.

"That's very thoughtful, Herr Gruber," said Herbert. "We'll do our best. My son and I had rather a heavy evening, celebrating my return, that's all." Mickey had removed his sunglasses, and now gave his father a brief, but very old-fashioned look. Ah, so he had not forgotten. "Actually a glass of fizz will probably do us good."

"Good, good," said Gruber. "This is, after all, quite a special occasion."

The blonde girl came in again, carrying a tray of bottles and glasses and put them down on Gruber's desk. Frances leaned forward and said;

"Herr Weiss, my husband said you work with the United Nations. It sounds most interesting."

"My work is mostly very dull, Lady Christie . . . But I am not working today. I was just so fascinated when my friend Gruber, here, mentioned that you were coming. I could not resist the temptation to invite myself. I really shouldn't be here, I know, this is a family occasion . . ."

"Oh no," said Elspeth, "It's really interesting that you're so, so interested. Is it possible we could talk, maybe later?"

"My wife is a journalist," said Mickey.

"Oh really? Well I can see that this would make a very good story for a magazine. However my presence here is of no interest to you, I'm sure. I am only a humble spectator."

"No, really . . ."

"And in any case, my work, you must know, is occasionally sensitive. I try to avoid publicity. I'm sure you understand."

Elspeth looked blankly at him for a moment, then said;

"Oh sure," and looked down at the carpet.

There was silence now, for some moments, while the Champagne was distributed. Everyone sat with their glasses and waited, as though for a toast. Mickey stared miserably at the wine, clearly not even tempted to drink it, though it was not any sense of occasion that held him back. Gruber opened a second bottle, and poured a glass for himself. Then he took a bunch of keys from his pocket, opened the deep bottom drawer of his desk, and lifted out a heavy cube wrapped in aged brown paper and string. Then he took a paper-knife from another drawer, placed it carefully beside the parcel, and stood back.

"Is that it?" said Mickey.

Gruber nodded.

"General. Please use my chair."

Herbert got up, and hesitated. Toasts could wait. He took a long, unceremonious drink from his glass, and walked across the room, around the desk to the swivel chair.

"Well chaps," he said, "This is it."

He picked up the knife, cut the string, and pulled the paper apart. Books. One, two . . . Six books, leather bound, each of them a foot square and two inches deep, unmarked. He opened the one on top. Handwriting, old fashioned but not good, an undisciplined hand, writing in German. The translation was not difficult.

I was born on the First of January, 1848, perhaps the most extraordinary year in all our history. The place of my birth was Vienna. . .

"Good Lord," said Herbert, "It's his autobiography."

Nobody spoke, although everyone was now sitting forward, except Gruber, who stood and craned absurdly from a respectful distance. Herbert lifted the first volume from the pile, and opened the second. Here the story began in 1869, with Wolf studying music in St Petersburg. Volume three opened in 1895, in Belgrade. Volume four began with a lengthy description of Bombay in 1912; Herbert gave up before the end of the first sentence, lifted the book, and stopped. It was heavier than the others. He put it down again, and flipped through from the back.

All but a handful of pages at each end had been cut to form a square hollow space, containing a slim automatic pistol, a cluster of tiny bullets, and perhaps twenty large gold coins. Herbert heard the others gasp, and looked up. They were all standing round the desk now, and only Weiss had managed to keep his mouth closed.

"Well, well," said Herbert. "I believe this is a four-shot Derringer. Not even rusty."

"And the coins?" said Weiss. Herbert looked at the gold carefully.

"Well, I'm no expert . . . But that is the Romanov eagle. They're Russian. This is most interesting. You see, all the pages were covered in writing at one time. Wolf obviously considered that this hiding place was more valuable than his memoirs. Remarkable."

Weiss nodded slowly, his eyes still on the coins. Mickey said;

"But why should he have wanted to keep these things hidden for fifty years after his death? The memoirs I can understand, but the gun?"

Herbert hesitated, feeling that he ought to know the answer to that question. Somewhere, somewhere . . . He gave it up.

"I don't know. Maybe we can work it out."

Again he lifted the fourth book from the pile, and opened the fifth. London, 1917. London, in the middle of the war? Between the fifth volume and the sixth there lay a faded brown envelope, the size and density of a school exercise book, flattened hard over the years, with the single word 'Herbert' written in large long-hand on its back. Herbert's heart twitched as he saw it, but he put it on one side, and opened the last book. The narrative commenced back in Vienna, in 1928, and ended, only forty pages later;

I have lived a long life, and I am content to be left undisturbed, with my memories and my teaching. I have a pupil coming in half an hour. Who knows how many more lessons I shall teach? As I write I can smell Mariangela's cooking...

"Mariangela! The housekeeper, of course. I'd completely forgotten about her."

"Is that important?" said Mickey.

"Well... Yes, yes of course. Wolf died suddenly, you see, unexpectedly. It was Mariangela who took these books to the lawyer. She probably didn't bother to look inside, or perhaps she didn't want to. Anyway, she might not have known about the gun and the gold crowns. She just knew what Wolf had proposed to do with his memoirs, and carried out his wishes. Yes. That's it."

Weiss said; "You don't seem to be very surprised by all this, General Christie."

"Well, no. I can't say that I'm truly surprised. Whatever it means, you see, I'm sure it's quite in character. I think I remember Wolf actually telling me that he had been an agent of the Czar. There were always stories in the family, one never knew quite what to believe. Gosh, it's going to take some time to get through all this."

"What about that envelope?" said Mickey.

"Ah, yes . . ." Herbert picked up the envelope, turned it over in his hands, and opened it. It was a letter, dated Sunday, 11th February, 1934, and written in English. He felt his heart thump like a fist on a table, a demand for attention, and realised it was beating fast.

> *My dear Herbert,*
>
> *I do hope you have kept your promise, and kept this packet unopened until your return to England. When you have read it, show it to your father, he will know what to do. I am afraid it is most likely that we shall not meet again, but I am thankful that we were able to spend these few days together. The fact is, Herbert, that I must run away. I must leave Vienna, and hide in some other country. I have run away many times before, I know how it is done. Don't worry about me. It seems that there is one lesson I have still not learned, that life will always find new ways to surprise. I had not expected this to happen in my eighty-seventh year. Nevertheless, I must respond as I always have. While I still live, I must be what I am . . .*

Herbert reached the bottom of the first page, and let his eyes rest there. They had misted over; he wouldn't be able to read any more, anyway. Instead he repeated to himself the words he had read, conjuring his uncle's voice into his mind, brushing into its eye the details of the old man's face as he talked, and the mannerisms of his stubby hands. Then there came, unbidden, the background of the picture, the study on the ground floor of the house, full of dark furniture and murky sunlight, thick with the air of a room where the windows never opened, the dust and smells still lingering from a different century.

"General Christie?"

"Herbert?"

"Dad, are you all right? You've gone pale."

"Herbert, what is it?"

He looked up at them, took a breath, and realised that he must have stopped breathing for a few moments. He felt giddy and faint.

"I'm sorry," he said, and paused to breathe again. Frances took his hand and said;

"Herbert, you're shaking. What is it?"

"Mostly hangover, I expect. It's a letter. A letter I should have got before I left in '34. Got mixed up with the books, I suppose. It's a funny feeling, getting a letter that way, fifty years late."

"What does it say?" said Mickey.

"Well it seems . . . Yes, it seems Wolf was planning to do a bunk. He says he has to clear out for some reason. I think he must have written it the day before he died."

"Clear out?" said Mickey. "Why?"

"I don't know. It's a very long letter. I'll finish it later. After all, it's not really very important now."

Gruber said;

"General, would you like a glass of water?"

Herbert swivelled around in the chair, and looked up to smile at Gruber—so worried, and so young.

"Thank you, no. I wouldn't mind another glass of Champagne, though."

He sat back, and watched them all as they took their cue to look away from him, to look relaxed. Frances once more attempted to engage Weiss in conversation, Mickey talked to Elspeth, and Thorne to the secretary, in German, politely but obviously flirting. Gruber handed Herbert his glass, and set about opening another bottle.

"Have you thought about what to do with these things, General? If you want to leave everything here for a few days, naturally we are at your disposal."

"Thank you, yes. That might be a good idea. I suppose there might be complications about simply walking out of the country with this lot."

Gruber, bottle and glass in hand, gave a leisurely shrug.

"We'll sort it out. In the meantime, perhaps we might discuss your wishes over lunch? Your family, of course they are all most welcome."

Herbert smiled again.

"I think they can make their own arrangements," he said.

"As you wish."

"And what about Herr Weiss?"

The question clearly surprised Gruber, but before he could answer Weiss himself turned towards them.

"I am afraid I must leave you, gentlemen. I have another appointment. It was truly fascinating, though. I am most grateful to you, Sir Herbert. Berni, let me know the end of the story."

"Of course, Herr Weiss."

"Goodbye, General. Perhaps we can meet again before you go."

Herbert rose to shake hands, and tried to stuff Wolf's letter into his pocket as he did so, but it was much too big.

"It was a pleasure, Herr Weiss. Yes, I hope so."

He watched as the big man gave his polite farewells and then left, to be shown out of the building, and possibly the street, by Bernhard Gruber. Of course they would not meet again, not in the next few days. Herbert was not even sure that he would welcome the chance to talk again to someone with whom he could reminisce, although it did seem strange, now, that they had made no effort to establish common ground.

"What a curious man," said Frances. "Do you suppose he's a spy?"

Herbert laughed.

"Well, you know, Vienna's always been that sort of place." Probably not any more, though, he thought, reflecting also that he and Weiss might still be bound by the etiquette of a time when it had been bad form to ask too many questions.

10

. . .While I still live, I must be what I am.

Herbert, I have told you very little about myself, but I have to confess that something I have told you. is untrue. I did not retire from my political work in 1918. I kept in touch with the Emperor in exile, and I agreed to work for the Bolsheviks, who have made good use of many of us who had owed their livings to the Czar. Maybe you will not be surprised to learn that it was I who drew young Becker into the circle, and made him, as one might say, my heir apparent. His infiltration of the Schutzbund, and reports on its organisation, have made me a popular man in the Kremlin. But now there is an irony. Although I have received no money from a Habsburg for seventeen years now, for God knows they have had a hard enough time feeding themselves, my occasional correspondence with that family has been discovered, and Becker himself has denounced me to the Russians as a monarchist. He has grown ambitious, and wants our little empire for his own. I have been warned that someone is being sent, all the way from Moscow, especially to murder me. That is the way they order things there, but it is not my way. Incredible, isn't it? Eighty-six years old, and still I must be eliminated as an enemy of the Revolution. That is why I'm going. I can't just sit here and wait to be murdered. I will escape, even if it kills me.

Meanwhile—this will amuse you—I have used my savings to employ your magpies, the one who knows all about our operations here to use his assassin's knife on Becker, the other to get you out of Austria and then disappear from your life. I am praying, if I can dignify an old man's curse with such a word, that there can still be some honour in this treacherous world.

On the following pages I have written everything I know about our network here in Vienna. All the names, all the petty crimes—everything I can remember. Keep it safe until you reach England, and give it to your father. And remember our –their—code word, God forgive, is Anastasia.

Goodbye, Herbert. I hope our conversations have helped you in your search for understanding. It might comfort you to reflect that my own faith will be put to the test very soon. Don't drive yourself mad, remember the futility of inquiry, and remember above all that God is the answer, and that this is why He has created nothing but questions.

I remain, for as long as I remain anything at all, your loving uncle,

Wolf.

HERBERT LOOKED QUICKLY THROUGH THE LIST OF NAMES ON THE REmaining pages, and recognised none of them. Then he read the letter again, and again. Becker. Becker, to whom Wolf had referred as someone familiar to Herbert. So who was he? The mere idea of scrutinising his memory for a clue made him weary. Just now all he could think about was the terrible irony of it all. Wolf had died, his body had failed him, on the eve of his proposed flight from his home, and he had not even been able properly to arrange his act of vengeance. Herbert remembered well enough the Englishman who had put him on the train out of Vienna, and who had indeed disappeared. But why was he described as a magpie? And who was the other one, the hired assassin? He felt he should know, that he did know but didn't want to, that the images would soon rise again, expected and feared. He had forgotten it all so well that he had become complacent, he should have known that the life he had had still lived, that he could not get away forever with reducing it to a handful of pictures, however painful. He had to get it all back.

When the shooting started in the street they had been celebrating something, dining frugally and by candle-light. Where? At whose house? What was the name of the pretty girl who had been hit in the face by the glass? She was wearing a blue dress, and standing at the window in a room which he now remembered only as being not in his uncle's house.

Herbert sighed. He must let the answers come of their own accord, or they would not come at all. He put the letter back in its envelope, got up from the lavatory lid on which he had been sitting, and automatically pressed the flush lever. It was time to go back.

He paused at the doorway leading into the main body of the coffee house, and looked across the room to his table, soaked in sunlight by the window. There was Gruber, still being perfectly charming to Elspeth. Ah, that girl. Frances had happily gone off to take her ride around the city, Mickey had sensed well enough the lawyer's wish to have a private conversation with his client. All Elspeth had done was to ask if she could come too, and the poor man had smiled and said, but naturally, she would be very welcome. Surely Mickey could have steered his wife away without embarrassment, instead of leaving her to damn herself? One would have thought so. Clearly the man suffered from a fault in his upbringing.

"Ah, Sir Herbert. Would you like something else? A brandy, perhaps."

"That would be very welcome, thank you. All right, Elspeth?"

"Oh, I'm just fine. Berni's been telling me about his childhood, in Innsbruck."

"Innsbruck? That was Schuschnigg's home town, I believe."

Gruber sat down with his guest, and then bobbed half way up again, to catch a passing waiter.

"They settled there after the First War," he said. "Schuschnigg was born in South Tyrol."

Elspeth said;

"Herbert? Ah, who . . . ?"

"Schuschnigg? The last Chancellor before the War, poor man. Hitler had him locked up. When I was here first, in '34, he was Minister of Justice, which was a bit like being a Swiss admiral. Then he took over after the Nazis killed Dollfuss, in July of the same year. Had an awful time, apparently. Schuschnigg was a lawyer, wasn't he Berni? Do you think you'll be Chancellor one day?"

"Undoubtedly, when Elspeth is President of the United States. Ah, here's our brandy. Cheers."

"To your political careers."

Herbert drank, savoured the spirit for as long as he could, then forced a giggle to prolong the joke. The lunch had been full of nonsense like that, light banter to entertain the lady. Now Elspeth drained her glass, looked squarely at Herbert, and said;

"So what are you going to do about the books, and the other stuff?"

"Well . . ." Herbert offered an apologetic look to Gruber, and received a blank face in return. Well, why not? "I don't know, quite. I've just had a look through the rest of this letter, and . . . It might raise one or two problems."

"What sort of problems?" said Gruber.

"Well, it's difficult. You see, Berni, my uncle appears to have been something of a master spy, a double agent. It seems he was working for the

Habsburg emperor, before and after the First War, and for the Russians, Romanov and then Bolshevik, apparently over the same period." Gruber raised an eyebrow. "Yes, quite. But it's more interesting than that. The letter includes a great long list of names, people who were working for Stalin in Vienna, in various ways. Now, I don't know how important that is. I don't know anything about these people, whether they were caught anyway, what they did later, whether they're still alive. None of the names even rings a bell from '34, or '45, when I was actually involved in this sort of thing. Chances are it's all dead history."

"But," said Gruber, "It will all have to be checked. Yes, I see that. Well, I suppose we had better bring in the police. No?"

Herbert hesitated. Gruber had picked up the reservation in his face, but how to explain it?

"To tell you the truth, Berni, I'm reluctant to let this go. You see, when I was here in '45, this information would have been right up my street. Maybe, if I sit on it for a while, I can make sense of it. Actually the most sensible thing I can do is pop down to Whitehall when I get back, and go through the records. Then, if any action needs to be taken, our people can fix it with the Austrian government, through the proper channels. So. You hang on to the memoirs, and all the bits and pieces, and I'll hang on to this letter. I imagine everything will be safe enough with you?"

"Of course, of course . . . That is . . ."

"Yes?"

"Oh, it's nothing. Actually the building was burgled last night—you may have noticed the repairs when you arrived—but the men were stopped by the night watchman, and they didn't take anything."

"Do you know what they were after?"

"I have no idea. Perhaps they thought there was money in the safe. Of course we have papers, wills, contracts . . . But, Sir Herbert, I must say that I am not entirely happy with this. I think I may have a duty . . ."

"Berni, I didn't have to tell you what's in this envelope. As far as you're concerned it's just a letter to me from my uncle. It's not a weapon, it's not made of gold, there can be no complications about my taking it home. Clear?"

Herbert continued to look at Gruber, while the young lawyer considered his position. There was surprise in his face, a new, almost fearful look, a look of reappraisal. *Yes*, thought Herbert, *it's a long time since you've used that tone. But it still works.* Finally Gruber leaned forward, picked up his glass, and smiled weakly.

"As you say, Sir Herbert. It is your property. You may rely on my discretion. Some more coffee?"

"Thank you. Thank you very much. I'll let you know how it all turns out."

Gruber shook his head.

"Thank you, Sir Herbert. I don't want to know."

"As you wish. Oh, Elspeth, you will keep quiet about this, for the moment?"

"Oh sure. Anything you say, Herbert. Relax."

"Good. After all, stick with me and you'll have a much better story at the end of it."

"You're telling me!"

"Fine. So that's settled."

He leaned back then, and stared lazily out of the window, allowing the young people to resume their conversation. Of course there had been no need to tell them anything about Wolf's letter. He had created a small problem so that he could congratulate himself on a small triumph, albeit tinged with shame. He could quite easily have handed it over to the police, and let them make of it what they would. It was nothing to do with him any more. Yet, somewhere in all the chaos a dead uncle had stirred up in his heart over the last few hours, he realised he had found again something of the bitter relish of secrecy. It was like the rekindling of an old infection, that automatic concealment, flaring now to preserve the privacy of his own thoughts. Even on such a tiny scale, the thrill of the deception made him tremble. It was a young man's game, after all. There was no peace in it. Wolf had died in the grip of the very same habit. It would be a terrible state in which to die.

> *It might comfort you to reflect that my own faith will be put to the test very soon . . .*

There could be little comfort to be derived from wondering how that old man had fared in such a test, weighed down as he had been by suspicion and fear. He had dragged a whole life of secrets with him to the grave, and left behind only six volumes of memoirs, and a futile scrap of ponderous English. This was not the life to which he had looked. All that mass of paper amounted only to pagan immortality, a barrow on a hill. Whatever it might mean to his nephew, sad and old in a time he could never have dreamed, it had meant nothing to Wolf himself.

Herbert said;

"Oh, Berni, I was wondering—how did the embassy get on to this? Did you inform them?"

"Not exactly," said Gruber, "That is, not formally. Peter Thorne is a friend of mine, and he was there at the reception when I was talking to Herr Weiss. He felt that it would be appropriate for the ambassador to be represented."

"I see. He must be more senior than he looks."

Gruber shrugged, and said;

"He is a commercial secretary."

"And Weiss?"

"Intercultural affairs, I believe."

"That could mean anything," said Herbert.

"And everything, indeed. I don't know. But he is always at the best parties."

Herbert turned back to the window, and recalled for a moment his meeting with Weiss, and the look of recognition they had shared. Yes, there had been another, younger face behind that glance, another memory layered down deep in the past.

Herbert looked away from the amblings of tourists in the street, back to two people who would one day hold his memory, and puzzle over the dark patterns left swimming there. What would they make of him? Could they ever understand the things that moved him, things he could not even see? Why should they try? They would have their own riddles to solve, their own secrets to hide. Maybe they, too, would yearn, in old age, for a weariness with thinking. Maybe they would find it, and be sleepily content.

"Elspeth? Do you think perhaps we ought to be going?"

"You think? Oh sure. No problem."

"Must you go?" said Gruber, looking at them with a disappointment which surely transcended mere courtesy. Herbert looked at his watch.

"I thought we must be keeping you from your work," he said. Gruber chuckled mischievously.

"Sir Herbert, you are the guests of Sturmer. I am working while I am here with you. Besides," and he waved a hand towards the quiet city outside, "this is Vienna, you know. Please, finish your brandy, and have another.

And I will have one too," he added, "to help me forget what you have told me. Fair enough?"

"Very well," said Herbert. "Here's to your memory, Berni."

"Thank you, Sir Herbert. And here's to yours."

11

"THANK YOU SO MUCH FOR THE LUNCH, PETER. I MUST GO BACK TO work now."

"Margarita, it was Her Majesty's pleasure, as well as mine. We must do it again."

"Uh yes, please, I would love to. Goodbye then, for now."

A kiss on each cheek by way of farewell was standard in this city, a continental commonplace, but the final kiss on the mouth was special, an invitation worth following up. Peter Thorne enjoyed watching Gruber's secretary walk away, and thought; *Ah yes, but in Vienna these perfect blue-eyed blondes are two a penny*. Even the glorious cat-walk gait was ordinary here, astonishing at first to a man from England, where women seemed to have forgotten the technique twenty years since. But the novelty soon wore off. Now, that American woman, Elspeth, so improbably married to an Englishman just like himself, but so dark and warm, so intriguing—she was something else. He hadn't tried to work the charm on her, as he had on Margarita—noblesse oblige, after all—but it was good to know that he could, if he had to. He had long ago realised that it was charm that had got him into the Foreign Office in the first place, not just the easy social grace of the bright public schoolboy, but its intellectual corollary, the lazy wit that hinted at a hidden brilliance. It had really been too easy to bag Margarita for lunch, and widen her eyes with stories of glamorous nights in the West End. She was only a secretary, and he was a British diplomat in a city where Englishmen were almost embarrassingly fashionable. Not that he'd say no . . . But Elspeth. Now, there was a challenge. Not on.

Thorne shook himself and realised, with gratitude at the distraction, that his shoe-lace had broken. Two doors away was a shop that dealt in a variety of everyday things, much like an old-fashioned English Post Office, but even as he knelt on the pavement he noticed the sign on the door, bearing the single word *"Urlaub."* The shopkeeper was on holiday, probably for two weeks, in April. And anyway, of course, it was only 2:45. Up here in the Eighth District, oh, at least a quarter of a mile from one of the greatest cultural meccas on earth, the commercial imperative of tourism cut no ice with the tradesmen. Lunch was lunch. There was no point in trying to buy anything here until at least 3:00. *Schlamperei* was what they called it, the distinctive Viennese blend of *Mañana* and the "West Highland Rot," and "Never do today what you can put off until tomorrow." Sure, we'll overthrow the Emperor, or build a modern industrial economy—just as soon as we've finished all this beer. Sit down, relax, have a drink. There's always time.

Thorne dragged his mind away from the beguiling curves of spring-clad women, and concentrated on the business of the morning. Weiss. He had heard about Weiss as soon as he arrived in Vienna, and for over a year now he had secretly cherished the idea of leap-frogging his colleagues, of somehow strolling in with that vital connection that everyone else had missed. To have found it by bunking off work to get drunk with Berni Gruber would be particularly sweet—and very Viennese. He knew that for more than a decade, in this uneasy meeting-place of east and west, there had been too many potential defectors from the Soviet side who had disappeared or relented at the last minute, and that Weiss had been too close to too many of them, too soon before the event. There had also been too many leaks in the other direction, but again the evidence that pointed to Weiss was circumstantial, the stuff of wishful thinking. Like many young Schutzbund fighters, Weiss had been driven out of Austria by the fascists, and had returned via Czechoslovakia after the War, to begin a distinguished career in government service. His record bore none of the tell-tale contacts of the Cold War KGB recruit.

And yet . . . Why should he be so interested in the visit of a retired British general, and in a legacy fifty years old? Could he have been recruited so young, and kept the secret so well for all that time? Thorne needed proof, and it might just be that the only proof surviving had been kept alive, for half a century, in the bottom of a lawyer's safe. At least the problem had a name, conferred in wry, parodic reference to the conventions of popular fiction. It had become known as the Anastasia Ring, from the only word consistently offered, in desperation, by the freelance couriers who had been daft enough to get caught—though whether there really was a ring, an organised espionage network, was still uncertain. Thorne looked at his watch, and shuffled his foot uselessly in its crippled shoe. Perhaps another coffee, and a drink . . . ? An empty taxi crawled up the hill towards him, and he hailed it on impulse. No, no. Back to work. He hadn't quite gone native, not yet.

12

THE GIRL IN THE BATHING SUIT WAS STILL SHINING DAMP FROM THE water, and perched, somehow gracefully, on the lip of a quayside bollard under an evening sun. She was staring away from the light, across her left shoulder, proud and humourless, a great beauty, severe in her bathing cap with her straight back and jaw, and her straight arms maintaining the poise that emphasised the perfection of her body. The front, larger than life-size view of her was curved around one half of the pillar, the rear view pasted to the other side, with the single word "Palmer" printed above her head. She was all over town. Mickey stood staring at her for the fifth time in an hour, and wished that Palmer, whoever they were, had not bought up every cylinder on the Ringstrasse that week. Most of the effects of a hangover he could accept as just punishment for excess, but the blind and bursting lust that accompanied them had always seemed needlessly cruel. The poster entranced him. Such erotic power was eerie in a figure so still and hard, an allegorical bronze, a virtue personified. It was a maddeningly good piece of advertising.

He pulled the cigarettes out of his pocket, looked at them, and put them back. There were dozens of ways in which a man with a hangover might peacefully waste an afternoon in this city. There were art galleries, museums, shady gardens, quiet cafés. Anything ought to be better than walking around the busiest streets in the sun, aching with stupid desire for a blown up photograph. He looked at the pillar again, and drove himself a little more mad, imagining what it would be like to ease one of those straps across the tensed muscle of the shoulder, to release a pillow-full of hair from the German order of that bathing-cap. Yes, she did look very German.

Once again, Mickey dragged himself away from the girl, and continued his walk. He didn't know where he was going, but he knew that if he stuck to the Ring he would eventually come back to the bottom of the hill leading to the hotel, past the street where Gruber worked. He would then have walked all the way round old Vienna. He neither knew nor cared how long that would take, he just didn't want to have to talk to anyone until he felt a great deal better. Talking to his father was going to be awkward, anyway, after the miserable time they had had together the previous night. Better to keep walking, and to avoid, also, for a while, the irritating things his wife and his mother would have to say about the morning. Guns and foreign gold, the memoirs of a spy . . . Revelations of that sort would draw platitudes from anyone. With a twinge of resentment Mickey acknowledged that his father had been young in a different kind of time, and had lived in a more colourful world which, for his son, resided only in history and fiction, a world of heroes. Such a world was more alien to someone of Mickey's generation than any foreign country could be, and it had produced a breed of men who had become more and more out of place as they aged. Men like his father were uneasy men.

On impulse, and not caring much about getting lost, Mickey turned left, towards the centre of the city, and found himself in an area dominated by bookshops. It was cosy here. On the Ring, with its trees and width, the pedestrians had been lost in the scale of their surroundings, detached from the huge imperial buildings at their side. In this intricate quarter the blocks looked as though they had been built and used by human beings, each floor and window crafted to the form of a man. Mickey stopped, and slowly turned around in a circle, keeping his eyes above the ground floor level of the streets. He could see nothing, absolutely nothing, that could have been built after 1800. Such a view was not uncommon in grimy old London, but this was different, because he was in no way a part of it. He was a stranger here, as his father had been fifty years before. Now was the time to strain at catching a sense of what it had been like to be the young Herbert Christie, to take a shallow breath and chase the giddy vertigo that made all distances the same. The people who ignored him on every side could be at home in any age. While he stood and stared like a lunatic, they worked and ate and walked in and out of ancient buildings, forgetful alike of the antiquity about them, and of the mass of the future bulking low above their heads. Mickey breathed again, and moved on. Now was no longer just the present, but the vivid present, a tense narrating the reaction that precipitates the past. He could imagine himself young in a younger time, at the beginning of a story, with a whole saga of world events yet to happen. It was a stirring illusion while it lasted. Perhaps being young in the 1980s really would turn out to be that exciting. Somehow, it just didn't feel like it.

At the corner of a narrow side-street made dark by the height of its buildings, he suddenly stopped, halted by the smell of cooking. He had been unable to face breakfast, he had been walking for nearly two hours, and all at once his system, washed clean and numbed by alcohol, had come alive and started screaming for food. The smell coming out of the café was a school dinners reek of dark gravy and meaty stodge. He had to go in.

The place was cramped inside, badly lit and full of rickety old furniture. Mickey ordered by pointing, at random, to a line on the menu, forced himself to return the waiter's smile, and found himself rewarded, after a few minutes of desperation, with a plate of rich stewed offal supported by a dumpling. It was exactly what he needed. He finished it quickly, and signalled to the waiter with the word 'encore' drifting uselessly through his mind.

"Mein Herr?"

"Ah . . . Do you speak English?"

"Yes, of course."

"Oh good. The same again, please. And a beer."

"Very good."

The waiting wasn't so bad this time. He had now reached the stage at which his body was crying out for a cigarette, while remaining terrified of alcohol. But he knew from experience that a glass of cold fizzy beer taken now would greatly accelerate his recovery, while a cigarette could be fatal. With difficulty he fought down the urge to try it anyway, and concentrated on his surroundings.

The place was not modern. It was easy to romanticise here, to imagine his father, uncomfortably dressed in the drab, heavy clothes of the '30s, sitting awkwardly over coffee with his enigmatic Uncle Wolf. After the shocking display of uncertainty he had given the previous night, the idea of a nineteen- year-old Herbert Christie had acquired a new plausibility. Mickey had often heard that children matured more quickly these days. At nineteen his father had been virtually an adolescent, a gangling, innocent minor, two years away from the vote. Mickey found it hard enough to recall his own experience of that phase. Perhaps it was not yet far enough away to be distinct in his memory, long ago as it seemed.

Feeling much better now, and tucking thoughtfully into his second plate of stew, he found himself catching easily again that peculiar sense of the school year's end, the gentle imminence of change. The recognition of his father as a fellow man was a last rite of passage to the plateau of adult life. It could happen late, and without warning or ceremony, and it was happening now.

He became aware of a presence loitering at his side, and looked up, quickly debating whether he should order another glass of beer, but it was not the waiter. It was a woman, about his mother's age, wearing a plain summer dress and carrying a canvas shopping-bag. She must have been staring at him, because she blushed and backed away when he caught her eye. Rising clumsily, he started to babble the automatic apology of the Englishman caught unawares, and cursed himself for a caricature of his race. The woman looked at him steadily.

"You're English?" she said.

"Yes . . ." Helplessly, he glanced around the café, in search of distraction. It was nearly full. "Did you want to sit here? Please . . . I don't mind."

"Why, thank you. It is getting a little crowded."

She sat down opposite him, and ventured a gentle smile as the blush began to fade. Mickey smiled back, and looked around again for the waiter. He had caught a strong hint of the United States in the woman's voice, and he had no desire for company, particularly that of a tourist—a fellow tourist. It was time to go.

"I'm so sorry to have disturbed you in the middle of your lunch," she said.

"Not at all. I was just going."

"Oh, but you'll stay for some coffee? The melange is particularly good here."

In the act of signalling to the waiter, Mickey froze. The diversity of Viennese coffee was a mystery to him. Perhaps this was something more interesting than a tourist.

"Is that what you're going to have? Well, all right. Ah . . . Perhaps you'd like to order?"

She did so, fluently in German, addressing the waiter as 'Heinrich'. She said something else as well, in which the only word Mickey recognised was '*Engländer*'.

"You're well known here," he said.

"Oh yes, I come here most days."

"So you live in Vienna?"

"Yes, I've lived here for nearly ten years now. I grew up here, of course. That's a long time ago," she added, smiling more openly than before. "I'm Sophie Miller."

Mickey took her hand, familiar with the curiously abrupt American style of self-introduction.

"How do you do. Mickey Christie."

The hand tightened for a moment around his, and the blush flooded back into her face. Mickey raised his guard. The face was friendly and reasonable, full of intelligence and the balanced wisdom of age. She didn't look mad, but you could never really tell.

"I'm afraid you caught me staring at you just now," she said.

"Oh, ah . . . "

"It was very rude of me, I know, I'm sorry. But now that I know your name, I really have to ask you something. Did you . . . Do you, by any chance, have a relative called Herbert? Herbert Christie?"

"What? He's my father!"

"Your father? Oh Lord . . ."

She was visibly excited now, and Mickey felt it catching. He hoped she was not going to burst into tears.

"How do you know my father?" he said.

"Oh my! I'm not even sure he'd remember me, it's so long ago. But your face . . . You're very much alike, you know."

"Yes, I know."

"That's why I was staring at you like that. I just couldn't believe it. But your father! That's incredible."

"Quite a coincidence, certainly."

"We met here, in Vienna. He came to stay with his uncle here, oh, I don't know when . . . "

"1934?"

"Why yes, it must have been. When all the trouble began. So you know about Wolf? Yes, that's when it was. We didn't know one another for very long, I but I've never forgotten him. He didn't write, after he left. We were very young, of course. People change quickly at that age. But do tell me what happened to him. I would like to know."

"Gosh. Well, he joined the army, and had rather an illustrious career. Victoria Cross, knighthood. Married my mother in 1945, I was born in '56. Only child, like him. He's really quite famous, in England." The coffee arrived, and Mickey stopped to think while Sophie exchanged some more words with Heinrich. Should he tell her that his father was here, in Vienna? Perhaps he should just take her address, and let him make up his own mind. An old acquaintance, even, in the language of their generation, an old flame, might not be a welcome surprise.

"Please go on, Mickey," she said. "Tell me more, tell me everything. I want to know everything."

He paused to collect his thoughts, and started again, disarmed by the naivety, the girlishness of her, and summarised his father's career. He had never had such a good audience. She was fascinated, amazed that the young man she had known had become a professional soldier, was moved and stirred by the glories of his life. She nodded, and gasped, and looked steadily into his eyes while he gave his account, smiling encouragement whenever his knowledge became uncertain. He quickly began to feel uncomfortable under that look, so full of pride and love he had not earned, drawn only by the shape of his face. When he finally stalled at the years of retirement, he was no nearer to solving his dilemma, though conscious that one alternative had honesty on its side.

"And what happened to you?" he said. "I mean, after you knew my father."

She sipped her coffee, and looked down at the table, sadly, for a moment.

"Oh, I stayed here, through the Anschluss, and the war. I met my husband when he was stationed here in 1946, and we moved back to West Virginia."

"Ah."

"Then . . . Well, he died, and I stayed on for a while, but I decided to come back. It's still my home."

"And is it very different now?"

"Different? Mickey, you should have seen Vienna after the war. It was a bad time, for all of us. I was glad to get away. A lot of girls were. But I never forgot Herbert. He was so young, and so serious-looking — just like you. He loved Vienna, you know."

"Oh, I know. I'm getting quite fond of it myself."

"Strange, that he should have been back here, in the occupation. Oh well, it wouldn't have been the same." Still solemn, she glanced quickly around at the old café, then looked at her watch. "Heavens, Mickey, I must go. I'm very late. But I wouldn't have missed this for the world."

She got up from her seat, and Mickey rose with her, his heart thumping. Whatever the merits of his decision, he couldn't let her go like this, so soon and probably for good. She must know so much that he needed to hear. She had taken, and given nothing back.

"Look, Sophie . . . I don't know why I didn't tell you this before . . . I'm here with my parents, and my wife. My father's here, in Vienna. We ought to arrange something."

"Oh my gosh, Mickey, I don't know. Do you think your father would want to see me?"

"Heavens, I've no idea. Yes, of course, I'm sure he would. I mean of course, why on earth not?"

She looked away from him, and chewed her lip, clearly afraid, and torn. *Go on,* thought Mickey. *It's their problem.*

"Look," he said, "Why don't you give me your address, phone number and so forth . . . "

"I don't know, Mickey . . . Well, all right. I'll give you a card . . . "

"I know! I won't tell my father I've met you. You call the hotel, and surprise him. I've got a leaflet here somewhere . . . All right?"

"Yes, all right."

"Promise?" She looked at him squarely again, and smiled, the same soft smile of recollection.

"Yes, Mickey. I promise. Your mother . . . "

"She'll be delighted to meet you."

"Really? Curious, anyway. Me too. OK. I really do have to go now. Thank you, Mickey. Goodbye."

"Goodbye for now."

He watched her as she made her way, clumsily, still shaken, to the door, and waved when she turned to look at him, as he had hoped she would. Only now did he notice how short she was, and how much older her body seemed than her lively face. He sat down again, and gestured for the bill. He felt cheerful, almost excited. The week was turning out to be a good deal more entertaining than he had dared to expect. He was actually glad that he had come. Rising again, this time to leave the café, he stopped short, alarmed by the glimpse of a familiar face he could not identify. Then it came. The dark, pudgy man who sat reading by the door was the solitary tourist from the previous night, the one who had followed them from the hotel. He was even wearing the same tie. Filled with unaccustomed good will, Mickey squeezed between the backs of half a dozen chairs to reach the table, and slowly bent forward.

"Excuse me," he said. "I believe we're staying at the same hotel."

The man looked up, without interest or warmth, from his newspaper.

"I do not stay at a hotel," he said. "I live in the 4th District."

Mickey stood up straight again, and removed his friendly smile.

"I'm sorry. Surely, though, you were in the bar last night . . . I didn't notice what it was called . . . You know, the new place, across the road from the hotel."

"Last night I was at home with my wife. Do you want to know what we did?"

"Good Lord, no. I'm sorry, I seem to have made a mistake."

"I think so." He returned to his paper, and Mickey walked out into the street, feeling decidedly put out. Nobody had been that rude to him since he had left the office, four days earlier, and his defences were down. Of course, he had frequently been just as offensive to presumptuous tourists in London, but this was different. He had been perfectly polite, he had acted in good faith, and anyway, he was sure he had not made a mistake. He doubled back a few steps, and peered in through the window. The man was still there, paying his bill. There was no doubt about it. It was the same man.

Mickey turned, and started walking again. He had better things to do than worry about a rude man in a café. Sophie Miller was going to occupy his thoughts for as long as it took him to find his hotel. Sophie Miller, and his father . . . The scope for speculation was staggering. He took her card out of his pocket, and read it through, over and over. Even if she didn't call, he could always find her. He could come back to Vienna, if necessary, to hear her story and find out exactly what part she had played in his father's life. Now that he was out in the sunshine once more, his conversation with her was a full and vivid dream, remembered in astonishment after a few seconds of feverish sleep. It had been over so quickly, and he had never regained his balance, he had wasted the time, and not thought about what he was saying. *"He loved Vienna, you know." "Oh, I know. . ."*

How did he know? His father loved Vienna, not as the tourists loved it, but as a man who is bound to a living thing that has held and inspired and hurt him for most of his life. Now Mickey, too, was feeling the grip of it, an inescapable inheritance, a family obsession, feeding on itself from one generation to the next. The gothic conceit made him laugh aloud, when he looked about him at the pretty, light-hearted town. He was starting to feel at home. And Sophie hadn't even asked him what he was doing here.

Elspeth was waiting for him in the lounge when he got back to the hotel. She was sitting on her own with a long drink, rather noticeably dressed up in black silk. He wondered what she would look like in a Palmer bathing suit, and realised he must have passed a few more of those posters on his way back.

"What's this?" he said. "Got a date with that nice Mr Gruber?" She grinned, and kissed him on the mouth as he bent towards her.

"Well, he's pretty cute. But you're taking me out tonight. He was busy."

"But darling, the museums are closed now."

"Funny guy."

"That's me. Where's Dad?"

"Upstairs with your mother. They're going out together, some place else. Don't you want to know where we're going?"

"Yes of course." He sat down, and waved at a passing waiter to order two more drinks. Elspeth opened her bag, and handed him two small pieces of paper.

"We're going to the opera," she said. "I got two returns from this place in the subway. Tell me I'm a clever girl."

"You're a clever girl. What is it—not Wagner?"

"Mozart. The Magic Flute. Good, huh?"

"Terrific," he agreed. "Have I got time for a bath?"

"Oh, sure. I just couldn't wait to dress up. Mickey we had a really great afternoon. Berni took us to this place near the cathedral for lunch, and it was really good . . ."

"Berni?"

"I told you—he's cute. Then we went around the cathedral, which was just amazing, and then we went into the subway where they have this really big shopping mall with cafés and everything. It's a really good idea, you know, because all that stuff would just look trashy up on the street. They really know how to do things right here."

Mickey nodded.

"It's quite a town," he said.

"And you know what? That letter your father found this morning could be really important. It's full of stuff about people who were spying for Stalin here in 1934!"

"Good Lord. But they'll all be dead by now, surely? I know Dad's still with us, but he was only, what, twenty then. I suppose there's a chance . . ."

"Right. We have to keep quiet until he checks it out."

"Fine by me."

"So what have you been doing all day?"

Mickey hesitated. Much as he wanted to match his wife's breathless enthusiasm, he just didn't know how. It was a convention in their relationship. She was the one who gushed, he was the one who was always unimpressed. It was a good game, and a daily vehicle for their affection, but now he wished they could swap. There was nothing for it, though. He sat back and reached lazily for the drink at his side.

"Well, something pretty amazing happened to me," he said. "I met a woman who knew Dad, back in 1934. They haven't seen each other since."

"Oh, wow!"

"Yes. I was just sitting in this café, and she spotted the family resemblance. Quite extraordinary. I'm not going to tell him. She's going to telephone here, and surprise him."

"Mickey, that's wonderful! What was she like?"

"Oh, just a charming old lady, rather shy. Rather American, as well. She married a G.I. after the war. I hope to God he remembers her."

"Well look, if she remembers him, just like that, then . . ."

"Yes. I expect it'll be all right. How was he, this afternoon?"

"Fine. A little tired, maybe." She stopped short, and smiled past him, towards the lifts. He deduced that his parents were about to join them, and turned around in his chair, to see his father strolling across the lounge, alone, and still clutching the brown envelope containing his last letter from Wolf. He didn't look fine. He looked pale, and older—much older, of course, than Mickey had been remembering and imagining him all afternoon. He touched his son gently on the shoulder, a vestigial gesture that said 'don't get up', smiled at Elspeth, and flopped into the chair beside them.

"Hello, Mickey. Where have you been?"

"Just wandering around, working off the hangover. It was a pretty heavy evening." His father nodded wearily.

"You can say that again. I feel pretty washed out myself."

"Funny thing happened, though," said Mickey. "I saw that bloke, you remember? The one who followed us to that bar across the road here."

"Oh yes?"

"I went over to say hello, and he isn't a tourist at all. He lives here, apparently. He tried to tell me I'd made a mistake, too, but I know I hadn't. He was really quite rude about it."

"Perhaps he's a secret drinker, didn't like being found out."

"Yes, perhaps."

"Well, we've had an exciting time. Elspeth tell you about this?" He waved the envelope, and put it down on the table. Mickey nodded. "All under wraps for the moment. Extraordinary business, though." He tipped his head back to rest in the armchair, and stared at the ceiling in silence. Mickey exchanged a glance with his wife, then said;

"I thought it seemed to hit you pretty hard, at the time. You looked scared out of your wits."

"Did I really? Funny. I hadn't even read it then, not that part. I must have been thinking about something else."

"Like what?"

"Oh, you know. Just remembering. Damned funny feeling." He sighed, and his eyes dropped a little, towards the chandelier hanging above the reception desk.

"Go on," said Mickey.

"Well . . . I was expecting a surprise of some sort, of course. But when I opened that envelope, that letter from Wolf, well, I got something I hadn't bargained for. The most peculiar thing. It must have been the smell, I think."

"The smell? What smell?"

"I don't know, quite. But I do know that smells are the only completely accurate memories we have. Everything else is mostly inference. Doctor told me that, last time I went in for the annual once-over. Smells. My God. It really hit me. You wouldn't think a letter that old would smell of anything, and it didn't, not that I noticed. But somehow, it took me right back. And I got the strangest sensation. I felt as if I was actually back there, or at least that I could be, as long as I kept my eyes on that letter, and forgot about Gruber's office, and you, and everything. It was a chance to go back. If only I could concentrate, and forget, and believe, I would look up and be back there, starting all over again. If only I could believe . . . "

"Dad, that's ridiculous."

"Is it?" He sat up suddenly, shaking himself out of the mood, and forced a smile. "Quite right. Snap out of it, Christie. It doesn't work like that, not in this world. No second chances."

"Who wants one?" said Mickey. "If I'd been through everything you have, I'd be glad it's over."

"Ha. That's a point. I see you believe in destiny. Yes?"

Mickey thought about it.

"I don't know," he said.

"Well, I suppose I do. But one has to believe in free will, as well. You see the contradiction? I'd like to meet someone who could solve that riddle. Wolf did his best, of course, and I think I was convinced at the time, but it soon wore off."

"Wolf?"

"Oh yes. Quite the theologian, was Wolf, a philosopher as well as a spy. You can see how he'd be able to take a simple paradox like that in his stride. Destiny and free will, the dual nature of Christ, the Atonement. He had it all worked out. In theory, that is."

"I had no idea," said Mickey.

"Oh, I haven't thought about all that for years. And it used to worry me so much. But then, somewhere along the way, I stopped trying to work it all out for myself, and just held on to my faith as best I could. I realised it was all pretty daft, in the end."

He reached forward, and picked up the envelope, and Mickey watched his father's face as he stared into its depths. So serious-looking . . . Would Sophie recognise this man as easily as she had seen him in his son? Yes, he knew she would, and he knew, as well, that he could see himself just as clearly in his father's face, now, and at the other end of his life. Perhaps that was a destiny in which he had always believed.

"Daft?" he said. "You mean your faith?"

"No, no. You see, at the end of the letter, Wolf said 'Don't drive yourself mad, remember the futility of inquiry . . . ' You see? ' . . . God is the answer, and this is why He has created nothing but questions'. Nicely put. If there are questions, there must be an answer. Doesn't matter what it is, as long as you know it's there."

"That's one way of looking at it," said Mickey. His father looked at him, hard, for a moment, then returned to the packet in his hand.

"It's the best way," he said. "It's the only way that makes sense, in the end. Anyway." He held the envelope out to Elspeth. She looked at it, and then at him, mutely out of her depth. "Go on, Elspeth, take it. Not for public consumption until further notice, but there's no reason why you shouldn't look at it in your own time. Give you something to chew on."

She took it slowly, and thanked him, and he sat back in his chair again, suddenly chirpy and self-satisfied. It's not real, thought Mickey, it's an act. But what lay behind it?

"Ah, here comes your mother. Not before time. I'm afraid we'll have to be going, or we'll miss our table. Probably won't see you later. I need an early night. Well, have fun, won't you?"

"You too." Mickey got up to greet his mother, then stood and waved as they hurried out of the door, and into a taxi. Then they were gone. Elspeth stood behind him, and wrapped her arms round his waist.

"You're worried, aren't you?" she said.

"Yes. There's something wrong about this. It's eating him alive."

"You too."

"Yeah . . . " He turned round and hugged her, but his thoughts were still elsewhere, and she knew it. After a moment she pulled away, and gave him a sad smile. Embarrassed, he bent down and picked up the opera tickets from the table.

"The Volksoper," he said. "Do you know how to get there?"

"We could always get a cab."

"Yes, of course."

"But we can get on a tram just across the street, and it'll take us right to the door. More fun."

"Right. I'd better go and have my bath. You coming up?"

"No, I'm going to stay here and have another drink. You'd better hurry if you don't want your wife to get smashed."

"Right."

"Mickey?"

"Yes?"

"I love you."

"Oh hell, Pet, I know that. I'm sorry. A bath will cheer me up. I'll be all yours again when I come back. I promise."

"Can you take the letter with you? It won't fit in my purse.

"Sure."

He caught the lift by running for it, and leaned against the wall as it went up, sighing miserably. His father was upset, so he was upset, so now Elspeth was hurt as well. That was love, but it still made him feel mean. One of them was going to have to be stronger than this. His father had his hands full. That, if not the reason, was clear enough. Even now he was faking the party spirit for the benefit of his wife, protecting her, shutting her out, and

Mickey had just promised to do the same. For the first time he realised how his mother's character must have been limited by that principle, that men must keep from their wives the things that torment them, for fear of corrupting the innocence in which they find release. It was an old-fashioned idea, stupid and insulting, and he longed to defy it. But how could he explain to Elspeth what was going on, when he didn't know himself? The frustration of it hurt him, to be bound by rules not of his making, laid down by the dead in that other world, before his birth. He could tell her all about it later, perhaps, but for now he could only perpetuate the destructive secrecy that had made his father so difficult to know all these years. It seemed it was his turn to be strong.

13

SOPHIE KNEW SHE COULDN'T WALK MUCH MORE. SHE DESPISED HERSELF for showing the symptoms of old age, the weakness in the knees, the imminence of tears, but she would have to give in, and soon. Her apartment was ten minutes away, but the Bar Nimitz was just across the street. She had been to the bar too many times, but her apartment, so large, so convenient and so well appointed, held the menace of the call she dreaded, perhaps even a visit from her brother or some leering stooge. She turned into the doorway of the Nimitz, this flashy nonsense of a place, named for an American admiral whom nobody here remembered, geared for the market of visitors with more money than taste. She had carefully eavesdropped on the cocktail chatter of embassy staff, and then got quietly, decorously drunk here a hundred times, and made it the couple of hundred yards home in a cab called by the help. They listened to her stories, but didn't believe them. Who cared, as long as she paid her tab? They were nice. And the most important thing, for her, was that she could be an American here, her husband's widow, her German unusually good, but otherwise a harmless crazy Yank lady who always tipped well.

As usual, she hoisted herself onto the bar-stool designed for the young and tall, and ordered a schnapps.

"Good evening, Frau Miller. And how are you this evening?"

"Not so good, Jurgen. Are you busy?"

"Not too busy for you, Frau Miller. Is there something troubling you, gentle lady?" Sophie smiled involuntarily at the courteous form of address, so natural in the German of her youth, so quaint in English.

"There is, Jurgen. My brother . . . "

"Ah! Your brother the spy?"

"That's the one."

Jurgen. He was maybe forty, Viennese born and bred. He'd been around, he'd learnt not to believe everything—or anything—he heard across the bar. But he'd also learnt how to listen, and his blanket scepticism made him safe. What a way to live, when a man who believes nothing you say is the only man you can trust.

"So what has he done now?" Sophie took a long, un-lady-like gulp of her drink, and waved a finger as she swallowed, ordering another.

"He called me today. He does that, you know? He pays for my place, he pays for everything, he can call and ask . . . " Jurgen nodded, slowly, pouting sympathy, as he poured the second glass.

"And so?"

"So he says, 'Are you lunching at your café today, Sophie?' You know, I normally go there around One. And he says, 'Go there now. There's a young Englishman there, my man has followed him. You'll have no problem finding him. Introduce yourself and find out whatever you can.' "

"And did you?"

"Sure I did. I had to. But . . . "

"Another, Frau Miller?"

"If that's OK."

"Of course, of course. And so?"

"So . . . The bastard, he didn't tell me."

"Strong words, Frau Miller."

"You don't know my brother. The bastard, bastard, didn't tell me, that this young man was the son of someone I had . . . known, a long time ago. Someone I cared about."

"Ah, ja?"

"Yes. And this man, not the man I saw today, his father . . . "

"The one you had cared about?"

"Ja, yes, his father is now a general in the British army, well, retired now, but really important, in some way, to my brother . . . " Jurgen flapped a hand at her, to postpone her monologue while he served another customer. She was trembling now, and her heart sank as she caught sight of herself in the mirrored wall behind the bar, a sad old lady clinging to the attention of a barman who believed nothing except his tip, a conversational whore, listening patiently to the rambling of a lunatic. He returned and smiled, and she said; "You don't believe any of this, do you, Jurgen?" He shrugged, and opened his eyes to the width of innocence.

"But, Frau Miller, why should I not believe you?"

"I guess you worked out a long time ago that I was born here. I'm not really American at all. Except by marriage."

"Frau Miller, my mother was a novice nun, raped by a Russian soldier. What do I care?"

She gasped, and drained her glass, and said; "Jurgen, that's the first time you've told me anything about yourself. I guess I never asked. I'm sorry." He smiled gently, and shrugged again with a spreading of the hands, and she said: "But is it true?"

He held the pose, and she realised it was the one she had seen many times before, and meant the same as always. Enough. Go home.

"Call me a cab, Jurgen?" He relaxed, and signalled to another barman.

"Of course, Frau Miller. Some coffee while you are waiting?"

Miserably Sophie let her eyes drift out of focus over her empty glass, and felt the tears begin to well. No, she couldn't bear it, the thought of poor gentle, frightened Herbert, after all this time. A general . . . Could he have changed so much? In any case, she decided, she would keep her promise to Mickey, and keep it better than he could know. She would call Herbert, and warn him, tell him everything, and be free. She gulped her coffee, and slid from her stool, gathering her bag from its hook.

"I'm not going to take it any more, Jurgen. I don't care about the money. I'm going to turn him in. I know I say that every time, but this is different."

"I'm sure you will one day, Frau Miller."

"No, not one day. Tomorrow. I'm going to do it tomorrow."

14

"It's only ten o'clock," said Frances, dropping her bag on the bed and yawning wide across the room. "We must be getting old."

Herbert sat down and failed to smile tolerantly at the truism. They had spent most of the evening reminiscing about the childhood and adolescence of their son. To be tired before midnight was only a petty symptom of advancing age. He watched his wife, and wondered if it had always taken her this long to prepare for sleep. Probably not.

"It's the journey," he said. "We still haven't caught up."

Frances emerged from behind the wardrobe door, only half undressed, and sat down at the dressing table.

"You didn't give yourself the chance," she said, "Painting the town red. Silly boy. Mickey looked dreadful this morning. He's not as strong as you are, you know."

"That's probably not true any more." She was silent for a moment, while the cold cream went on. He lay back, and waited.

"I've never been able to understand why men have to get drunk," she said. "It's so silly. You can't enjoy anything properly in that state."

"I don't do it very often."

"Not now, no. But before you retired you did. All those dinners."

"Oh, that was different. It's probably very necessary, you know. It lets off the steam, releases the tension every so often. Call it the male period."

"Herbert, don't be crude." He closed his eyes and said nothing. They had had this conversation many times. "I think this evening was much nicer. Just a quiet dinner and a glass or two of wine. That's all you need. It was nice, wasn't it?"

"Oh yes, it was very pleasant."

"Well, then." He waited, but she said nothing more. Apparently she had won the argument. He felt himself drifting into sleep, and got up quickly to change into his pyjamas. Frances was now wearing her night-dress, and was settling herself in bed with a magazine. She started to read, then looked up at him suddenly.

"Did you talk to Gruber about those books?" she said.

"Well, yes. How do you mean?"

"Are you going to be able to take them back, when we leave? I'd like to read them."

"They're all in German, my love."

"We can have them translated, can't we? You must know someone."

"Oh yes, I'm sure. I don't know. I'll have to talk to him again. The letter's the main thing, for the moment."

"That can't be important after all these years. But the memoirs must be fascinating. Just think! Herr Weiss said they'd be a national archive."

"Yes . . . " Herbert froze for a second, suddenly alert. Weiss had actually said that this might be the resurrection of a national archive. Resurrection, *Auferstehung*—Anastasia. It was the same word. Surely it must have been a coincidence? It just couldn't be . . .

"They can't stop you taking everything home, can they?" said Frances.

"I don't think so, eventually at least."

"Why eventually? It belongs to you doesn't it? Well then. What can they do?"

"I don't know, Fran. I'm not a lawyer, am I?"

"There's no need to snap."

He got into bed beside her, and lay still on his back, waiting for her to turn out the light. If Weiss had used that word deliberately, then what did it mean? What was his interest? The word could have been a signal, or an experiment, or nothing at all. There was no way of knowing. But if it did have an intended significance, and if the man who had followed them to the bar had also followed Mickey all over town the next day, and if the burglary at the Sturmer building should turn out not to be coincidental, well, then there was something to worry about. It began to seem possible, even likely, that Herbert and his family had become the objects of unwelcome attention from this Weiss. But it was also possible that Weiss was playing a game of his own, or that Weiss and the burglars were on different sides — or that Herbert's imagination was getting the better of him. But if he was right, then the interest being taken in him and his inheritance must, for safety's sake, be regarded as hostile pending evidence to the contrary. That meant that the only sensible thing to do was to go back to London at once. They would do best to travel separately, the two women together, as lady and companion, Mickey and himself independently, at different times. They would leave most of their luggage behind, and leave the bill unpaid. With luck they would be over the border before anyone noticed they were gone. As for the letter, he could post it, before he left, to a family in Italy, with instructions to send it on to London. With a sudden twinge of panic, and shame at his faltering memory, he realised he could not remember where he had put his revolver. An idea came that he had hidden it by cutting a hollow space in the pages of a book. But that was ridiculous, because the Webley was far too big for that.

He awoke to darkness, aware that his wife had just spoken, with his left hand fumbling around under the bed.

"You were talking in your sleep," she said. "Something about furniture."

"I was dreaming."

"Thought so."

He relaxed, and laughed at himself for dreaming such nonsense. Then he remembered, with a sudden chill, that the dream had begun in reality, and that while he slept a buried memory had crept back into being and now stood over him, an urgent presence.

He had probably never used her surname, except to address her father. She had only been—it still hurt him even to think the name—Sophie, a little bundle of smiles and giggles and innocent hope and romance bound up in an eighteen-year-old Viennese girl. In truth he had hardly known her, but still he had loved her, as far and as much as a daft, lost English boy could. And so her elder brother Joachim, that big blond oaf with the loathing in his eyes, must have been Joachim Becker, *young Becker*, Wolf's protégé and betrayer. But there was more. For he knew, now, he was sure he knew, that he had seen Sophie's brother again that morning, that Joachim had somehow escaped the magpie's knife, whatever that meant, was here and face to face with him again, and calling himself Weiss.

So Wolf's letter was not ancient history after all, and the burglary at the Sturmer building, and Weiss's, Joachim's presence there today were not accidents. The thing was alive. Could Sophie be alive as well, and still in Vienna? He didn't know what to hope.

Herbert turned, and looked at the digital bedside clock glowing in the dark. It was nearly four in the morning. It would keep until breakfast. Another four hours wouldn't hurt, not after fifty years.

"Fran? Are you awake?"

"Yes. What is it?"

"I'm afraid there's a chance we might have to leave early. I've just been thinking about it."

"What do you want to leave early for? I thought you liked it here."

"You're half asleep, my dear. We might have to go, because of that letter." There was a long pause, then she said;

"Oh."

"You are asleep, aren't you?"

"Yes."

He turned away from her, howling inwardly at the thought of going away again so soon. During the journey there he had even fantasised about finding ways to stay behind at the end of the week. Twice before he had been driven away by circumstance, forced out by fighting and intrigue, ordered back to Berlin. There was so much that he wanted to do here, things the others would not understand. He wanted to pace the streets, and enjoy the scale and the air of the place, to sit still in the gardens for hours at a time, to read the papers in a coffee house, and know that he could stay there all day if the fancy took him. Most of all he wanted to leave only in his own time. He had had enough of being told where to go and what to do. He would stay this time, no matter what they said at the embassy. He had earned that much.

The city was at peace now, and he wanted so much to be part of it. That he had revived the unhappiness of the past, just by coming back, was a hard thought to bear. Of course Wolf had started it, by vaingloriously making a time capsule of his memoirs, and by dying before he could deliver that letter. Mickey said he looked scared when he opened it. Well, and why not? To be brought face to face with himself across fifty years, to see again his own youth and naivety, so clearly but so far away—that would be enough to scare anyone. But as though that were not enough, it had to happen in Vienna, where, long ago, he had somehow glimpsed a clarity in his life that had eluded him before and since. Wolf and Sophie had shown him the sense and the order of it, and he had managed to hold it steady for a day or two, until the sense and order all around him had been destroyed. At that moment he had been thrown headlong into a career in which there was only darkness and blind faith. He had never recovered the balance of that little time in Vienna. He had never been still.

Now Herbert knew that he must finish the business Wolf had begun, and feel the satisfaction of rest. He must lay the ghost—except that he had never thought of the old man that way, never talked to him again in a dream, or caught the whiff of his tobacco in an empty drawing room. He had never been prone to superstitious fancy. He sensed rather that the living made a mark in the course of time that was not erased, but that even the longest life became a story that was over before it was fully told, leaving nothing but its footnotes to a thousand others. There were no ghosts.

15

HERBERT REMEMBERED THE SILENT DREAMS OF EARLIEST CHILDHOOD, the friendly gloom and peace of an old house in the English countryside. It was a time when every sound had stood alone in emptiness; nailed shoes on polished boards, the creak of panelling in the night, the rattle of his pram on the gravel outside, and the rooks' complaint above. During the day the voices of women echoed in the tall rooms where he crawled and played, the only child, the only man. The life had seemed endless, there was so much stillness in it.

Now he leaned out of the carriage-door window with his face to the smoke, aching for sleep but eager for excitement, mesmerised by the platform oozing toward and underneath him while the station hardened into focus all around. His calves and feet were numb from the cold, and the fog chilled the prickly sweat on his back. A pretty girl on the platform smiled at him, and he thought the train would stop just as they were level. The blush brought pain into his face. Then, as the engine crawled through the last few yards of its journey, he tugged at his suitcase and staggered to the ground with his left hand guarding his hat. He was nineteen years old.

There was only one old man, standing alone among the people hurrying in and out of the station's drifting murk, and looking perfectly the part of someone's family sage. Short and red-faced, he wore two overcoats—one buttoned up, the other open at the chest—a bowler hat, and many grey scarves plaited loosely around his neck. Herbert swung the suitcase, and bent the effort of his senseless legs to matching its rhythm. Soon he could make out the regular pulse of steam from the old man's lips, the thickness of his spectacles, the density of fine lines on his face. Herbert's heart was racing. It had been a long, sleepless haul from London, a fidgety day and night of fear and daydreams.

"Herr Winkler? Uncle Wolf?"

The old head twitched round in its cocoon, and smiled.

"Herr Christie, I presume? Herbert, welcome to Vienna."

"Thank you. Thank you, Uncle. How do you do?"

"Yes, yes, delighted to meet you, Herbert, I'm sure, and you must tell me all the news of your family, but later. Let's get home, out of this cold. Come along, the car is waiting."

Marching to keep up as Wolf led the way through the station, Herbert wrestled from his coat pocket the bottle of scotch he had brought as a present. Somehow he felt he must be abreast of his uncle before he could offer it, not stop him as though playing for time to catch up with his great handicap of a suitcase. But Wolf turned and said;

"You seem to be struggling, Herbert. I suppose that case is full of books, young philosopher that you are. Or so your father tells me you are. So did you come all this way to read books?"

"I did bring some books, but only to read on the journey. Of course I came here to talk to you, Uncle."

"Oh, well I hope it's worth it."

"But actually I didn't read anything on the boat except the paper. There's quite a lot about Austria in the *Times*, because of the Austrian Exhibition in London."

"Yes? Have you still got it?"

"Oh, gosh, no, I left it on the train. Sorry, Uncle."

"Don't call me Uncle all the time, Herbert, it makes me feel so old. Call me Wolf, everyone does."

"Oh, right-o, thank you . . ."

"And what have you got there?"

Beaten, Herbert stopped, panting, and put down the case.

"It's for you, Uncle, Wolf. I got it in London. I hope you like whisky?"

Wolf unwrapped the bottle and held it in both hands, beaming.

"Herbert, thank you. I'm glad you didn't leave this on the train. Are you ready to walk again?"

"Perhaps, if there's a porter . . ."

"Porter? For a strong young man like you, with one suitcase? Ah, the pampered Englishman! Come along, we're nearly there. Look, there's the car."

Herbert looked up, to the station's open forecourt. There was a Rolls Royce standing there, gleaming and new, with a uniformed chauffeur in the front. This was a shock. He had been warned not to expect even the modest opulence of home, that his relative, like the rest of Austria, had been through harder times than the Christies had ever known. But his father's Austin was ten years old, and never looked clean. Without thinking he said;

"But it's a Phantom!"

"So I believe. Well don't just stand there, Herbert. I'm an old man and I'm freezing to death."

The chauffeur turned lazily in his seat as they approached, and grinned. Why didn't he leap out to take the case and open the door? Could Wolf be so eccentric, or the customs of a foreign country so different? Puzzled, Herbert hesitated for a moment, then let himself into the back of the car, pushing the case ahead of him, while Wolf pushed him from behind. The car started at once.

"It's a long time," said Wolf. He sat facing ahead, with his eyes closed.

"What's a long time, Wolf?"

"Ah . . . A long time since I saw your father. Before the war, of course. Twenty- two, twenty-three years. I went to his wedding."

"Oh, really?"

"It was the only time I've seen your mother. A beautiful English lady."

"It's kind of you to say so. I must remember to tell her, when I write." Herbert felt himself settling into the deep-buttoned leather as though it were a bed, and breathed in the stirring smell of it, mixed with the hint of petrol vapour and hot oil, that was almost as good as warmth itself. Through the clean window at his side he could see the western districts of Vienna opening their streets to him as he passed, and here and there a patch of sunlight brushing on hoary stone.

"I shouldn't bother. I don't think she liked me very much. I must have seemed very strange to her. I think I drank too much. A funny old Austrian man, drunk at her wedding. And your father, so splendid in his uniform—he had just been made a captain then, I think—and all his friends, from his regiment, with their swords shining in the sun outside the church. My wife had just died. Your aunt, Herbert. I was there for her."

Herbert said nothing, but looked at Wolf's profile in the patchy light of the car, and away to the window, and back, and away. After two minutes or more he gently cleared his throat. Abruptly Wolf spoke again, his face still calm, as in sleep.

"Yes, she was too young. But what you said just now, it amused me. You said 'What's a long time, Wolf?', and you see I took it the other way, I thought, ah, the boy is so young, he doesn't know what a long time is. So I shall tell you. Are you ready? A long time, Herbert, is the distance between the time in which you live, and a time in which you have lived, and each can be as long as you like, and divided from the other by a moment. There, how's that?"

"I think it's quite poetic," said Herbert. Wolf laughed suddenly, and opened his eyes.

"Poetry or philosophy, Herbert, it's not bad for three minutes' work. Why, what would you say?"

Herbert looked out of the window again. They had been driving along a broad avenue of shops and cafés, and had turned left, into a network of narrow streets where bourgeois houses rose straight from the pavement, naked, to his eye, without the familiar area railings in between.

"It's the time it takes to get from one place to another," he said.

"Ha. Children's poetry." Wolf closed his eyes again, and Herbert blushed unhappily. He knew that he too easily slipped into the hot shame of the schoolboy—a cause of shame in itself—and fought against it. But he had been told many times how quickly he became tiresome when he talked. Much better to shut up, to cause no fuss, invite no derision. He had come here to learn—what? An old man's wisdom? Or just to listen? Or not to think? Maybe to be happy, among strangers. Wolf said;

"So you like the car?"

"The car? Oh yes, Wolf, very much. I've never driven in a Phantom before. It's beautiful."

"Good. Unfortunately it does not belong to me. But I have a great many friends. I'm lucky that way. Very useful for a poor man, Herbert, an old poor man like me. I don't know what you'll think of my apartments. I'm afraid you'll find them filthy and damp and full of rubbish . . . "

"Oh I'm sure I shan't . . . "

"But it was a fine building once, before the war. It belonged to your aunt, actually, she had property over here before we were married. But then, you know, the war. I have managed to keep two floors to myself until now by being my own caretaker, but the rent I get is not much, and never on time. Everybody thinks I must be a rich man, to live in two apartments, but it is not so. I have nowhere else for my books, and my books are my life, here and hereafter. I cannot sell my own eternity. Next year, perhaps, I must let the upstairs, bring the books down, and move myself into the street to make room. I have made up your bed upstairs, above the stove. It should be warm enough."

"Please don't worry, Wolf. I'll be fine."

"I hope so. Anyway, here we are. Don't forget your case."

Herbert stumbled into the street, and crouched as the wind cut through his coat. Wolf already had his key in the door, and turned to shout a few words at the chauffeur, who laughed back. Straightening, and preparing to lift the case once more, Herbert said;

"Thank you for coming to meet me, Wolf. I wouldn't have liked to walk all this way."

"We do have trams and buses in Vienna. Anyway, Käsemann is the one you should thank."

Herbert turned back to the car, and waved at the driver's window.

"Dankeschön, Herr Käsemann!" The chauffeur put the Rolls into gear, and drove away, laughing.

"Come along, Herbert, you're letting all the cold into the house. There. This way."

Herbert followed his uncle into a dark hallway that had once been carpeted, but where they now stood on the bare stone, with their voices echoing thickly in the damp. High above him a stain on the ceiling recalled the presence of a chandelier, and ahead a broad, shallow staircase coiled lazily upward, decorated now by only a stubble of wrought iron at its edge. Shivering, Wolf struggled with his keys before a thin pair of double doors that rose needlessly to twice his height.

"I hope Mariangela is better, or we will have to cook for ourselves tonight."

"Oh, is she . . . ?"

"My housekeeper. She's not well."

"Oh, I'm sorry . . . "

"*Ach*, it's nothing. Don't worry, we'll be inside in a moment. I should get this repaired."

"Why did Käsemann laugh, Wolf? Did I say something wrong?"

"Käsemann? Oh, you young fool! Käsemann owns half of Europe, as well as another dozen of your Phantoms. Damn this lock. My friend Siletsky is his chauffeur. He had a spare hour. Ah! Now at last we can get warm."

The first room of the apartment was nearly filled with books, the rugs all but invisible beneath them, the old dull furniture distorted under their weight. Rusted swords and tinted photographs faded to velvet brown hung on wallpaper stained beyond recovery by the damp that filled the air. Herbert breathed in, and shivered from the shock of it; damp cloth, damp leather, old cooking, old tobacco, damp, cold, dirt. Dispirited, he looked around the room for a fireplace. There was none, just a baroque stove on tiny legs in the corner, its flue rising naked to the ceiling, soot-black and coffin-cold. My God, what a place, he thought. Wolf was stamping through the other rooms, calling for Mariangela. Was this her idea of housekeeping? Was this the Austrian idea . . . ?

He sat down on a dusty cane chair, and looked about him at all the drab salvage that made up his uncle's home. It struck him as peculiar, now, that Wolf should have mentioned the war, twice in only those first few minutes. People still talked about it a lot, of course, in England, but not to visiting Austrians. Perhaps Wolf just couldn't help himself, perhaps the war, for the defeated, was still a present bitterness, like cold and poverty, striking its leaden theme through their conversation and their thought. And how would he feel now, if Wolf had been young enough to fight, twenty years before, as his father had? There was no answering that question.

16

WOLF HAD SAID; "VERY ENGLISH, ALL THIS MUCKING IN." HERBERT lay tense beneath crisp, heavy bedclothes, in a room dense with books ranked floor to ceiling like grim squat warriors poised for battle in the coming pagan dawn. He was warm at last but unable to sleep, his brain and body thrilling with strong coffee, his mind alert and racing in the dark. They had cooked incompetently together, hard pork and soggy vegetables, adding too much paprika too late, all acrid and gritty in the mouth. Freezing cheese followed, with only scotch and coffee to drink. Still he had been grateful, selfishly, for Mariangela's illness. He was not at ease with strangers, particularly strange women. "Terribly, terribly English." The ground floor's second room was warmer and more orderly than the first, but there was no escape from the smell, made heady with hot smoke from the stove. His eyes watered at the memory.

"So, you are worried about God?"

The question was ill-timed, an impulsive attempt by the host at distraction from his embarrassment. They were both shivering, and needed to bolt the food before it cooled. Herbert filled his mouth and gasped, as much at the taste as at the burn it gave him, and chased it with a gulp of whisky that took his voice away. At last he said;

"Not exactly."

"You believe there is a God?"

Herbert nodded.

"The Christian God?"

"Yes, I think so."

"You have doubts?"

"Well . . . "

He winced, and squirmed into his pillow at the image of the earnest child he must have appeared at that moment.

"Tell me, Herbert, what it is that troubles you."

Confident that he had forced the initiative onto his guest, Wolf attacked his meal with no apparent distaste. Now Herbert ate guiltily, every chew a postponement of duty.

"Well . . . I just can't seem to make sense of it." Wolf waved his knife in encouragement. "I mean . . . How can we have eternal life? It would drive us mad. Everything's got to have an end. Hasn't it?" Still eating furiously, Wolf gave a look, arch, humorous, affectionate, over his glasses. His fork loaded, hovering, Herbert went on; "Well I think it has. For us, I mean. I know space goes on forever, and time. But we need endings, we need to know where things begin and end, all of us, it's like we need to know what the rules are, in a game. But it's not just that. Why do we have free will so that we can do wrong? And do we really have free will anyway? And if Christ was a man, how could he be without sin? Surely that's the whole point about man, that's why we're not God, that's why we need forgiveness. And why are we here in the first place?"

"Stop, stop, Herbert, please, one thing at a time. Now. Where shall we begin?"

Wolf's plate was empty. Herbert looked at his own, still piled with dark slop, and said;

"Do you go to church, Wolf?"

"No. I don't need Catholic guilt or Lutheran misery, and I can't kneel or sing any more. My prayers are my own."

"So what do you believe?"

"What, or why?"

"Both."

"Very well." Now, while Herbert applied himself to the pork and cabbage, Wolf leaned back, pulled the cheese towards him and regarded it blankly, tapping his thick, blunt fingers on the edge of the dish. "So. I believe in God, of course, Creator, Father, Saviour. You will ask me what these words mean." He spoke lazily, as though the subject bored him. When he looked up to continue, it was with the same mild affectation of uninterest that he might have applied to an embarrassing memory, or a present lust. "You see, Herbert, you have to understand that we can only know of God what he chooses to reveal to us, and also that there is nothing about God that we can understand. Nothing. So we see him only in metaphor, that is how we comprehend such things, all the time. Do you see? Does the temperature go up, or down? Does the inflation, an abstract idea, rise and fall like an aeroplane? Of course not. But we confine these things in our imagination, so that we can use them, remember them, make sense of them. All the time we use metaphors like that. So, it's like that as well, with God. Only with God we must remember what is metaphor, and what is real. When we speak of God as our Father we are expressing a reality. The human family, the state of fatherhood, is the metaphor by which we grasp such a relation. Do you see?"

Herbert nodded, swallowing, wide-eyed.

"All right," said Wolf, "So that is also partly the answer to your problem. As we confine ideas, we also confine our own being in this present state of life. You must not think of eternity as endless history, or infinity as endless travel. These things are finite by nature, that, if you like, is what they are for. You say we cannot live forever, because it would drive us mad; but that's because you think of eternal life as an endless career, accumulating an unbearable weight of memory and experience. Of course such a prospect is maddening, it is our very confinement in time and space that puts eternity beyond our comprehension, and man always fears what he cannot understand. He may even try to destroy it, like the atheists do. But when we face eternity, we will no longer be bound in our understanding. So there is nothing to fear."

Herbert stared at his plate for a moment, grappling with this new excitement. He was not sure that he understood; yet there was some joy, some hope, even in the discovery of ideas beyond his knowledge. Perhaps that was the point, or part of it. He looked up in time to catch a twinkle in his uncle's eye, as he popped a slice of cheese into his mouth with something of a flourish. The old man had found his stride.

"Now, if you're ready, consider, in such a scheme, the place of free will in this eternal life that bothers you so much. It must consist, must it not, in our ability to participate in the nature of God, a life outside time and space. We might feel that we are bound, like animals and inanimate things, by the force of circumstance, of one thing always leading to another. But we are not. Our minds, our imaginations, are free, because they are the spirit that God has placed in us. And faith translates this freedom into action. Our faith is our power, and our life. Yes? And the greater our faith, the closer we are to God, the greater our power. But to achieve a perfect intimacy with God—perfect, mind you—must be a logical impossibility, except . . . ?"

"Except for God?"

"Exactly so. So Christ, God made man, the fulfilment of man, is not a paradox at all, but a tautology. It has to be so. Do you agree?"

Thinking hard, Herbert sipped his whisky, playing for time. He must find something intelligent to say, anything to make his uncle feel that his explanation had been worthwhile. Leaping blind, he said;

"Does that mean that only Christians have free will?"

Wolf jerked forward in his chair, with a sudden smile like a grimace against pain.

"No, no! Well, there are some who would say so, perhaps. No. I said we only know of God what he reveals to us, and that it is all metaphor. Remember? So. There can be any number of metaphors for a given truth. We, we Christians, know God this way, through Christ. Other peoples may know him in a different way, find their faith by a different route. Who knows? Not me. It's none of my business. But I don't think we can deny salvation to the Jew or the Turk, who worships God in his own way, the way given to him and his ancestors. I don't really know, but I do know this, that though God may judge him, I cannot. Do you see?"

"Yes, I see that."

"Good. Here, have some cheese. So does eternity still frighten you?"

"Yes, I think it does. Oh, everything you've said makes sense, Wolf—and I'm grateful, I really am—but, well, I suppose it just hasn't sunk in yet. Or maybe there's a difference between theory and practice."

"No. There is a difference between thought and faith. You are convinced, but you don't believe, eh? 'Lord, I believe, help –' what is it?—'help *thou* my unbelief'. Ah, the wonderful old language of your Bible. So much more force than the modern tongue. Don't you agree?"

Herbert said nothing, avoiding the distraction. Eventually he said;

"You've given me quite a lot to think about, Wolf."

"Oh, don't think. Thinking will get you nowhere, you'll just drive yourself mad like before."

"But you've got it all worked out, it makes sense to you."

"I can say things that sound as if they make sense. That's not the same. When I face eternity I shall be just as surprised as you. You asked me another question. You wanted to know why we are here in the first place."

"Yes?"

"I haven't the remotest idea. I don't know, I don't need to know, I don't want to know, and I would not understand if I were told. There. Chase that little demon halfway into the night."

Coiled in the warm bed, Herbert started at the ferocity of that last remark. Did Wolf really say that, or had he invented it, memory drifting into dream? No, that was not how the conversation had ended.

"Herbert, if you fear eternity, you already know that you are part of it. Terror is an emotion we reserve for reality, for things that are happening to us. Fear is of the future, it requires imagination, the intimation of the immortal soul beyond the senses of the present. I'm tired, Herbert. We must talk again."

He realised his eyes were aching from the effort of clenching them shut, opened them and stretched out on his back, his lips moving silently to the phrases as he recalled them. Then he started to breathe harder, as the old anxiety began again, as the darkness started to move past him, a scenery of emptiness on a journey without destination. At least he could try to stop it. He reached out and turned on the lamp, but immediately found in it the hallucination he dreaded, of an image impossibly close, exploding all proportion. For now he was not looking to the length of his arm, but only from the retina to the image upon it, a tiny distance that blew the eye, the face, the self, to vastness. The process accelerated, hypnotic and inescapable, the self expanded, and the image grew nearer and smaller, until the tension exhausted him, and he fell back on the pillows, scanning wildly for release across the walls and ceiling of the room.

"You're mad, Herbert, you're mad, oh dear God . . . "

Sobbing, he closed his eyes, and found, as he knew he would, the same effect in the blackness between the eye and the eyelid, a negligible distance yet divisible to an infinity of fractions. The self was inert, its progress across the fractions illusory, numbering them one, two, by tens, by thousands, then flying across imponderable divisions of space, no nearer than before, futility without rest. He opened his eyes again, as desperation ebbed with the energy for it, as it had a hundred times, and turned out the light. He could stare at the ceiling in the dark, for now he knew what it looked like, and it gave the darkness form. And so he lay, until the shock of unfamiliar sound and creeping light told him that he had been asleep. There was someone tapping at the window, insistently, but so lightly as to be hardly audible. Frightened and half awake, he crept to the window and peered into the gap behind the curtain, holding his breath. Then he sighed aloud, with joy and relief. Why had he not recognised the sound? It was snowing, that was all, and he loved the snow. Relaxed, he went back to bed, happy like a child, and lost himself in warmth and sleep, cherishing the sound of the snow, a friend in a strange place.

17

THE NARROWNESS OF THE STREET MADE ALL ITS TRAFFIC ALARMINGLY loud, the engines echoing back and forth between the tall houses making every window buzz in its frame as they passed. It was a steam lorry that woke him, the sound of it already immediate four doors down, and growing to a scary pitch before continuing harmlessly on its way. After that every passing taxi was a fair-ground thrill.

He got up and drew the curtains, noticing for the first time the shutters that should have been closed all night. It was cold in the room, and the sun lost all its warmth in the clean snow outside, shining white off the ornamental sills of the houses opposite. Herbert went back to bed and lay still, revelling in soft warmth, counting off the chimes of some nearby church. Eleven. He had slept deeply at last, and now wondered at all the strange images he retained from the previous day. Fatigue brought an oblique view of life. He felt content now, pleased and excited to be so far from home. This was going to be quite an adventure. There were all kinds of people in Vienna; philosophers, musicians, to say nothing of spies and foreign assassins. There would be girls, too, delectably European, innately glamorous, and for whom he would also represent the glamour of the visiting young Englishman. They would all want to talk to him, there would be no place for shyness, no competition to fear . . .

The door opened with a creak and a rattle of china, and Herbert immediately tensed, checking that no part of his body below the chin lay exposed. Wolf's voice, shouting over the sound of a piano, wafted in from below. He knew who this must be.

"Good morning, young sir. Will you have some chocolate?"

She held a familiar, almost patronising warmth in her eyes, this dark, blousy woman with the broad, slack smile. His pyjamas safely buttoned to the neck, Herbert pulled himself half upright, more as an absurd gesture of respect than for practicality, and said;

"Thank you very much. You must be Mariangela."

"And you are Herbert, from England. How do you do?"

He offered his right hand, cradling the chocolate in his left, and Mariangela bobbed like a parlour maid, her hands at her lap, and laughed. She sat down on the bed, bulky and unselfconscious, still beaming at him with some secret joy. Then nodding, as though speaking to a child or an idiot, she said;

"You slept well?"

"Oh yes, I was very comfortable, thank you. Ah . . . My uncle mentioned that you were not well. I hope you're quite better?"

Mariangela pulled several faces, rocked on her hips, blew at the window and flapped a hand, before reverting to the old smile. Perhaps her English was exhausted. Herbert took a long drink of chocolate, hoping to cover his amusement. Then, surprisingly, she said;

"It's a terribly long way from England, and the trains are so cold and dirty. I hope it wasn't too beastly for you?"

"No, no," said Herbert, "I quite enjoyed it. I've never travelled this far before. Have you visited England?"

"Unfortunately, no. But Wolf has shown me all his pictures. I would like to see London one day. So big! It's the biggest city in the world, isn't it? It must be wonderful. Do you live in London?"

"No, I live in the country, in Worcestershire. But I know London quite well. I'm very much looking forward to seeing Vienna, though. I hear it's more beautiful than London."

She blushed and waved again, as though deflecting a personal compliment.

"No, London must be more beautiful. It's so big!"

"Well, it's big all right, but it's very dirty, too. And it's mostly suburbs, you know." Instantly, the smile collapsed in puzzlement. "Suburbs? You know, where people live. Nothing but houses, and gasworks, that sort of thing."

The smile returned, after just the wrong amount of time, and Herbert smiled uncertainly back, wondering where to go from here.

"Do you like my English?" said Mariangela, nodding again.

"Oh, gosh, yes. You're quite fluent. I feel ashamed. I don't speak German, you see."

"Italian?"

"Italian? No, I'm afraid not. Just some French. Latin, of course . . . "

"I am Italian."

"Oh really? How interesting."

"I came to live with Wolf, after the war. We fought with you, we Italians."

"Yes. Yes, I know."

"So it was hard for me. But Wolf is a good man, a real friend. He taught me to speak German. And English!"

"I see. Well, he's a very good teacher."

"Oh yes. But he could not teach me to play the piano. I have no talent."

"Ah. Well I never really got on with the piano, I must say. But I'm sure you sing."

Bullseye, he thought. Though it had seemed impossible, the smile broadened, the eyes widened and shone, the bosom rose.

"Oh, I love to sing! Do you love to sing?"

"Well, ah, I enjoy singing, yes."

"It's a wonderful thing. All music is wonderful. We must sing together. You must come to see me, when Wolf is asleep. I have my room, downstairs. You would not mind coming to my room?"

"Gosh no, of course not."

"Then you will come, and we will sing. And I have something you'll like, something special. From a friend," she added, and gave him a nod accompanied by a wink and a pout, a combination of which he could make nothing; but he kept on smiling anyway.

"I'm sure you sing very well," he said. She flapped a hand at him again and laughed, rocking forward and back. Then through the chill of the room he caught her warm breath, already loaded with some heavy spirit. He dismissed it, shocking though it was, but she must have caught the spasm on his face, with a sly glance moved by some heightened sense, because she stopped laughing at once, and stood up, straightening her face and her skirt.

"Well I must not sit here when you want to dress," she said. "I have so much work to do. I must fetch your water now."

"Thank you for the chocolate," said Herbert, "and we must talk again soon . . ." She was nearly out of the door. "And I can't wait to hear you sing." If she had not turned and smiled again at that moment, he thought, he must have died of guilt.

He slid back into the pillows and drank the dregs of the chocolate. So that was Mariangela, the tipsy housekeeper. How old would she have been when the war ended? Twenty, twenty-five, perhaps. It occurred to him that he had never before considered the living casualties who had only lived where the armies marched, not fighting, but running and hiding, starving and crying in the night. Mariangela was one of them. Maybe her home had been destroyed, her family killed or scattered, and she had found her only refuge among her enemies. Even if she had already been living here, she had certainly spent her best years as an exile in a nervous country. No wonder she drank.

It was exciting though, undeniably, shamefully thrilling, to meet someone like Mariangela, after so many years of living in England, where the war was something that had happened somewhere else, and where the noise and the blood of it were only stories. Englishmen went abroad to fight. Then he remembered, from a cold Sunday morning two or three years before, the rector's sermon on the text "the abomination of desolation standing where he ought not," recalling to the minds of a congregation depleted of its men the terrible sight of Zeppelins over London, not just the fear and the damage they caused, but the blasphemous affront of those slow vile slugs of war defiling the blessed skies of the new Jerusalem. Even then it had shocked him, the arrogance, the damnable self-righteous pride, as though the country that had been the calm eye of a storm of bloody conquest for two centuries could claim any God-given right to peace. And yet it had worked. The congregation saw the meaning, felt again the fear and pain of loss, the violation of gentle and sacred things, as they pictured the face of the bestial demon hanging in the sky. It was their metaphor, if not his, and some of them had wept at the force of it, thanking God for His victory.

He realised he was thinking about the war again, that Mariangela had mentioned it at their first meeting, as Wolf had. It was inescapable here, at least in this house, seemingly still run down and rationed sixteen years on. The company of these people was going to make demands of sensitivity, of vigilant tact, far greater than he had expected, even while he learnt from the strange preoccupations of their lives.

He heard the grinding of china on stone as Mariangela lowered the heavy jug and basin onto the landing outside, leapt out of bed and grabbed his dressing gown. But she was already at the bottom of the stairs again before he reached the door.

18

VOGLERGASSE IS VERY NARROW, BUT QUITE PRETTY, ALTHOUGH A LITTLE run down, like so much here, and in a most respectable area, called Josefstadt. Wolf's house is quite large, although he only occupies the bottom two floors and lets the rest to tenants. His apartments are terribly damp and dirty. . .

Herbert paused, and sucked his pen like a schoolboy, realising he had made a mistake. "Terribly damp and dirty," gosh no, that wouldn't do, not in a letter to his mother. If she read that he would be ordered home by telegram. Then inspiration struck.

. . .terribly damp and dirty compared to our home, though much better than school was. Of course it's not Wolf's fault, because he is very old, and his housekeeper, to whom he gave shelter after the war (she is Italian), would never be able to keep a position in England, because she drinks.

There, Wolf was absolved.

She obviously made an effort with my room, though, because that at least is clean and warm. The weather is bitterly cold, but quite beautiful. I haven't seen anything of the city yet, but Wolf is going to ask one of his pupils to show me the sights. I know nothing about her, except that her name is Sophie.

Herbert stopped to look at his watch, and felt his lips tighten with the twinge of an apprehension he despised. In five minutes he must go downstairs again to the room where his uncle taught, and then spend untold hours in the company of a girl he had never met. Of course he couldn't help hoping for a beauty, even though he knew it would be much easier for him if she were plain, but he had no idea at all of what to expect. Wolf had not prepared him. All he had said, as they shared a late breakfast of fresh rolls and stale cheese, was;

"Come down again in an hour, and I will send you out into the city with a guide. Sophie is a good girl, you'll like her. Why don't you write to your mother while you're waiting? Let her know you're comfortable here."

He folded the letter and put it in his pocket, straightened his tie and squared his shoulders to the mirror. He did not feel comfortable.

The study door was open as he made his way through the outer room, and as he reached the threshold Wolf looked up from his desk by the opposite wall, smiled and beckoned. Advancing, he caught the sound, then the sight of movement to his left, and turned. The girl was standing with her coat open, piling her shining black hair into her hat, and smiled politely at him while he stood there overcome, not hearing Wolf's introduction. He had never seen anything like her. The hair, cream skin, blue almond eyes, high cheekbones, the perfect carriage, the improbably voluptuous figure . . . She was a living Dual Monarchy of fabulous beauty, now gone with another smile, and a word he didn't catch.

"Well, Herbert, you might have said something to her. You could have said hello, she would have understood that."

Mortified, Herbert flopped into a battered armchair in front of his uncle's desk, and blushed horribly at the warmth that lingered there.

"Oh gosh . . . Didn't I . . . ?"

"You did not. Of course, she's used to being stared at, I suppose."

"Did I stare? Oh no."

"Well, don't worry about it. She doesn't speak English anyway. Not a word. Ah, I see. No, that was not Sophie. Didn't you hear? That was Eva, come to invite me to a little party for her father. You can come too, if you like. I thought, for a moment then, that you were entertaining hopes?" He laughed, and Herbert forced a sickly smile in return. Hopes? No, he hadn't got that far. "Ah, Herbert, no, she wouldn't do. Not for you. She's far too beautiful."

Too beautiful? This was a new idea. Herbert repeated the words silently, searching for their meaning, while his uncle rose from behind the desk and walked to the window. There he leaned with his back to the brightness, and crossed his legs at the ankle, a young man's pose.

"Wolf, what do you mean, too beautiful?"

"A contradiction in terms you think, eh? Not at all. I think you might understand, when Sophie comes. Oh, not from her. She won't take your breath away. More like an English girl, to look at, I mean, and her English is very good. No, I was thinking of the city. You might find that Vienna is too beautiful. I think so, sometimes, and I was born here. But for you . . . All our wonderful grand buildings, all our music, our beautiful girls, like Eva. Even our cakes, when we can afford them, all that pastry, all that cream, too much all at once, too much for the lean, ascetic Englishman. We get fat, we Viennese, on cream, and music and too much beauty all the time. You'll see."

"It's another metaphor, then?"

"Metaphor? Ha!" The old man laughed again, and held his stomach affectionately for a moment, as though it were a child in his lap. "What, am I metaphorically fat? No, Herbert, there is some reality in this world. But this beauty we have been discussing, the curve of an archway, or a woman's breast. Reality! Illusion! Snap your fingers and it's gone."

"But it can't be reality and illusion, surely?" said Herbert. Wolf gave a dismissive wave of the hand, and crossed his legs the other way.

"Ach! You know what I mean. Here today, gone tomorrow, what kind of reality is that, something that exists ten times longer in your memory than it did on earth. Forget it, and it was never there. So forget it now, and be done."

"It seems rather a shame."

"But you're thinking of Eva again. What do you want from women, Herbert? A pretty picture to look at for ten, maybe fifteen years? Or are you a ladies' man who will catch a hundred in their prime, and die without a special name to whisper to the priest? Eh?"

"I certainly hope not."

"So. Don't be afraid to admit what you want. You want love. Don't you?"

Herbert fidgetted for a moment, while his uncle stared down at him, then said;

"Well, I suppose I do, yes."

"Yes." Wolf paused, upright, for a second, then returned to his place behind the desk. Standing in front of the window he had been little more than a silhouette. Now Herbert saw that his face had changed, earnest when before it had been humorous, and straightened a little in his armchair.

"Love," said Wolf. "We should have talked about love last night. Let me tell you something, Herbert. There are no metaphors for love. It is the one thing we have which is beyond our comprehension and yet can still be known for what it is. We know it in our hearts. Tell me, what is love?"

Herbert opened his mouth and stalled, surprised by the question. His mind was blank.

"Love," he began, "Well, love is . . . caring for someone . . . "

Wolf's hand slapped down on the desk, a pistol shot in the gloom.

"Think! To describe is not to define. Yes, to care for someone, to feel their joys and their sorrows as your own, to know that their life and yours are not distinct but bound together, yes, that is *to* love, that is the symptom, the expression of it. But what is it, Herbert? You cannot say, I cannot say. It is not to be defined, because it is God in us, his greatest gift, a holy truth on earth. These feelings we have when we love, a wife, a friend, a child, this is how God feels about us, and how we also feel about him, if we have our faith. Think of it this way. The perfect love of God for man, in God made man. That was no metaphor, Herbert. That was the truth itself." He stopped, and leaned back in his chair, relaxed and smiling gently again. "So. What do you think now, about beauty?" Herbert drew a deep breath, playing for time, but before he could answer Wolf spoke again, shaking his head at the sunshine outside. "You are a young man, Herbert, you see with a young man's eyes. You know more about beauty than I do. I'm afraid I've spoilt it for you, for today at least."

"Perhaps you've just given me a sense of perspective, Wolf."

"I hope that may be so. As for love, you know very little, and I can't really help you. You have to find out, and you will. You'll be married one day, and have children, and maybe even a young fool of a nephew who blushes at pretty girls. No, don't blush again, Herbert, that was unkind, and I'm sorry. But you will find out. Maybe your wife will be beautiful, who knows? And you will love that beauty because it's hers. But beauty cannot make you love. Beauty will only make you fat. . ."

Then Herbert started at the sudden brush of heavy cloth across his hand where it rested on the arm of the chair, and looked awkwardly up as Mariangela swept past him to her employer and friend, to take his face between her hands, and kiss his forehead as though he were a baby. Herbert thought that he would always remember this scene, this reality, as a brilliant dream, and would every time have to convince himself anew that it had truly occurred. While Mariangela prattled her endearments in Italian and German, he wondered if he should look away, or even try to continue the conversation as before. This only made it harder not to laugh. His fingers hovering impotently above the desk, Wolf caught a glimpse of his nephew's face, coloured and protested—"Bitte, Mariangela, Cara, bitte,"—but to no effect. At last, still cupping the ancient face in her hands, Mariangela turned and settled her rump on the desk, and gave Herbert her widest smile.

"Such a lovely man!"

"Yes," said Herbert.

Finally released, Wolf nodded absently in agreement, and while Mariangela let out a huge and shuddering sigh of happiness, bowed his head in defeat. It was then half a minute, a long, long silent time, before anyone moved. When the bell rang Mariangela patted her lap and sighed again, then rose and left to answer the door. Still Wolf stared down at his desk, and Herbert looked about him for some distraction. He decided to go and finish his letter home, and got up, but found himself greeting another visitor, a trim little mousey blonde, her prettiness all in her smile and her grey eyes, in the tilt of her chin and her jolly, tomboy stance. Just like an English girl.

19

THE SNOWFALL HAD BEEN LIGHT, AND NOW THE STREETS WERE BARELY wet under the winter sun. By the time they reached the long downward slope of Florianigasse, Herbert had heard and failed to take in the whole, chatty history of the girl's family and schooling, and had rehearsed that of his own without interest, or the slightest concern for whether his companion understood. His mind was elsewhere, trapped in a circle drawn around beauty, love and fat. Wolf was fat, Mariangela was fat. Mariangela loved Wolf, Mariangela had made him fat, but Mariangela was not beautiful. Maybe love was beautiful, and love had made them fat . . . No, no, beauty and love were distinct and not to be confused, as Wolf had said, so why was there all this fat? He screwed up his face and shook his head, as though still stupid from sleep. He couldn't think properly. He couldn't think at all. The girl's Viennese voice, grinding away like gravel in English that was rapid if not quite fluent, was getting in the way. He couldn't very well tell her to shut up, so he said;

"Tell me about Wolf, Sophie. How long have you known him?"

She looked up at him, all startled innocence, and said; "Does that mean something?"

Oh God, was she turning philosophical as well?

"Well, yes," was the best he could do, and there was a brief silence.

"What I mean," said Sophie, "Is it something I don't know? Tell you about Wolf? He is your uncle. Yes?"

"Ah, I see. Yes, but I only met him for the first time yesterday. You certainly know more about him than I do. Do you see?"

"Ah." She paused again, and stared ahead at the pavement, considering . . . What? Philosophy? Propriety? Subjunctives? "Wolf is my teacher," she said at last. "He teaches me the piano, and English." Another pause. "Perhaps it would be better, " she added, "if I play you some Chopin."

Ambushed in the rut of boredom, Herbert stopped dead and rocked backwards, laughing aloud. And now Sophie made him feel very grown up, laughing too, but nervously, like an unspoilt child.

"Very good," he said, and, without thinking, gave her his arm. She hugged it close, still laughing, and so they walked on down the hill, while Herbert realised that he had forgotten to be shy for a moment, and immediately lost his nerve. Then, inspired, he said;

"Where are we going?"

"Ah, soon you will see the Ring. Then we start."

"And what is the Ring?"

"The Ring is a wide beautiful street in a circle around the middle of Vienna. Inside the Ring is the First District, and everything, nearly everything to see is there, or on the Ring."

"Ah. So what are we going to see?"

"First you must see the Ring. Where we are going, there is the University on the left, and the Rathauspark, where is the Rathaus, you know, the city parliament, on the right. Then we turn right of to, no, on to the Ring, and you see across the Ring a very famous coffeehouse, the café Landtmann, and then the Burgtheater, a theatre, you know . . . ?"

"I know."

" . . . and then on the right is the Parliament, and then the Museum and the Art Museum and Maria-Theresia Platz, and now on the left is the Hofburg which was the palace and the gardens of the Emperor in the old days. Then on the left is the Opera House, and then I think we will leave the Ring and walk along Kärntnerstrasse where there are shops and coffee houses and so, and then we find the cathedral of St Stephen which is exactly in the middle of all. It all," she added, and muttered to herself in German.

"But can we really see all that today?" said Herbert. Sophie laughed.

"Of course not inside, but you will know where all the buildings are. And they are beautiful on the outside, I think."

"Right. Could you tell me once more?"

Happily, Sophie began her monologue again, occasionally correcting herself, and adding more detail as she went along. As they marched together to her step between the high shadows of grimy and innominate façades, Herbert began to imagine the city she described, of galleries and pastry-shops and parks where lovers walked at dusk. He smiled and started to love the idea of it, of a vast pleasure-garden in the heart of Europe, appointed with the finest music and art; or a rambling art gallery with gardens and cafés at every hand; or an enormous café set in an ornamental landscape dotted with theatres and galleries for the entertainment of its patrons. In this little plot of a city was a whole world of joyful life, awash with food and wine and innocent romance, love and beauty and Viennese fat all swirling intertwined around a magic circle called the Ring. How lucky they were, Wolf, and Sophie, to be at home in such a place!

At last they walked from the quiet of narrow streets to the full noise of the boulevard, where the traffic of the city swarmed, sun-lazy, across their path. The Ring did not disappoint. Herbert stopped and looked slowly from left to right, grinning, thrilled by the sight of gentle elegance on such a scale. All about him, and farther along the easy curves of the Ring, stood huge buildings inert and intimate in their splendour, each one adorable as a bride. Wolf was right; it was too much all at once, this vastness crammed with decorative detail, this tangible proximity belied by the haze of distance. Herbert blinked, his sense of balance failing. With difficulty he focused again on the little girl beside him, and said;

"Sophie— What do you think about love?"

She looked up at him for a moment, half smiling.

"Do you like the Ring?" she said.

"Oh, it's wonderful, quite wonderful."

"Yes, I think so . . . Why do you ask me about love? What should I think?"

"Wolf was talking about love earlier, that's all. I wondered what you thought."

"Ah, Wolf. Wolf is old-fashioned. This part of the Ring is named the Twelfth of November, from the revolution. But the old people, like Wolf, still call it the Franzenring, from the Emperor."

"And over there, that's the theatre?"

"Yes."

"And the café Landtmann over there?"

"Very good. And up there, on the hill, behind the trees, is a house where Beethoven lived. He wrote *Fidelio* there."

"Really?"

"Now! Run!"

Without warning she grabbed his hand and ran, laughing, into the road, across bridle paths and tramlines and the noxious wake of the cabs, to the low wall of the café forecourt opposite. Gasping, Herbert said;

"What did you do that for?"

"For fun, you Englishman!"

On the other side of the Ring, the pavement they had just left looked half a mile away. She pirouetted across his view, unwinding, and came to rest leaning on the wall beside him.

"I think I like the old name better," he said.

"Yes? So . . . And what do you think, about love?"

"Oh gosh, I don't know. But Wolf . . ."

"Wolf has Mariangela. Are you surprised?"

So, it was not a secret.

20

He was still tired from the journey. In the sudden warmth of this cheap café in the city centre, the thrill of his guided tour was lost, and he could only sit and smile at Sophie while she chattered on, waiting for the coffee she had ordered. But now she suddenly rose to meet a tall, burly young man who was marching towards them, unsmiling, with his coat still buttoned from the street, and Herbert snapped awake again, alert for the demands of social duty.

"Herbert Christie, this is my brother, Joachim."

"How do you do?" said Herbert. Joachim took his hand and nodded stiffly, rattling out some Austrian greeting, a brutal sneeze of the mouth. Then he lowered himself, as though with distaste, onto a chair beside his sister, and said;

"You are the nephew of Wolf, yes? From England?"

"Yes, I arrived yesterday. Your sister has been kindly showing me something of the city. It's very beautiful."

"You should say that *she* is beautiful."

"Oh, ah . . . "

"Or are you afraid perhaps that I will hit you?" He smiled broadly then, but without warmth, and Sophie laughed nervously.

"Well," said Herbert, "You would have something of an advantage, I think. Do you box?"

"Yes." The smile was gone. Sophie began to say something, quietly, but he ignored her. "Did you stay in Paris?" he asked.

"Paris? You mean recently? No, I er . . . "

"In Paris the government is frightened of the fascists. Also here, and in England. Did you know?"

"Well I don't know about Austria, but . . . "

"Then you must know about England. Are you on the side of the people?"

Herbert thought for a moment, then said;

"Against whom, exactly?" The question seemed to surprise Joachim, not for its cleverness, which had anyway been unintentional, but for its naivety. His pale blue eyes widened as he continued to look straight at Herbert, fixed, it seemed, on something pitiful, and hating it.

"My brother is very interested in politics," said Sophie.

"Yes, so I realise. I feel quite ignorant. Ah, shall we order another cup . . . ?"

Joachim stood abruptly, and again bowed from the neck. His coat was still buttoned.

"We must leave," he said, and turned for the door. Blushing unhappily now, Sophie quickly gathered her gloves and bag, and rose again with a weak little smile.

"He doesn't mean to be rude, Herbert . . . His English . . . I'm sorry, I must go. I enjoyed this morning very much. We must meet again."

"Oh, of course . . . Thank you very much . . . Goodbye."

She was gone, a distant dream.

Alone with two cups of coffee, Herbert realised he didn't know where he was, or even how to ask for the bill. Then, reaching into his pocket for the bulge of Austrian money, he felt the cold-hot flush of doubt and reassurance, followed by the chill fatigue of courage spent. He sipped the coffee, knowing that when it was finished he would have to stand up, clear his throat, and make a speech to the whole place. *I say, does anyone here speak English?* His heart was hammering already.

Then a man scraped his chair from the next table without getting up, and said;

"Is the lady coming back?"

"I don't think so. I say, are you English?"

"Absolutely, old boy."

He spoke like a public school man of the lower sort, about forty, with a moustache, and a dull club tie under his coat.

"Gosh, that is a relief. I'm afraid I'm rather stranded."

"What, no money?"

"Oh yes, I remembered to bring money. It's just that I've rather lost my bearings, and I don't speak German."

"New in town?"

"I arrived here yesterday."

"Got a name?"

"Oh, forgive me. I'm Herbert Christie."

"Felix Dangerfield. So, who's the popsy?"

Herbert felt the warmth leave his handshake, and hoped the other man hadn't noticed. Doubtless he hadn't meant to be rude.

"I wouldn't call her that, exactly," he said gently. "She's one of my uncle's pupils. She was showing me round, but she had to go."

"Sorry, old boy. No disrespect. And what about the gorilla?"

"The . . . ? Oh, that was her brother."

"Ah, I see. Bad luck. Pretty little thing, though, isn't she?" Herbert said nothing. "So, you've got family in old Vienna."

"Just my uncle Wolf. He lives in Voglergasse, in Josefstadt. Perhaps you know it?"

"Voglergasse? Not old Wolf Winkler?" In one movement Dangerfield turned back to his table and snatched a paper out of the hands of the dark, grizzled man behind it. "Isaac! D'you hear that? Old Winkler really did have an English wife after all! This young chap's his nephew! What do you make of that?"

Slowly, the other man nodded at Herbert and smiled wearily, with his lips closed, a smile so wide that it made the tips of his ears tilt inwards. Then he looked down again at his paper, while the Englishman swivelled back to face Herbert, with a new warmth in his eyes. "Well, it's a funny old world," he said, and lit a cigarette, chuckling to himself through the smoke.

"Is your friend English too?" said Herbert.

"Isaac? Well, he was born in Whitechapel. Not what you'd call an Englishman, exactly, though, is he? I mean, use your eyes, old boy."

Irritated, Herbert said; "I simply meant, well, perhaps . . . "

Dangerfield leaned forward, and lowered his voice.

"Introductions? Not just now. Isaac, you see, he works for me in a manner of speaking. That's different. It looks mean, I know, but take it from me— you're new here, after all— it doesn't do to get too chummy with our Hebrew brethren, not in public, not here. Especially with those chaps about. Nazis, I mean."

At another table nearby a group of young men in leather shorts and white stockings sat noisily drinking beer, their big knees red from the cold. Each one, though his blond colouring made it absurd, also wore the toothbrush moustache of the German chancellor. With the smallest, barely noticeable gestures—a grimace at the mouth, a crisp straightening of the fingers holding his cigarette—Dangerfield quickly parodied the new German salute, and laughed softly.

"Harmless enough," he said, "but—well, they've had a few, and there are five of them."

"I see."

"So. Where are you from?"

"Worcestershire."

"Ah. Not my patch, I'm afraid. City boy. London born and bred."

"I often wish I lived in London. It's very quiet where we are."

"Oh, you're not missing much. I didn't go back after the war. No jobs, you see."

"Were you in the army?" Dangerfield nodded, then hurried on;

"I moved here in '22. It's a fine old town, Vienna, once you know your way around. How long are you going to be here?"

"I don't know. A month or two. Perhaps longer."

"Well, you must keep in touch. Maybe I'll show you a few sights the little lady wouldn't know about." He winked as he said this, and produced a dog-eared calling-card from his waistcoat pocket. Herbert shuddered inwardly.

"Thank you, that would be very kind," he said. "But, Mr Dangerfield, do tell me . . ."

"Felix."

"Felix, do tell me. How do you know my uncle?"

"Oh, seen him around, you know. He's quite a popular character round the coffee houses. Interesting chap, I've always thought."

"Yes, I think so too. But why were you so surprised that he had an English wife?"

Felix shook his head, and swallowed some coffee.

"No reflection on your uncle. Not a bit of it. It's just Vienna, that's all. People say a lot of things, and you learn to take it all with a pinch of salt. It's nice to know things for sure. Anyway, it's my job, in a manner of speaking. Not so much a job, really, just . . . what I do."

"I'm sorry, I don't think I understand. What is what you do?"

"Information, old boy. Finding things out. That's just between you and me, of course. Say no more."

"Oh, of course," said Herbert, suddenly grateful for his upbringing and the easy grasp of protocol it gave him. But this was thrilling. One way and another he had quickly grown to dislike this Felix Dangerfield, but that no longer mattered. He had met a spy, a real English spy, on his second day in Vienna! Working hard to appear unimpressed, he found he could think of nothing more to say, and, worse, felt a childish grin distorting his face against his will. In search of distraction while Felix sorted out another cigarette, he turned again to look at the five drinking, laughing Nazis, one by one, with a tourist's curiosity. With their silly clothes and loud manner, they made a comical tableau. Then one of them caught his eye, and now they were all looking at him, menacingly still, united in drunken arrogance. He turned away, but a moment later there was a glass of beer swaying in front of his face, and a big blond Hitler towering over him, challenging him to drink it.

Felix got up and spoke quickly, lightly, his hands open at his side in conciliation. Herbert caught the word "Engländer," and at once the mood changed. Now these five were his greatest friends, squeezing his shoulder and shouting at the waiter for more beer.

"They're buying you a drink," said Felix.

"But I don't want a drink."

"Don't be difficult, old boy. Just take your medicine like a brave little soldier. Down in one, if you can."

Herbert took the glass, waved it around the company with a mild smile, and drank. It was surprisingly easy. Compared to English bitter this thin, yellow stuff was like water. As he drained the last of it there were cheers, applause, the sound of empty glasses slammed on wood, and movement. They were leaving. Then a strange thing happened. The man who had first challenged him pointed to Isaac and spoke to his companions as he passed, and then, as friends would, they all laughed and slapped the Jew on the shoulder on their way out, an affectionate farewell. Still reading, Isaac ignored them all.

"What was that about?" said Herbert. Felix leaned back in his chair, and took a deep drag on his cigarette.

"They said he's the kind of Jew they like—poor and harmless. They said they'd never see him flashing his money around in nightclubs, picking up under-age girls. That's what they said."

"Oh good Lord. That's terrible!"

Felix shrugged. Then Isaac spoke, in the clean carrying drawl of the Jewish East End, without looking up;

"They also said I don't smell too much. Nice fellows."

"Oh, look here," said Herbert, "I'm . . . terribly sorry."

Now at last the Jew raised his eyes again. "You should be sorry? You've got friends for life. You just drank to the health of their beloved Führer."

"But I didn't mean to do that!"

Twisting in his chair, Isaac glanced through the café's full-length window to the street, where ten white stockings still shuffled for warmth under flapping green coats.

"They're still there," he said. "You want me to go and tell them?"

Embarrassed, Herbert sat back and drank the last of Sophie's coffee, while the other two gently laughed at him. He was out of his depth. He would have to go. Then, turning miserably in search of a waiter, he found himself staring straight at his uncle Wolf, wrapped up as he had been the day before, now standing at his side, a miraculous vision, a wheezing, shabby angel.

"Well Herbert, I see you've made some nice friends. Dangerfield, Greenbaum. I met Sophie and Joachim in the street, and they told me you were here. I knew you would never find your way home by yourself. Come along, let's go."

"But the bill . . . "

"I've paid it." He turned at once and led the way to the door, while Felix and Isaac casually waved goodbye. Herbert barely had time to grab his hat before they reached the street. Then, trotting awkwardly beside Wolf, he said;

"I don't think Joachim liked me very much."

"He watches out for Sophie, as a brother should. But also he thinks the English are useless and decadent. A little rich, coming from a Viennese, I know. But Joachim is an idealist."

"He was talking like a communist," said Herbert. Wolf paused, then said;

"Don't ever say that, Herbert. Joachim is with the socialist club, the Schutzbund. You must not confuse the two. The Schutzbund are not internationalist revolutionaries. They are Austrian patriots, in their way. But that is another reason why Joachim was so anxious to take Sophie home. There were Nazis in that coffee-house, and he will not stay in the same room with them. Quite right too."

"Are they really dangerous?"

"Not to you, not to me. They are very small, but they make a lot of noise, and they are the only club who wear their stupid uniforms in public all the time. They're an irritation, that's all."

"Where are we going?"

"You'll see. No, they're not dangerous—not as dangerous as that scum I found you with."

"What? Really? But Felix Dangerfield's an English . . . an English agent, isn't he?"

Wolf laughed bitterly, a locomotive gust of steam in the freezing air.

"Is that what he told you?"

"Well, no. Not in so many words."

"Don't let your imagination lead you astray, Herbert. Agent! Such a grand word for a cheap informer who scrapes a few *groschen* from the police and the foreign press. An agent for himself."

"And Isaac?"

"The same, more or less. But Felix can make the contacts with his fine English manners and his old school tie. A lovely partnership they make, the grand Englishman and the sly Jew with the knife and the pistol under his coat . . . "

"What?" Herbert stopped dead, shivering, and Wolf turned to him with a gentle smile.

"Keep moving, Herbert. It's cold. Oh yes, I'm afraid you've had a dull day. You might have witnessed five murders, and the last appearance in Vienna of Isaac Greenbaum. He's a man who knows how to disappear, and live somewhere else with a different name. Didn't you wonder why a Jew should leave London to live in Vienna?"

"But Wolf, are you saying those men are criminals, wanted by the police in England?"

"I'm saying Why are they here? No more than that." He stopped, and, placing one hand on Herbert's shoulder, gestured with the other into the square before them.

The cathedral had appeared so suddenly, as though the buildings round about had stepped back to reveal it, unmistakable, rising huge on its rolling plain of cobbles. But how foreign it looked, with its steep roof patterned in gaudy herring-bone, and its single crooked spire. Herbert stared and grinned, while the words of the other Englishman still repeated in his head; *"People say a lot of things, and you learn to take it all with a pinch of salt."* And it was hard enough to credit that he had even met Felix, and Isaac, and a socialist and five Nazis, in so short a time in one little place. The sheer concentration of experience here was a shock, like the relentless huddling of detail in the streets behind him. At least the cathedral square gave some perspective, the relief of open space. Wolf said;

"It's funny. All over the world you find them, the charming *Engländer* with his striped necktie, the silent Jew hiding in the shadows, both with names they were not born with, both with no future, and no past they can admit to. Parasites, living off the grit between the cobbles of crowded streets. Be careful of those two, that's all. Anyway, here we are. Forget those filthy magpies for a moment, and look on a holy thing."

21

THERE WAS SNOW ON THE STREETS OF JOSEFSTADT. IN THE EARLY MORNING Herbert stood at his window and watched it fall, luminous in the grey light, dampening the waking noises of the town. Then a gang of shabby men, hired for the day, would appear and shovel the stuff into mounds to keep the streets alive, hoping for a steady fall through the night and another job in the morning. Herbert became fascinated with the snow, with the crystals dying spread-eagled on his window, and the perfectly even fall of them in the street. They drifted down at random, but no intelligence could have enforced such ruthless order as that of their distribution on the earth.

Every day he walked through the freezing wet with Sophie, tightly arm in arm against the cold, laughing and shivering at once, and shortening his stride to match hers. He looked forward to her smile and the sound of her voice. He had never been friends with a girl before.

Outside the centre there were few people abroad, and many of these were poor, mostly the old or mad. But there were war veterans too, some blind, some legless and trolley-borne, a brick in each hand, and occasionally a prostitute, a thin bright-eyed nocturnal thing left over in the bitter morning. Herbert looked twice at everything, determined to remember every street sign, every stray cat and human face, to lose nothing. And even in the grand sweep of the Ring, where ragged demonstrations railed against authority, he forced himself to catch the detail in the crowd, a coat patched from an orange blanket, or a laughing child amidst the rage. He had never felt so aware of the world as of these present memories, or so content.

"You look so much happier than you did when you arrived," said Wolf. "I was concerned. Such a serious young man here, under my roof. It made me wonder what was the point of being old."

Herbert laughed. They had been silent for many minutes, while Wolf read a Hungarian newspaper by the dim electric light over the table.

Mariangela entered quietly, lowered the huge old dish, with great care, onto its place, and began to ladle stew and dumplings onto their plates. She said nothing, but smiled at Herbert the same grand smile of delight that she always gave him. Even now the old man did not look up.

"Are you getting to know Vienna a little?" he asked.

"Bit by bit. I can find my way home from the centre. And I keep seeing buildings I've seen before, but thought were somewhere else. It's really quite small, isn't it?"

"The First District, yes. And you haven't asked me to explain the meaning of the universe all day. Don't you care any more? Or have you found out? If that is so, please tell me."

"Oh no, Wolf, of course I still care. There's so much to learn, I know. I suppose I've relaxed a little since I arrived. It's all so far away, and it's so nice here."

Now Wolf looked up.

"So? The universe is a long way away, and Vienna is not part of the universe? And my poor crippled home, freezing and hungry and at the mercy of the whole world, this is paradise? You could teach our Viennese philosophers a new kind of knowledge, Herbert. You are wasted here, spending your afternoons in the coffee-house with me."

"Oh, Wolf, you know what I mean. I know things are pretty rough here. It's just that I'm a visitor, all my problems are at home. And you've helped me so much, I'm really grateful."

"And Sophie?"

"Sophie's been very kind, as well, showing me round the place. I can't possibly take in everything she tells me, but I'd be lost without her. Of course I must thank you for arranging that, as well. I think I needed to meet new people, you and Mariangela, and Sophie, and Felix Dangerfield . . . "

"Ha! Have you seen him again?" Herbert blushed guiltily. He had dreaded having to mention Felix.

"We've met him by chance a couple of times. I don't think he can do me any harm, Wolf. I am an Englishman, after all, like him."

"Not like him, I hope. Ach, you must learn. Buy nothing from him, avoid his friends. If he asks you to do anything for him, refuse. And stay away from Greenbaum. This is good advice, Herbert."

"But you don't mind if I meet him, I mean, casually? I'm sure we could never really be friends, but . . . "

Wolf's shoulders sank.

"Oh God," he said, "What is coming?"

"Well, he did say he'd take me to a night-club this evening . . . "

"You wouldn't understand a word."

"But apparently there's an English place, well, English-speaking . . . "

"Ah ja. More than one. Some tourists, some American correspondents, some crooks and some prostitutes."

"Oh Wolf! I wouldn't, I mean I would never . . . "

"All right, Herbert, I believe you. Stay sober and hold on to your money. But I hope you would not take Sophie to such a place?"

"Gosh, no. I hadn't even thought . . . "

"So what does that tell you?" Without waiting for an answer, Wolf turned again to his paper, the subject now closed. Mariangela raised her glass for the ritual pre-dinner toast—*Mahlzeit!*—, leaned towards Herbert, and pressed the hot, female weight of her hand onto his arm.

"Eat, Herbert," she said. "I have never been to a night-club. It must be so much fun."

The remark was an encouragement, not a complaint. He shifted around in his chair, and prodded his food. Did Wolf expect him to reject every new experience? Ignorance had brought him nothing but confusion and misery. How could he grow if he was not allowed to learn? But Sophie . . .

"Anyway, I'm glad you like Sophie," said Wolf. "A good girl, intelligent and charming. Do you agree?"

"Of course, Wolf. I've had more fun walking the streets with her than, than I can remember."

"Good. Why don't you call on her one afternoon?"

"But I'm seeing her every morning."

"Quite so. A nice surprise. Then ask her father if you can take her somewhere. Perhaps the cinema. She tells me she enjoys the Marx Brothers."

Herbert froze, and now Mariangela nodded urgently at him with her mouth full. Had she never seen the Marx Brothers either?

"Wolf! I couldn't possibly! I mean, I hardly know her, and . . . "

"And? You will go drinking with thieves and murderers, but in a cinema your courage fails you? We should have had these Marx Brothers in the War. See Tommy run!"

"Wolf! Please!" The old man leaned back and laughed now, a gentle, good-humoured laugh, while Herbert squirmed, breathing hard, angry at the vicious jibe and hating the truth of it. Then he said;

"Would she come?"

"Of course she would, you young fool. And don't you want her to? I'm not asking you to marry the girl. She likes you. Don't be ill-mannered, Herbert. Play your part, or she'll think there's something wrong with her. Or you."

"But what about Joachim? I'm sure he doesn't approve of me."

"Then you must earn his respect by behaving like a gentleman. Anyway, it's the father who decides. Joachim will do as he's told."

This seemed unlikely. On his visits to the Voglergasse in recent days, Sophie's brother had barely spoken to Herbert, only looked down at him with braggartly contempt. It was hard to imagine him taking orders from anyone, even Wolf. Still, Herbert said;

"Very well. If you're sure it would be appropriate."

"And as for the night-club, permit me to assist you. You should go, and observe. You cannot love virtue unless you have seen vice. The one is meaningless without the other. So go and look, experience the dirty underside of this paradise you love so much. Find out what ugliness looks like. At worst, find out how much of a fool you really are. Oh, and I hope you enjoy yourself."

At last he dropped the paper on the floor and bent, with the concentration of old men, over his plate. But Mariangela leaned back for a moment with her hands in her lap, smiling the gentle smile of love at his wispy head, and, turning to share it with Herbert, winked.

Half an hour later Herbert let himself out of his uncle's apartment house, and hoisted his coat collar as close to the brim of his hat as it would go. Already the ground was frozen knobbly hard, and the cold of the air was deadly. It was snowing again, and he could barely see the street ahead through the steam of his own mouth.

"*Herbert!*" Mariangela stood, hunched but still massive, in the doorway, beckoning him back.

"Mariangela! Is something wrong?"

She reached out and pressed something into his gloved hand as he approached, and whispered;

"Enjoy yourself at the night-club! Wolf won't know what time you come home. Don't worry!"

Herbert looked, and found that he was holding a banknote.

"Mariangela! No! Please! I have plenty of money . . ."

She flapped her hands to silence him, and shut the door.

Appalled, he set off down Voglergasse towards the Ring, already groping for the words with which to give her back the money without causing her pain. Then he stopped, a new thought dawning. So far he had spent his evenings at home. Now Mariangela wanted him to come back in the small hours, and Wolf told him he must take Sophie to the pictures. They wanted to be alone. But here he stuck. He could imagine an embrace, but Wolf, and Mariangela, unbuttoned, flesh on secret flesh . . .

Soon he found again without difficulty that special one of Vienna's thousand coffee-houses where the man who called himself Felix Dangerfield smoked and eaves-dropped through his afternoons. There were no Nazis this time, and no murderous Jews, only a sprinkling of idle Viennese and the Englishman, in a cleaner suit than before.

"Ah, young Christie. Well met. So, you managed to get the old mountain-top sage off your back for the evening."

"Felix, please don't talk about my uncle like that."

"No offence, old boy. I'm sure he says far worse about me, eh? Have a drink?"

"Not for the moment, thank you. Felix, this place we're going to . . ."

"What about it?"

"Well . . . What sort of people go there?"

"Oh, press boys, F.O. types, the odd lonely Yank trying to pick up a decent tart. Oh, I see. Never play poker, young Herbert. You've got a face like a music-hall billboard. So Uncle Wolf tried to warn you off, did he? Yes, there are some low-life types about, to be sure, but they're no bother to the likes of you and me. And you know why not? Because they need us more than we need them, that's why. And anyway, you're different. Nobody's got a thing on you. You're safe as houses. Parsifal the pure, the holy fool, that's you. No offence. By the way, have you got any English money?"

"No, I changed it all. Why?"

"Oh, no matter. I could have got you a better deal this evening, that's all."

A waiter arrived with a cup of coffee, a glass of water, and a measure of pale spirit for Herbert. He did not protest. Instead he said;

"Felix, what did you do in the War?"

"Got shot at, like everyone else. Played cards a lot." He paused. "Oh, all right, I'll tell you the story. While I was in France I saw just about every device for killing men ever invented, and all of them pointed straight at me. They all missed, except one. Know what that was?"

"No?"

"Bow and arrow."

"Oh, Felix . . ."

"No. Promise. Sure as I'm sitting here. I was just wandering up to this farmhouse in search of a billet, and this wretched French kid, about twelve years old, let fly at me with a home-made bow. Thought I was coming in to rape his sister, which I wasn't, as it happened. Anyway, the thing hit me in the stiff upper lip at about half a mile an hour, but it still left a scar. That's when I grew the moustache. Satisfied?"

Herbert smiled. "It's not really what I meant," he said.

Felix leaned back, drained his glass, and lit a cigarette.

"Oh, I see," he said. "You want to know how I kept my reason through the hell of war, and all that. Well, I told you. I played poker."

"Poker? How did that help?"

"It did and it didn't. But I played, every chance I got, every spare moment. And when I won, I thought: well, that's all right, my luck's in, I'm not getting blown up today. Then I'd think: but hang on a minute, maybe soldiering's like love with cards, maybe you're lucky in one and not the other. So when I lost, I thought: fine, I've got all my luck saved up for the push. But then I'd start wondering whether losing to a flush in spades was just a bad omen, and I'd be done for anyway. So it drove me mad in a way, but it passed the time, and it stopped me thinking properly, which was what I needed. Chaps who really did stop and think went right off their heads, for good. *Herr Ober! Noch an Schnapps bitte! Nein! Zwei Schnapps!*"

"Did you pray?" said Herbert.

"Pray? Oh, we all did that, all the time, if you can call it praying. Sheer bloody rubber-spined begging would be nearer the mark. No, it was superstition that got me through, not religion. Until the end, that is."

He stopped, and sipped his drink, and stared into his glass. Herbert drank too, barely noticing the raw fire in his throat. The man certainly knew how to tell a story. At last Herbert said;

"And what happened at the end?"

Felix sighed.

"The thing you've got to remember, young Herbert, is that poker isn't just about luck. There's an element of science to it. Look. You've got a pack of cards, all right? You pick a card, you shuffle the pack, and deal ten off the top. Your card's not there. So you put them back, shuffle, deal ten off the top, shuffle, deal ten off the top, and so on. Sooner or later, your card's going to be in the top ten, yes?"

"Of course."

"All right then. I started totting up the casualties in my lot, how many chaps had come in and copped it, how long they lasted and what hit them, and all that. Wasn't easy, either. I did my best, but I couldn't keep up, and I wasn't sure I knew the whole of it anyway. But the point was I knew that if I stayed where I was long enough, sooner or later my card would come up. And then I started worrying about it all the time, knowing I was overdue for a pine box, or at least a leg off, or something. Finally I convinced myself that I'd been too lucky for too long, and my last night on earth had actually arrived. And then the very next day it was all over. Just like once in London, when the club got raided while I was well ahead, and I didn't have the chance to lose it again. What do you think? The triumph of luck over the odds, or did God stop the War just to save my skin?"

Herbert had no answer to that question. "Felix, that's an amazing story," he said.

"But I'll tell you something else," said Felix, "and you can pass this on to that uncle of yours. It's not just whizz-bangs that follow the odds. I've been thinking about that ever since. No, it's everything, your whole bloody life. If you lived forever you could pick and choose a bit to start with, and have your run of luck. But the odds would get you in the end. You know they say that if you stand on Westminster Bridge for long enough, you'll see everybody in the world? It's like that. Live forever, and absolutely everything that could possibly happen to a man would happen to you, and on every spot of soil on earth, over and over again. But if you pop off after your three score years and ten, you've beaten the system. See? In the War they used to say that death makes us all the same, but that's rot. It's death that keeps us different. So stuff what you can into your own little time, and try and make sure it's fun. You especially."

"Why me?"

"Because it's going to happen again, isn't it? Everybody knows that. I don't want to be a wet blanket, old boy, but if I was your age I wouldn't be taking my three score and ten for granted."

"I hadn't thought about it."

"Oh, well don't then. Christ, I've had enough of this. You know how to get a chap going, Christie, you really do. Let's go and have some fun, put you ahead of the game. Nobody took me to a night-club when I was nineteen, I can promise you that."

Herbert got up, folded his scarf across his chest, and buttoned his overcoat. Then it happened; a brutal twist of the light, a change of pressure, caught in a moment with a Christmas cracker snap in the air. Now the voices all around were loud and thick, and pale Felix murmured "Steady on, old boy. Nothing much," from far away. Herbert leaned on the table and lowered his head, and felt a hard grip on his shoulder.

"All right. It's all right, Herbert. There was nobody sitting at that end, the window's gone, that's all. Nobody hurt. Come on, let's go. *Let's go!*"

Herbert obediently tottered into the street, but faltered, retching, and fell almost on purpose to his knees on the cobbled ice.

"For heavens' sake, man," said Felix, "What's the matter with you? And what would that nice little girl of yours say if she could see you now?"

Sophie. Herbert's hands were sticking to the street, and the nausea bloated his face and filled his eyes with tears. But Sophie, and Wolf—no, this wasn't good enough. He stood up, leaning on Felix, and his head cleared.

"I'm sorry," he said. "Oh, I left my gloves in there."

"Forget it. If we run into the *Polizei* we'll be here all night. And you need a proper drink. Come on, quick march. It's not far."

"What happened?" said Herbert. Felix shrugged as he walked.

"Home-made bomb. Not much more than a jumping jack, but it knocked the stuffing out of you, all right, didn't it?"

"I've never seen anything like that before."

"Yes, well . . . That's what it's like here at the moment," said Felix. Presently he turned and led the way through an entrance decorated with flickering neon, and Herbert found himself descending into a fetid well of noise and colour, thick with cigarette smoke and the sickly fug of the crowd. A waiter spun him out of his coat and hat, and a negro sitting at a piano gave him an easy smile and wink as he sang. Automatically he smiled back, but then his view was obscured by a rush of eager, jostling men, a couple of them in evening dress, all shouting in English;

"Dangerfield—he might know."

"He won't know."

"Ask him. He's a lucky devil at times."

"He'll make it up."

"How do you know? Get him a drink."

"Look, I've got to file in half an hour, is there anything in this or not?"

"Felix! Felix, old man. What about this bomb? Got anything?"

"Chap just ran in and said there was a bomb at Reiner's. Three dead."

"I heard five, all Nazis. What about it, Dangerfield? Got anything?"

"I was there," said Felix.

"What?"

"Told you he'd make it up."

"Oh rot, we can check it in the morning."

"So what's the story? How many dead? Who did it?"

"No casualties," said Felix, and there was a general groan. "No Nazis on the premises, tiny bomb. They did it themselves, to blame on the Reds."

"You're sure?"

"Is that horse's mouth, or are you making it up, as usual?"

"Shut up, man. Ignore him, Felix, they've just cut his retainer. What about it?" Felix slowly lit a cigarette, and nodded the last reporter into the corner, behind Herbert.

"Stable cat," he said. "Sources close to Starhemberg. They're losing their grip, and it's going to get worse. And that's gospel. Ten quid."

"I can give you Austrian. . ."

"Oh no you don't," said Felix. "Ten quid. And a couple of chairs near the stage wouldn't come amiss."

"A fiver, and you can have my table. There's a bottle of bubbly on its way."

"Done."

"And I want all the chapter and verse first thing. I'm not forking out a fiver for an educated guess."

"Done, I said."

There was applause now, as the pianist rose from his seat and bowed, and a small jazz band started to play in his stead. On the stage four girls danced in tiny satin dresses, each of a different shocking colour, bending and twirling and kicking high. Felix took his chair and leaned forward as the bottle popped, eyes flicking from one girl to the next—blonde in blue, chestnut in red, jet-black in yellow, red-head in green—and grimaced around his cigarette.

"Damn it," he said, "I don't think I can stretch to caviare."

Herbert watched the stage, only feet away, and realised that he was staring through flapping skirts at naked womanhood, times four. He gulped down the Champagne and clamped his lips tight on the taste, lest his jaw drop and dribble it. Secret pictures dusty-dry in a tuck-box had not prepared him for such an unsurprising thing, so casually worn.

"Enjoying yourself?" said Felix. Tongue-tied, Herbert nodded, and felt a headache stirring in his brow. "Which one's your favourite? I'll introduce you."

"Felix, please don't make fun of me."

"Sincere offer, old boy. They're not all tarts, you know."

"I'm sorry."

Deliberately he looked away from the stage. Behind them the crowd drank and chatted and watched, old men with young women, old women with young men, nervous touts moving urgently from table to table, waved away like flies or entertained for as long as it took to strike a deal. At the back of the room the English and American journalists queued for the telephones busy with pad and pencil, while through it all the team of blank-faced waiters kept up their seamless routine, trays glinting through the smoke as they spiralled down and up and down again. Herbert caught the eye of a heavy man in a dinner jacket, who at once made his way across the floor, and stood over their table, blocking the view.

"Herr Dangerfield."

"What is it, Franz?" said Felix, "Telephone?"

"Herr Dangerfield, you know that we prefer our honoured patrons sitting at the front of the house to be correctly dressed."

"Ah," said Felix, "Well my friend here is the son of an English duke, and he mislaid his bags in transit." A pause. "No glad-rags, you see. Naturally I didn't want to embarrass him by dressing up myself."

"Herr Dangerfield, I am not happy . . . "

"Oh, it'll do, Franz. It's a good enough story. Just bugger off, for Christ's sake."

"Herr Dangerfield . . . "

On impulse, Herbert pulled Mariangela's banknote from his pocket, and put it down on the table. Without changing his expression, Franz picked it up, and slowly bowed.

"Welcome to our establishment, your Lordship. I hope you have a most pleasant evening. Please ask for me if I can be of any service." He bowed again, and left.

"Are you mad?" said Felix. "You could have got in a magnum with that."

"It doesn't matter," said Herbert, "I've got plenty of money."

"No such thing, old boy. No such thing as enough, let alone plenty."

"Why did you have to lie?" said Herbert.

"What? So bribery's all right, but a little white lie's going to bring the roof down? Come off it. Anyway, I wasn't lying, I was just trying to let him off the hook. Franz knows the score."

"Obviously I don't."

"Well how could you? No reflection on you. Rather the contrary, I suppose."

"In what way?"

"I mean if your face doesn't fit in a place like this, then you're probably closer to Heaven than a chap like me. And that's all you care about, isn't it? That and your nice little girl . . . what's her name?"

"Sophie. But she's not . . . my little girl."

"No? Well she's pretty sweet on you, that's for sure."

"Do you really think so?"

"Plain as the nose on your face. And you've got it pretty bad, as well, haven't you? Anyone can see that."

Herbert thought about it quickly, as the girls arched their backs and shook their breasts in front of him, and his mind seemed to clear all at once. Then he said;

"Felix, I believe you're right. I believe I do love her, truly. I hadn't thought about it until now. Gosh."

"Well that's dandy. So you'd better get your skates on. You won't be here forever, you know."

"You mean . . . ?"

"I mean here, in Vienna. But what I said earlier goes as well. *Carpe diem*, old boy. Speaking of which." The band had stopped playing, and without warning the blonde in blue stepped lightly off the stage, and sat down in Herbert's lap, with her arm resting around his neck. "Looks like your mind's been made up for you. Lord Herbert Christie, allow me to present Fräulein Jenny Somethingorother, one of my closest friends."

Herbert gripped the back of his chair, and strained his neck to look up at the girl, too high, and much too close. She was still breathing hard from the show, and the perspiration shone all over her skin and trapped the satin where it touched. Knowing he could no longer reach it, she picked up his glass with her left hand, and raised it to him with a smile.

"Champagne?" she said.

"I believe 'plenty of money' was the phrase I heard," said Felix. "Herr Ober!"

Herbert felt stifled under the girl. He turned to Felix to mumble a plea for help, for release, but his voice was lost in a drum-roll followed by lengthy applause and cheering. Then Felix was laughing. On the stage a comedian was telling stories, in English, about the Chancellor who, it seemed, was unusually short. When he had a problem, he paced up and down under his desk. At the Hotel Sacher the other day, a woman with a small child had asked for a high chair, and been told No; Herr Dollfuss had a reservation. Herbert was not amused by the jokes, and couldn't see the stage anyway. But Jenny had heard it all before, and drained a full glass with the careless grace of a labourer sinking beer. Then she smiled at him again.

"Champagne?"

"You're wasting your time, sweetie," said Felix. "His Lordship is in love."

Jenny threw a *moue* of contempt at Felix, then fixed Herbert with an old-fashioned look.

"Champagne?"

He was lost. The girl's weight had numbed his legs, he was drunk and in shock, and now his head hurt, worse by the minute, a steel helmet-rim hot above the eyes. But there was no way out.

"For heavens' sake, Christie, you're not even holding the girl. Be a gent, can't you? She'll fall off."

He held her, clasping his hands on her hip. So close . . . In this place, with these people, what did it matter? He would be free of them, and clean again, soon enough. Easily he moved his hands, one after the other, under the high hem of her dress, and joined them again where they had been, on the angle of her waist, but a world away, on the flesh itself. Her right hand tensed, and awkwardly stroked his chin.

"And remember, ladies and gentlemen, the next time you're feeding the sparrows in the Ballhausplatz, watch out for the one with the moustache!"

The lights dimmed. Adjusting his hold, Jenny deftly high-kicked over his head and down again, and faced him, braced and balanced astride his leg. She began to rock, up and forward, down and back. His head filled with the smell of her, the sweat and powder and wine, and now a hot, cat-food stench, as well, cut through the sweetness, as she loosed his fly-buttons and groped inside, triggering mechanical desire. He felt her through the rough cloth on his leg, hot, then sticky, and suddenly a rush of liquid brimmed under his tongue, and he gasped for air.

She jumped aside at once—she knew the signs—and he ran from a crouching start to the door, up two, three steps at once, and cried out at the slap of the leaden cold on his face as he reached the street. He fell forward in the snow and heaved, but nothing came, only a long moan at the pain, and the unfairness of it. He got up, shaking and weak in the knees, and started to walk away from the club. Left and right and left again was Reiner's coffee-house, closed for business but brightly lit, with its shattered window already boarded up. From there the route was easy. Herbert stumbled and ran, north to the Burgtheater on the Ring, then across, and up the long dark slope towards Voglergasse. Footpads and prostitutes backed into their doorways as he passed, a fugitive madman, a wild white-faced stranger pounding random through the crunching slush without a coat. Then he remembered to do up his trousers.

In love—Herbert Christie in love. Was it true? He was afraid to believe it, afraid of the relief and the gratitude he longed to feel. But the passion was there, all right. He wanted to run to her now, to make any promise and mean it, and settle safe in her innocence forever more. Closer to Heaven . . . Yes, thank God, it was true.

He had to use both hands to get his key in the lock, and he nearly fainted from the warmth even of Wolf's chilly apartments. He leaned against the wall with his eyes closed while his breathing slowed, and prayed for the strength to get him up the stairs. Then he started, calm and alert all at once in the stillness. Someone was crying.

Ahead of him there was a tall strip of feeble light where a door stood ajar, and he moved silently across the few feet of boards and gently pushed, not knowing what he might see. On the wall a heavy wooden crucifix cast a flaring shadow from the candle at its side, and on the floor beneath it Mariangela knelt, hunched huge in her dressing-gown and rocking, forward and back, as she sighed and whimpered. Then she sensed his presence behind her and stiffened, and wiped her face with her hands, and her hands on the rug as she pulled herself upright.

"Mariangela . . . Is it. . . Is it Wolf?"

"Wolf is asleep, Herbert. Deep asleep."

"But is he all right?"

She laughed, though her mouth was still drawn in sadness, and hugged him hard.

"He's fine, Herbert. He is old, that's all. Just old. Poor boy, you are cold and soaking wet. What happened to your coat? You must have a hot bath before you sleep."

"What, now?"

"Do you want to catch pneumonia? Let me look after you, Herbert. I can't sleep now. And Wolf will not wake. Nothing will wake him. Go to your room. I'll call you when it's ready."

She released him, and sniffed, and patted her hair, dragging herself back into the habit of good humour that sustained her through the day. He saw her glance rest on the bottle by the bed, and turned quickly to save her feelings. But instead of the sound of glass on wood he was expecting, he heard only a gasp and another sniff as she blew out the candle.

22

THERE WERE ONLY ABOUT A DOZEN OF THEM AT FIRST, A MIXTURE OF unemployed men, hang-dog and stocky, with only anger to warm their bones; and students, taller, fresh-faced and fidgety with excitement, the affected workers' clothes hanging loose on their gangling frames. Together they marched south along the outer pavement of the Ring, and, finding themselves in front of the University, stopped raggedly, uncertain of where, precisely, they should make their stand. Then one of the students scraped a space in the snow with his boot, deposited there an empty packing case, mounted it and began to speak. At first his companions nodded impatiently, stamping around and flapping their arms against the cold. Then, by twos and threes, people of all sorts stopped to listen. Some hugged one another in fear, some wept, and ran back the way they had come. Others stood and stayed, insatiable even for the repetition of the awful news they were hearing.

The demonstrators started to feel important, and fell into ranks behind the speaker, cheering and nodding knowingly at the crowd, while kicking out at the stray dogs that danced, from a sense of the excitement only, about their feet. They were not an impressive group by revolutionary standards, but there was an air of moment to their gathering for all that. For in the early morning the word had spread from house to house; the police had attacked the Schutzbund at Linz, and it was time for Socialism to take up arms against the state. It was time for the shooting to begin.

Herbert had not seen Sophie for two whole days. His night out with Felix had left him chilled and feverish, the hot bath had come too late, and he had spent the weekend in bed, bloated and sweating from Mariangela's garlic soup. Now, on this freezing Monday morning, Sophie's father had confined her to the safety of home, and Wolf had taken Herbert to a coffee-house tucked away across the square from the Chancellery, where the best political intelligence was to be had. There they learned that the Vienna Schutzbund had indeed called its members to arms, though opinion was divided on what was the signal for insurrection to begin; either the arrest of the mayor, which was held to be imminent, or the general strike that would quickly follow in any case. Wolf finished his coffee with unusual haste, and led the way round the side of the building and up a steep, winding path to the summit of a thinly wooded slope overlooking the Ring. Here they stood and watched as the demonstration formed and swelled, marshalling revolution, boldly conjuring the demon of war.

But Herbert stood straight and breathed deeply with contentment. Though he had longed to explain his feelings to Sophie, and share the confidence of the new order he had found in their lives, he was happy to see rising all around him a drama to match his mood. Anyway, there was no hurry; love was eternal, and love was his purpose now, from which nothing could deflect him. He even felt a pleasant thrill of anticipation, awed by the imminence of great events tumbling rapid, hour by hour, across his view. Felix was right. Soon the peoples of Europe would be marching in their millions again, in all their splendour, and he, a young maverick Englishman, had found love a thousand miles from home, right in the foreign heart of all the action. He pictured Sophie and himself parting bravely and then reuniting amid the same weeping crowds. He did not fear for their survival. Love divinely given would sustain them, and draw them back together across the chaos. He shivered hard, and thanked God for the sheer grandeur of it all. Then Wolf said;

"You had better leave at once, Herbert. If the trains are difficult, go to your embassy. They will have to evacuate British subjects from Austria if this thing really happens."

"Wolf, I can't leave now!"

"Oh? And why might that be?"

"You might need me, you and Mariangela, if things get rough. I'm young and fit. And being a British subject could be an advantage. And I know how to shoot, from the Officer Training Corps at school. I can be useful here."

"Shoot? Who are you going to shoot? You don't know one side from the other. You can't help here, you stupid boy. And anyway, you only want to stay because you think you're in love with Sophie, God help her. You might well blush. Dangerfield told me when he brought your coat and hat. What do you think you are doing, Herbert? Can't you see it's impossible?"

"No. No, I can't see. You told me love is the greatest gift of God, the one thing we can truly know. And you were right, Wolf. I've found it and I believe it. I believe. It can't be impossible, don't you see? I can make it possible, I can make it true, because I believe!"

"Be quiet, Herbert."

"But Wolf!"

"Be quiet, I said. Look."

Directly opposite them, on the far side of the Ring, a tram had glided to a halt a hundred yards from its next stop. One by one, the passengers stepped down into the snow, and shuffled around, looking angry and foolish. Some stubbornly staid put, in the warm. Then the driver got out and walked, then ran, towards the demonstration, and the crowd there turned and cheered.

"The lights have gone out," said Wolf. "Look, in the buildings. The workers have turned off the power. This is it, Herbert. You must go."

"But I can't go home yet, Wolf. I love her."

Wolf hissed out a sigh through clenched teeth, and stamped his feet, more from irritation than cold.

"Have you told her?" he said.

"I haven't had the chance."

"You could try telephoning her now, if the lines are still working."

"Oh Wolf I can't say what I want to over the phone. I've got to see her face, and hold her hand . . . "

"Spare me, I beg you! Herbert I swear I liked you better when you were lost and miserable. This romantic nonsense . . . "

"It isn't nonsense, Wolf. It's the only sense there is. And I owe it to you. I'm grateful."

Herbert's voice cracked on the last word, and he coughed clumsily into his hand. This was upsetting. He knew he loved Wolf, too—for it was all the same, as the old man had said—and he wanted to share the joy of it with him, bonded and resolute through whatever lay before them. But Wolf stood stooped and weary, his mouth set, and stared bleakly at the mob spilling over the pavement opposite as though they were already just so many frozen dead.

"Ah well," he said at last, "Then I will tell you. Sophie will not be at home for very long. Her father and her brother are both with the Schutzbund. Today she is going to stay with her friend Eva and her father. And we will go there too, this evening, so you can make your declaration then.

For he tells me that his birthday dinner will not be cancelled for some petty riots."

"Wolf! That's the spirit!" said Herbert.

"Ha. Your bloody British spirit. How very top hole. But we shall see. You may yet be forced to love your girl from your home in England. Write to her and keep faith. You can do that, you know, if you're serious. Faith and patience are also part of love, and there is a heroism in these as well. Look away from these madmen, look behind you. We are standing outside a house of Ludwig van Beethoven . . . "

"I know, Wolf. It's where he wrote Fidelio. Sophie told me the day we met. I'll never forget that." Surprised, Wolf stared at him for a moment, then forced a smile.

Now a new sound rose from the crowd, an ugly whistling and jeering shot through with screamed abuse. A lorry laden with armed police was advancing at a stately pace towards them from the north, led by a whitewashed armoured car which slowly mounted the pavement, forcing the people to fall back and make room. The lorry stopped at the kerb, its passengers still but watchful. Then one officer stood precariously on the car's turret and started to declaim from a paper in his hand, while another patrolled around the vehicle, prodding people back with the barrel of his gun. Whatever the message was, it was not being well received. The yelling intensified, and a big young man climbed onto the car and abruptly pulled the messenger down into the street. The latter drew his pistol, and the two of them squared up, shouting, while the men in the lorry stirred, alert for the order to intervene. Herbert gasped, and grabbed Wolf by the arm.

"Wolf! That's Joachim! Down there in the street, with that policeman—that's Sophie's brother! We must do something!"

"Do? Do what? Stay where you are, Herbert. For the love of God, stay . . . !"

But Herbert was gone, running down the path and doubling back onto the Ring, heart pounding. Through stalled trams and idling traffic he ran, glancing now at Joachim and the policeman circling in the road, and the nervous men still waiting in the lorry behind them, now at the armoured car with its machine gun sweeping its aim across the crowd. From ankle-deep slush he lumbered, flailing, onto the pavement, and slid running along its edge.

"Joachim! Hi! You there! *Polizei!* Hey, you with the gun!"

He was getting close, now, elbowing past the stragglers at the edge of the crowd, aware that he was starting to attract some attention of his own. His anger was a curiosity here, a different thing, an English thing, fair play outraged by brutal bullying, and driven by chivalrous love. He would put a stop to this, he would make the brutish feel the wrath of a devoted heart.

"Hey you! Stop at once! I'm a British subject! I demand—I want—" The officer saw him, turned and aimed. Herbert stopped dead, skidding in the snow, and grabbed at a lamp post for cover, crouching and out of breath. Still the pistol pointed at him, and he tried to think of what to do next. But all he could do was stare at the gun, and suddenly there were no thoughts or words or memories in his head, and no movement in his body even to breathe or blink.

Then the machine gun blasted into the sky, and there were people running past him. The demonstration was over. The crowd had dispersed, the pistols were holstered again, and Herbert, ignored, took a rasping breath and started to shake. He held on to the lamp post, knowing that he would collapse quivering into the snow if he relaxed, and beyond that nothing except that he was alive. In his mind there were cities and people and emotions, but the words for them had gone. Only his name sounded there in the silence, urgent and distorted, and then he saw her in front of him, and ripped his hands from the frozen iron, tearing the skin, to make his own voice work again.

"Sophie! What are you doing here? You're supposed to be at home!"

She reached up and clenched her arms round his neck, pulling him down.

"Thank you," she said.

"What? What for?"

"Herbert do you know what is happening? They say they will kill anyone who helps the Schutzbund. And you will go back to England and I will never see you again." She began to cry.

"Where's your brother?" said Herbert.

"He has gone to join his friends, to fight. He escaped from here because of you, because you are so brave. And now he will be killed, and my father, and you will go too . . . "

"No, Sophie, I'm not going. I'm staying here with you. But Sophie, I'm not brave. I thought I was, but I'm not. I'm shaking, Sophie."

"How can you stay, how can you do this, if you are not brave? You are brave, Herbert, you are a good man."

"I love you, Sophie. I can't leave. I love you . . . "

He began to sob audibly, and shouted the words over and over into her neck, like a lament. Then he pressed his eyes, shut tight and hot, into her skin, and rocked with her where they stood, the voice in his head screaming prayers to beat the silence back. *God make it true, let faith make it true.* If he could fill the emptiness with faith, he could seal the love of God forever, and not be afraid again. *God make it true . . .*

23

SHE WAS STILL LOOKING AT HIM, TENSE AND WIDE-EYED IN THE CANDLE-light, with fear and with the hope she had found in him. She had been holding his hand so still, so tight and for so long across the table that he no longer felt her grip, just as anything he stared at for long enough, even her face, would eventually disappear. Beside him Wolf chattered idly, not really expecting their attention. But he listened anyway, to keep his senses alive.

"You know the curfew is for ten o'clock?" said Wolf. "But the coffee-houses can stay open until ten, as well. So we are supposed to sit and drink in the dark, out of harm's way, until ten, and then transport ourselves to our shuttered houses in an instant, like Indian fakirs. You see, not even Dollfuss can shut the coffee-houses. Ha! Only in Vienna . . ."

No, her face was different. If he held her gaze the eyes remained vivid, while the face around them swam and dissolved in a fluid ageing, fifty, seventy, ninety years old, until the eyes floated shining in a swirling dark. He could look away only to pick up his glass and drink, and at once look back to the young face fixed on his own; but if he moved his other hand she would think he wanted to pull away, so he let it sleep. They had all given up trying to eat, Herbert, Sophie, Wolf, Mariangela, Eva and her father, and the plates of cold meat, cheese and bread lay disarranged but scarcely diminished among them. There were empty bottles, though, the light native wine gulped nervously in desperate toasts. But it seemed that only Wolf still had the heart for conversation.

"Oh, I should have remembered," he said, "We must drink to young love."

"Wolf, I hardly think . . ." said Herbert, but it was too late. Another bottle of wine was gone, with a miserable murmur of assent to a Viennese article of faith. Now their host, a fat and crumpled widower in his seventies, began to speak to his daughter, quietly, with many wistful glances at the darkened ceiling—clearly a reminiscence, and clearly one she had heard before. Eva smiled softly, and looked at Sophie, weary and close to tears, on her right. Wolf leaned towards Herbert and said;

"Do you know what they did, these bold revolutionaries? They were supposed to print thousands of leaflets, calling the people to arms. So what is the first thing they do? They turn off the power! No printing presses! Genius! Only in Vienna . . ."

Sophie gasped, and began to tremble.

"I'm not laughing at them," said Wolf. "Sophie, your father and your brother are brave men. If I were not eighty-six years old I would be with them. But you mustn't worry. It might still come to nothing."

Herbert wondered. Would Wolf be standing, now, with the workers in the Karl-Marx-Hof? Would a man who still walked, in his mind, along the Franzenring really fight for revolution? Nobody knew. He peered at the face of his wristwatch, partly obscured by Sophie's hand. It was barely eight o'clock. They might be sitting here for another hour at least, even all night until the curfew lifted. Silently he longed for something, anything to happen, to break the tension. And then something did.

Echoing through the high narrow street below came the sound of marching, louder, closer by degrees, a column keeping dogged step, boots ringing on frozen stones. Then the distinctive beat of a taxi's engine slowed from the other direction, and stopped, idling, outside. The column halted, and two men began to shout while the engine ran.

Eva fidgeted for a moment, then leapt from the table and opened the shutters. Briefly she turned and spoke irritably to her father—she could see nothing. Then she leaned and cupped her hands around her face against the window pane. This was foolish. Herbert got up to pull her away, but before he could reach her the glass exploded all around him, and bullets whined and slammed into the plaster above his head. He thought his heart had burst as he spun round, crouching, with his hands up, he thought he would fall, and he fixed his eyes on Sophie and shouted her name with all his strength. But he didn't fall. Squatting and breathing hard, he saw Wolf stand ram-rod straight, the lines of his face wiped clean and flat with shock, then twist and fall on his back across the table and stay there, still and gaping.

Eva turned from the window, hunched and screaming silently, both hands holding her right cheek, the blood running down her arms. Herbert was bleeding too, from somewhere, but slowly he stood, and lowered his hands, and looked at Sophie. She was standing, calm and straight, and looking back at him from the other end of the table, waiting. There was a whole crowd shouting in the street now, but no more gunfire. Eva heaved and wept in her father's arms. At last Mariangela moved; not to wail and throw herself across her lover's body, or fall to her knees and berate a merciless God, but gently to close Wolf's eyes and mouth, and kiss his forehead once. Then she looked up at Herbert, and sadly smiled. *Nothing will wake him . . .*

He stood and stared at Wolf, at the blood-red wine spattered on his chest, and thought *This is death, this is death . . .* but it wouldn't register. And Sophie was tugging at his rigid arm and calling him, *Herbert! Herbert!* while the sound and light faded from his head, and his eyes began to stiffen in their roots.

"Herbert!"

Startled, he turned and looked down at her. She was breathing fast, and still trembling, but determined too.

"Herbert, I must go. Do you love me, Herbert? I must go to my father and my brother. North, to Heiligenstadt, the Karl-Marx-Hof . . . Do you love me, Herbert?"

He tried to hold her, but she stiffened against his touch. Then it dawned; she wanted him to go with her, to find Joachim, to where the fighting was.

"But, Sophie . . . " He glanced back at the body on the table. He felt he should stay with Wolf, but no one could stay with Wolf, not now. "But, Sophie," he said, "We could be killed!" *With Wolf.*

"And why do you want to live?"

That wasn't what she meant, but the constructions were beyond her: Why live, only to be with the dead? Why live, except to fight, and love the living? Still torn, he looked once more to Mariangela, now dabbing Eva's face with the handkerchief from Wolf's top pocket.

"Go, Herbert," was all she said.

So in a moment Sophie was pulling him by the hand into the cold of the street, and then he was standing alone, shivering by the taxi, while she cornered and harangued the driver. The marching column had been only half a dozen men, now dispersed and demoralised, each of them surrounded by angry householders abusing them in the headlights' glare. Herbert saw the cabbie duck around Sophie, and then run into the shadows, hunched, with his arms up, as though this little girl might attack him. She screamed something after him, then turned away.

"He is a coward!" Again Herbert felt that grip on his arm.

"What happened?" he said.

"He was driving home when he saw the soldiers. He was afraid, because he is a communist. They thought he would drive at them, and they shot in the air to frighten him. I asked him to drive for us, but he is afraid. Coward!"

Herbert looked past her at the soldiers, hemmed in now, and losing heart. They had killed an old man and mutilated a girl, and they would never even know. They had fired at nothing, and missed.

"Herbert, can you drive?"

"You mean . . .? Well, I think so, I mean I know how, yes, but . . ."

"Now. Drive."

He knew he shouldn't be doing this, as he climbed into the driving seat and fumbled for the pedals and gears, trying to relate his memory of the family Austin to this rattling cage of a thing. He knew he should be taking charge, dragging Sophie back to safety and keeping her there, hugging and calming her and waiting for news, fighting down her hysteria with manly common sense. But Sophie was not hysterical; she was sitting behind him on the edge of the seat, barking orders like a sergeant major. And as the taxi jerked and jerked forward, nudging a path through bleached and furious faces, he felt ever more strongly that he was going the wrong way. Soon there was nothing in front of him, no people, no solid objects to guide him, just the two beams bouncing up and down on the shapeless white. He steered between the pavements by instinct, speeding in awkward jumps, then braking when his nerve failed, and biting his lip to control the shaking and the flashing memories of life only minutes gone. His eyes filled with tears. Still he drove on, until a fleeting shape across the lights made him jump in his seat, and a sickening jolt to the car yanked the wheel out of his grip. Panicking, he grabbed it back and pressed down hard on the accelerator, and again they surged forward.

"Herbert! What was that?"

"I don't know . . . I think I hit the kerb. Maybe a dog. But I can't see, Sophie! Maybe we'd better stop, go back and look."

"No! We're nearly there. It must have been a dog, Herbert. It was a dog. Go on!"

He obeyed, but with a new and growing fear of what he might have done, and of what else might happen in this terrible night. He began to form a prayer for forgiveness—but forgiveness of what? He could never know, and the thought of it chilled him inside. He stopped shivering, and felt his face relax. If he was damned out of eternity there was nothing left to fear.

One by one, huge snowflakes began to settle on the windscreen. But Herbert peered and blinked, and realised that there was light in the sky ahead, flickering long like summer lightning. Then there was shape to the light as well, a pale hard bulk clearly defined, then vanishing.

"This is it," said Sophie. "We're almost there, Herbert. Go on."

There were other, nearer shapes appearing in front of them now, hard and black against the milky form in the distance, and soon the lights of the taxi brushed in the detail of lorries and tenders, and the awnings of a railway yard. And behind the fleeting silhouettes of the sheds beyond, the lines of the Karl-Marx-Hof became intermittently distinct, caught in the beams of searchlights flaring and fading at the generators' whim. Herbert looked back to the way ahead, and braked hard, stalling the engine.

Just thirty yards away, by a pile of sandbags on the edge of the track, four soldiers stood and gaped into the taxi's headlamps. Then, gingerly at first, they picked up their rifles and began to edge forward. Herbert leaned on the driver's door and dived onto the ground, then reached up to open the back and pulled Sophie after him. Together they crouched and ran into the blackness, tumbling painfully down onto the railway track, then across and up onto the opposite platform, where Sophie fell, sobbing and out of breath. The fire of machine-guns sounded clearly from beyond the low buildings ahead of them. Then Herbert heard the spasm of an engine starting, and looked back to see the taxi turning slowly away, with one of the soldiers standing on the running-board on the driver's side. But still it turned, crawling, and he realised the men were driving in a circle, using the headlamps to sweep the shadows for a target.

Again he grabbed Sophie's wrist and pulled her up, into a run for the cover of the railway huts, counting off the seconds before the lights would come round again and trap them. Nine, ten, eleven he counted, until their shadows streamed ahead of them in a sudden brightness, right into the shifting forms of another cluster of uniforms in their path. But now they were level with the huts, and stumbled hard round the first corner into shelter, blind again and startled by the noise of the gunfire channelled crisp and loud between the lines of wooden walls. Still they ran, but lumbering now, tired and losing heart, until they could see, on the open ground at the other end of the alley, field guns and idling men, and the great drums of the searchlights angled low at the long grey façade to their left. At the final corner they stopped, and held each other, crouching in the last few feet of the dark.

Herbert knew they were cornered. To advance or retreat again would mean capture, but if they stayed long, hidden in the shadow where they were, the cold would finish them. Already his limbs and back were numb, and every heaving breath hurt like a knife in the lungs. But Sophie was sobbing with distress as well, still anxious for her family, for the future, still with so much to fear. Her life couldn't end so soon, not like this, not here. He stood up, and began to walk. At once he felt the warmth of movement fighting back in his veins, and knew he must carry on. The voice of prayer was silent, but he trusted to the purpose that moved him forward, shielding, hiding her, towards the searchlights and the long-coated men and the guns. He squared his shoulders and stretched his legs to a march against the stiffness, and realised he hadn't said goodbye, or kissed her. But now he was in the open, with the light on his face, walking faster, getting warmer with every step. It would, it must be right. He could hear their voices now, between the bursts of fire, but they still hadn't noticed him. He made straight for a group of three who stood back from the guns, conferring and pointing with a map held between them, two officers and a civilian in a slouch hat and a coat shorter than the rest, who turned and looked, at last, with amazement into the gloom and the swirling snow. It was Felix.

"Herbert? Herbert! Christ, man, what the hell—?"

Then the firing started up again, but from a new direction, drowning Herbert's voice as he yelled for joy. Felix and the soldiers ducked and scrambled for cover, and Herbert turned to see scores of men running in waves from the Karl-Marx-Hof to take the station's open ground.

"Herbert! For God's sake man, get back! Get back!"

But from the shadows to his left, Sophie rose and darted across the ends of the railway huts towards the wide road and the archway on the other side, and Herbert followed, thinking only that he must catch her before she disappeared again.

"Herbert!"

Felix was chasing after him, he had a friend now, and he laughed as he dodged through the ragged lines of the counter-attack, running with a will, rewarded, forgiven, allowed to live again. Then the wind shot out of him as the blast caught him full in the back, he flew forward, limp and opened, and in the white flash of the instant saw his shadow hammered flat and huge across the wall of the Karl-Marx-Hof, and felt the hardness shatter the whole spread-eagled front of him. Then there was just the falling. Down, down. . . *with Wolf.*

24

IT WAS THE PAIN THAT SURFACED FIRST, A SCREAMING ANGRY THING alone in the dark. Then the faecal stench fed the pain and became part of it, a foul suffusing breath that was not air, sustaining an agony that lived instead of life. The pain rose and screamed in the void of the dark, then sank and lost its form again.

He was standing alone and in silence, in Wolf's study, peering into the deep dusk of the shuttered room. Then a panel cracked and opened, blinding him with a summer sunlight dazzle borne on stinking heat. He groped forward, fighting for breath, and forced the panel shut, but another one opened at his side, and another. Panicking, he lunged and thrashed at the walls to drive out the light, but the hot foul air sickened him and made his head swim, and he fell on his back, drugged and weeping as the glare overwhelmed him.

Now his head was full of the noise of people talking, and he was reeling drunk but sitting upright, and the glare was focused in the footlights of a stage. There were the girls again, in their gaudy slips, four of them, or was it five? He could see two pairs of girls distinctly, but when he counted from one end to the other there were five girls dancing there, and one of them had a different kind of face from the rest, younger and smaller and blank with fear. *Oh God, don't let it be Sophie, not here, not like this . . .* He looked away from her, and tried to fix on one of the others, but they were never still, and he couldn't keep up, always finding Sophie's face again. So he gave in and let himself miserably look at her, admit that she was here with him in this evil place, and immediately tensed with the fear that his eyes would be drawn down into the clipped and glistening angle of her kicking legs, and find it blind and sick like the others. He tried to look up above her, but his eyes pushed the whole stage swinging over his head, and when her skirt flew up there was nothing there anyway, just the washed out dirty whiteness of the snow at night.

So he listened for the sound of snowflakes on the window, but noticed the firmness of the surface under his back as he moved, and realised that he was stirring in and out of dream. But where was he? And were his eyes shut, or open in the dark, or blind? He fumbled for the comfortable texture of Wolf's blankets, and found only a thin greasy sheet that fought and squeaked against his grip. Then the pain caught up with him, and he choked and writhed back into the falling to escape from it again.

He knew it was a long time later when he half woke in the dim, musty room with Felix sitting by his feet, he could feel the weight of the hours piled up on him, squeezing out the strength. But he also knew that what he feebly saw was at least real at last, and it frightened him because his hold there was so weak, he was already fading back, maybe for good this time. Felix was slowly shuffling a pack of cards. He took the card off the top, and looked at it and frowned, and looked at Herbert, and put it back, over and over again. Herbert closed his eyes and felt the strength flow back a little, saved from the effort of seeing. He remembered Wolf's dying, and wondered if Felix were dead as well, caught with him in the killing, and waiting for him now. Did the dead feel pain, and think and puzzle so? He gave it up and slept, but when he woke again, felt his heart sink at the clear recognition of a consciousness still achingly, unhappily alive.

The room was strange to him, and he was alone, covered in coarse blankets on a daybed precariously narrow. It was a small and shabby place, chaotic in its clutter of open books, discarded clothes and dirty plates, with only lighter patches where pictures once had been to vary the sad floral pattern of the mildewed walls. This must be where Felix lived. He sat up painfully, groaning at the stiffness in his muscles, and swung his naked foot down onto a coffee-cup on the floor, noticing with distaste the moment it took to unstick from its saucer under his weight. Already trembling from the exertion, he made his way across the room to the door on the far side, and found it locked. To his right the pale light of winter day seeped through fastened shutters; but to his left was a door no taller than himself, with a latch and no keyhole. It opened easily, and he soon found and turned the light switch in the hanging filth of the wall inside.

Under the bare yellow bulb in the centre of this cupboard room stood a square table covered in green baize, and on it some hundreds of tiny model soldiers, perfectly ordered in the ranks of opposing armies. Napoleonic infantry, British hussars, standards and cannon stood in meticulous symmetry on the smooth and spotless cloth, the blue and gold and red of pinprick detail gleaming sharp in the dirty light. It was too much—he lacked the strength for the amazement demanded here. He turned off the light and shut the door, knees knocking, suddenly crying-tired again, and padded back, crouching, to the feral refuge of the blankets and the sleep.

Then the urgent smell of fresh coffee made him tense and gasp, and Felix said;

"Wake up old boy. Fever's gone. You ought to be ready for this." Herbert half sat up and sipped the coffee, too fearful to speak, wondering at the novelty of the taste and the presence of the living man beside him. "Before you ask," said Felix, "Sophie's all right. Got out with the rest of us, through the sewers. God, what a caper. That's where we had to take care of you, can you believe it? They had a bloody field hospital rigged up down there, in the middle of all the shit. Unbelievable." He shook his head, wide-eyed at the memory, and drew deeply on his cigarette. "Nothing much wrong with you, you'll be glad to hear. Just shock. A few nasty bruises. Hell of a night, though."

Herbert's head was throbbing from the coffee, and his whole body felt as if he hadn't used it for a month. Croaking and clearing his throat at first, he said;

"What happened, then?"

"Oh, it's all over," said Felix. "Order has been restored, as they say. The Schutzbund never stood a chance, though they made a pretty good fight of it here and there. Poor blighters. It was never worth it."

"Thank you for looking after me."

Felix shrugged and smiled, and looked at his feet. Then Herbert said;

"But what were you doing there, with the army?"

"Me? Just trying to do my job, from a safe distance, I thought. Then you turned up, and I found myself back in the trenches. Bloody Boy's Own Paper stuff, chasing after a girl with all that going on. You're lucky you didn't get us both killed . . ." His voice faltered on the last word, and he added; "Oh, sorry to hear about Wolf by the way. Rough on you. But he had a good innings, you know. Anyway. I'd better see about getting you some grub. Don't go away."

Herbert had no desire to go away. He lay back and stared at the plain yellowed ceiling, and listened first to Felix clumping down bare wooden steps, then to the passing of workaday traffic outside. Order had been restored. A good innings. A poor epitaph, that, for an Austrian, to be mourned in the private language of Englishmen, the grim flippancy of schoolboy cricketers at war, all padded up against the fear. Damned good knock, Wolf. Shame you were run out at the end. He imagined the old man in his two overcoats, stiffly mounting the steps of the pavilion to take his seat in the shadows of an English summer, and chuckled bitterly through the tears.

He was dozing lightly when Felix came back, and he sat up quickly and said;

"I need to see Sophie."

Felix paused lowering a tray with a stiff white napkin tented over it, then put it down on the seat of an armchair.

"Not such a good idea, old boy," he said.

"Why?"

"Look. " He tried, and failed, to flourish the rigid napkin. "Goulash. Good hearty peasant stew. Just what you need. Put some clothes on and sit properly, won't you?"

Herbert turned to the pile of clothes on the chair beside him, and added the trousers and socks to the shirt and underwear in which he had lain in the sweat of fever. It was an obvious distraction, a postponement, and he almost resisted it, but the smell of the goulash had started a savage hunger, eyes and mouth watering at once. He sat squarely on the daybed and bolted the food in silence, dribbling between mouthfuls.

"The thing is," said Felix, "you're none too popular with the little lady's folks just now. Joachim admits he owes you one for saving his skin at that barny in the street, but he's mad as hell about you dragging Sophie down to the Karl-Marx-Hof like that. If you wanted to play the hero you should have locked her up safe and sound before you left. You can see his point."

Herbert swallowed the last of the stew and said; "It wasn't like that."

"No? Well it doesn't matter, anyway. They weren't actually caught, but they've got to keep their heads down for a bit. Can't be seen consorting with dodgy foreigners. They've all gone off to the country somewhere. Sorry, old boy, but the sooner we can get you on a train to England, the better it'll be for all concerned."

"I don't want to go back," said Herbert. He looked down at his empty plate, and smeared the gravy away from the legend at its rim with his thumb; *Reiner.*

"No choice, I'm afraid. How was your goulash?"

Automatically Herbert said; "Very good, thank you. Did you go all the way to Reiner's to fetch it for me?"

"It's only downstairs," said Felix.

"You live above Reiner's?"

Felix laughed.

"No, not me. Not quite the thing. No, this is where Isaac lives, if you can call it living. He doesn't advertise the fact, but he owns the place, coffee-house, building and all." He looked about him with distaste, as though for the first time, at the dirty, meagre room. "You'd never think it, would you? Isaac's a queer fish all right. Just doesn't seem to care, somehow."

"Where is he now?"

"Out of town for a bit. Someone he has to avoid. It happens. Better not to ask."

"But don't you know?"

Felix frowned irritably.

"I don't need to know, damn it. I don't want to know. He's had a bit of bother somewhere, that's all, and he gave me his keys and said he'd be away for a while. Said I could put you up here while he was away, which was pretty decent of him, I thought. Isn't that enough?"

"But you said he worked for you."

"Well so he does, in a manner of speaking, from time to time. We help each other out. Anyway, what's it to you?"

Herbert leaned back again into the cushions and said;

"Oh nothing, I suppose. I should just be grateful and leave it at that, I know. It's just that you said . . . "

"Well never mind what I said, all right? That's your whole trouble, Christie, you always want to know, you've always got to find out. Asking me about God, me of all people."

"I'm sorry."

"Oh dash it!" Felix got up suddenly, and stood, swinging his shoulders in frustration. There was no room to pace; he kicked viciously at the chair legs, and sat down again. "Don't be sorry, don't be so wet, for Christ's sake. Just be grateful, like you said, be grateful you're alive, and let it go."

Herbert fell silent, puzzled, but angry too. There were a hundred questions to ask, and Felix, the spy, the informer, whatever he was, the man whose job was finding things out, was telling him not to be nosey, just like the rector at home. And soon he would be home again, quiet and powerless and letting it go, just letting things happen like before. Order would be restored, and the tangle of questions and memories and fears would be back where it belonged, deep in the dark inside, unvoiced and undisturbed. He knew he would have to go home, but it sickened him to know that he must slide so easily back into that bland and hopeless normality. He would be stronger now, he told himself; though he would have to go back for a while, he would escape again, he would be free . . .

"Herbert, you're shaking. Damn it, man, you're crying. Don't worry, it's just the shock. Get back under the blankets. Warmth, that's the thing for shock. Hot sweet tea, and lots of blankets. Best thing in the world."

Herbert tensed against the shivering, and allowed himself to be rearranged by Felix, prone and huddled on the daybed. He closed his eyes, and Felix said; "You'll be better tomorrow, believe me. I've seen it before, lots of times in the War, much worse than this. Just keep warm and rest, and you'll be home in a couple of days. Don't try to talk."

Herbert laughed at that, and realised that it must make him seem even more like all those poor, shell-shocked madmen, laughing and crying and quivering all at once with their eyes tight shut in forgotten hospital wards, and that made him laugh harder still. But he let the sleep come easily now, falling in with the retreat, knowing that he would soon be waking, in England, to a peace that was only life denied expression.

He thought of Wolf, clung hard to the image of the old man's face for company, and chased the echoes of his voice, and thought again, *I will be free.*

Then Felix was shaking his arm, and it was early morning, and the foul untidy room had opened its shutters, and lay balmed in the ordinariness of urban daylight. His suitcase had been retrieved and packed. They were leaving. Herbert rose and dressed without protest, sleepily taking in his last sight of the place where Felix had nursed him, and of the squalor of which he had been a part, the home of Isaac the Jew, the criminal, the man of property, the man who didn't seem to care.

"Is Isaac back?" he said.

"No," said Felix. "I'll thank him for you. Come on. You've got a train to catch."

As he followed Felix down the wooden stairs to the street, Herbert blearily thought that he would miss the place, and wondered at the idea, until the shock of the cold took away his breath, and he remembered to be anxious at the demands of the day, and the weeks ahead. But the taxi, and the grey ribboning of frozen streets, and the walk to the platform had drifted past before the truth fully dawned. He was taking his place in a railway compartment, facing west. He was leaving Vienna, and now the panic hit him.

"Felix, I don't want to go."

"Don't start that, old boy. You're still not well, you know." Again Felix was arranging blankets around him, treacherously calming and humouring him for a cruel departure. He fought against the tears.

"But how will I get in touch?"

"All in your coat pocket. Addresses, money, passport, it's all there. Trust old Felix. I've even wired your parents. Lucky that housekeeper found Wolf's address book. You'll be fine."

"But Felix!"

"Don't go on, Herbert. You're better off out of it."

Without another word, Felix left the compartment, and Herbert was still staring stupidly into the corridor when he tapped on the window from the platform outside, and pulled it down to lean on its rim.

"Write to me when you get back to Blighty, eh?"

"Of course. Thank you, Felix."

"Don't mention it. Quite an adventure you've had. Not sure you're built for this sort of thing, though. It hit you pretty hard. What are you going to do when you get back?"

"I don't know."

"Well, take my advice. Don't join the army. Whoops! There's the whistle. *Wiedersehen,* young Christie. Nice knowing you."

Herbert watched as Felix waved the train away, throwing his cigarette onto the track beneath it. Then the train quickly gathered speed, and he struggled to push the window up while the cold draught turned to a steel whip on the face. He was almost too weak, but he forced it shut at last, and fell back, gasping, onto the seat. It was then that he remembered Isaac's soldiers.

He was sure he hadn't dreamt it. The little room with its one dangling bulb was different from the snatches of delirium he recalled, it was firm and quiet and whole. In a dim corner of the slum Isaac had made for himself, he had also kept a pristine thing not even locked away, something to love, a paradox to relish. Felix was right. Isaac was a queer fish. But it did make a kind of sense that a man who lived with secrecy, and of a people without borders, should disregard domestic convention and yet keep private order in a cupboard, and treasure it in the obscurity of an inverted mind. Herbert could treasure the soldiers too, imagine them mutely peopling the emptiness he feared. He could count them forever, marking off the divisions of endless space, lending a still discipline to the madness of that minute infinity. Each one could be any one of them, each one was distinct, but also indistinguishable from the millions beyond. There was a glorious liberty in that . . . He would be free, and strong, and brave . . . He was sleeping again.

Part Two

September 1945

1

WALKER RECKONED HE MUST HAVE BEEN STILL IN BASIC TRAINING the first time he heard that 'Army Intelligence' was a contradiction in terms. He could no longer remember whether the joke had made him laugh that first time. He only knew that he had heard it, straight-faced, hundreds of times since then, had made a habit of repeating it to himself, bitterly, as part of his own routine. Tired jokes were as much a part of army life as orders and uniforms, companions as familiar as machine-oil and store-room dust, and the sticky film they made that clung to every soldier's skin. But in his current posting he had discovered a new truth in that hackneyed old line. It wasn't that the army lacked intelligence, but rather that an Intelligence officer was required to spend so much of his time dealing with stupidity.

Standing respectfully on the visitors' side of Walker's desk was a man called Sigmund Heuser, a middle-aged Viennese with a tubercular cough, like so many of them, who had dutifully informed on a neighbour suspected of a petty war crime. Now Heuser had returned, offering for sale the news that Adolf Hitler was alive and as well as any Austrian, and living in the Third District of Vienna, in the British zone, a stone's throw from Walker's office.

The coffee was ready. Walker tried to ignore the smell of it, wafting from the makeshift kitchen at his back, but the knowledge that it would soon be spoilt drove him mad, and made him want it all the more. He shuffled in his chair, and lit a cigarette, viciously shaking out the match.

"You're going to have to do better than that, Heuser," he said. "I've been through this a dozen times, Hitler selling pretzels in the Graben, Hitler hiding out in the butcher's back room . . . It's all nonsense."

"But I have seen him, Herr Major. In the apartment house near to mine. . ."

"No, no, *no!*" Walker sat back and looked up at the grey, starving supplicant on the other side of the desk, and shook his head. Poor sod. Heuser could smell the coffee too, and probably hadn't had any for weeks. To a Viennese that smell was torture. But Walker knew that if he cracked, and gave the man a cup, he'd never be rid of him, and soon there would be queues of slouching skeletons just like this one, all fighting to trade some cock-and-bull story for a taste from the NAAFI. Heuser's grimy fingers were clenching around his coat buttons, and his eyes were moistening, now, from the strain.

"You know me, Herr Major. I have helped you before."

"That you have, Heuser. That prison camp guard. You were paid."

"So you know I do not come to you unless I am sure."

"Or desperate."

A hint of burning had crept into the coffee smell. Walker snatched up a pen, and said;

"All right, all right. What's the address? I'll look into it, and let you know. They'll bloody well make you Emperor if you're right." A pause. "That's all."

"Herr Major, perhaps, in the meantime . . . ?"

"Absolutely not. Damn it, man, I'm not going to pay you for wasting my time. Now get out, or I'll . . . " What? Arrest him? Feed him army rations for ten days? That was hardly a threat, in the circumstances. "I'll never let you in here again. Go on, out."

Heuser hesitated, his mouth open for a final appeal, then bowed and turned, and closed the door quietly behind him. Walker dashed from his chair to the kitchen, and burnt his hand and swore grabbing the pan off the primus, where it bubbled with a liquid as thick as boiling mud. He was sweating, too, from anger as well as from the unseasonable warmth. The morning was already too hot, really, for the stuff to be enjoyable, and he knew it would be bitter and full of grit. But it would do, and at least he would have it all to himself. He sipped and grimaced at the taste, relishing the spite of a petty victory.

He loathed Vienna. Before Japan surrendered he had been able to tell himself that he was lucky to be here, well away from the fighting. But now, in the sallow heat of late September, the ubiquitous infection and decay of the city depressed him, and the lying, turn-coat Viennese made him sick with contempt. He had lived and served before, in Italy, among the tattered homes of the defeated, and had felt compassion, even a little shame. But

Vienna with her splendour, ever vainglorious, hammered by the bombs, inspired no more pity than an old tart caught without her make-up, or the sly and slovenly people who scavenged lazily through the tumbled stone.

It was nearly eleven. Any minute now, Sergeant Holmes would be back with the new bloke, Christie, some cloak-and-dagger specialist transferred from Berlin just to identify a suspect the Russians were keeping on their own turf. Bloody nuisance, but there it was. He went back to his desk to re-read the file, and whined aloud with anger as he spotted the words *Joe for King* scrawled in pencil on the edge of the blotter. Surely Holmes couldn't have done that? Voting Labour was one thing, but 'Uncle Joe' Stalin was a sight too popular among the men, and not just in Vienna. Sometimes it felt as if the whole army was turning Communist. But Uncle Joe's Intelligence officers had an annoying habit of picking up suspects by the lorry-load, anyone they could find with the right surname, and then holding the lot of them until Doomsday. Mostly it didn't matter much, not to Walker, anyway, but this one—he turned back to the file—this one was different.

John Green, aka Isaac Greenbaum, aka Grunbaum. Born in Whitechapel, 1902. Arrested for murder, 1916—*Dear God*—but released for lack of evidence. Active with fascist agitators in London until 1932/33, suspected of a series of back-street knifings, but vanished. Finally tracked down from captured Gestapo files, after a happy wartime career posing as a Jew and selling the genuine article in their dozens to the Germans. Nice little sideline in pimping to the officer class, mostly as cover. A regular charmer. Yes, the Comrades had caught a real prize this time, but they'd have to hand him over, because John Green was still a British subject, a murderous, treacherous, genuine piece of English filth. Walker was looking forward to interrogating him, always assuming they had the right man.

Fortunately, this Major Christie would know for sure, and the Austrians had supplied a friendly civilian, some ministry pen-pusher called Weiss, to conduct a preliminary interview and start the paper-work. The only drawback was that the whole thing could be wrapped up by close of play, after which Christie could be knocking around Vienna, getting under Walker's feet, for months before H.Q. got around to finding the blighter something else to do. Walker sighed uneasily. These fellows who'd spent their war in Special Ops could be pretty rum. Not quite right in the head, some of them. Not the sort to get chummy with, anyhow. Still, it was probably worth it, just to get Green away from the Russians. And maybe Christie would turn out to be keen on ping-pong. Ah, Army Intelligence.

2

THE PLANE WAS TOO SMALL, AND TOO HIGH ABOVE THE CITY TO BE identifiable from the streets. It was going nowhere, just circling and banking this way and that, skylarking in the blue, dancing like a kite tossed around in the wind. Herbert sat in the front of the jeep with his head tipped back, watching the plane, not really wondering why it was there or what it was doing, just glad to have something up above to watch. He knew what was passing on either side of him; damaged houses, whole terraces standing ruined or gouged brutally from the earth, and occasional fragile flights of decorative baroque still floating in the dust, miraculously intact.

He had seen it all before, and it no longer moved him. Only the fear that he might see something he recognised, whether damaged or not, gave him pause, and kept him craning his neck at the sky, while the sergeant drove and chattered at his side.

"The Frenchies are all right, sir," said Holmes, "and the Yanks, most of them. But these Russkies are a different kettle of fish. The men are fucking riff-raff. Fucking bastards they are, sir, pinch anything they will, as long as they're in the Russian zone. Find a granny pushing everything she's got in a pram, and pinch the fucking lot. You won't find any of our lads doing that, I can tell you, sir."

"I'm pleased to hear it," said Herbert.

"And the women, sir. Women officers, picking up men and forcing them to, you know, do it with them in doorways, at gunpoint. I'd rather get fucking shot. Fucking bastards, those Russians, if you ask me, sir." Herbert sighed, and said;

"Language, Sergeant."

"Sir?"

"Language."

"Russian, sir?"

"No, Sergeant, your language. Fucking this, fucking that . . . "

"Sorry sir. It's being with the men that does it, sir. Most of the officers, they don't seem to mind it, sir. Sorry sir."

"Oh, it's not important. It's not the profanity I mind, so much as the monotony, you know?"

Holmes said nothing, and Herbert realised that the meaning of that last sentence had been obscure to him. The rebuke had been mild, if unnecessary, not that it mattered. But it wouldn't do to alienate the backbone of the army by appearing unfriendly, much less intellectual. He forced himself to sit up, and knew at once that they were heading south along Wollzeile, towards the Third District, with the shell of St Stephen's Cathedral, still with its spire, to their right. Reiner's coffee house would be somewhere in the streets behind them, and Josefstadt, in the American zone, lay a quarter of a mile to the west. Herbert drew a breath, and rubbed the stiffness out of his neck.

"Still, I'm sure you're right," he said. "About the Russians, I mean. High Command have behaved pretty well here, I'm told, but the rest of them . . . It's the same in Germany. Have you dealt with their Intelligence units?"

"Not me, sir. But the Major does, all the time. Awkward, lying bastards he says, begging your pardon, sir."

"I'm sure. Well, I've come heavily armed." He reached into his bag for the half bottle of Teacher's, and hefted it like a stick-bomb. "This should do the trick. Cream, Highland, Teacher's. Allies, Soviet, for the buttering up of. They love this stuff, I can't imagine why. But you can't get a damn thing out of them without it."

Holmes laughed long and hard over the wheel.

"Oh, that's a good one, that, sir. 'Allies, Soviet, for the buttering up of.' I'll have to remember that one, sir."

Cordial relations had been restored. Herbert replaced the bottle, and settled comfortably again in his seat. Soon, this very day, perhaps, he would be using that bottle to establish the necessary rapport with his counterpart on the Russian side, just to secure an interview with a prisoner. He wished now that he had never listed his Viennese contacts from all those years ago, he should have known he'd be dragged back here somehow, forced brutally into the pain of remembering. Filing clerks could be extraordinarily diligent when they had some really obscure cross-referencing to do, and if it meant helping to get someone hanged, so much the better. But Isaac, if it was Isaac, would be hanged anyway by someone, here or in England. One traitor more or less—there was no point in this. But when Herbert asked them, perhaps because he asked them, to find Felix Dangerfield, they drew a blank. An American reporter had seen him, used him, last, just before war was declared; after that, nothing. He could be running a poker game in Soho now, he could be dead or living anywhere in this bombed wide open windy hell of a world. Good luck to him. He had never written, and Herbert had found no address for the man who had saved his life. He could have tried, through a London paper, to trace Felix, it would have been easy, and the right thing to do. But in the introverted depression of his return to England, such initiative had been beyond him, like Vienna and everything he had felt there, suddenly impossibly remote. His memories were dominated by vanity, naivety, cowardice and shame, and he knew he could only be strong by leaving them far behind, by turning his back on the guilt. He had become very good at that. And for eleven years he had not even voiced in his head the name of the mousey little girl who had come so close to bringing him to life, so close to getting him killed. If Isaac mentioned her, when and if they met again today, he might just shoot the bugger on the spot.

With familiar effort, he forced his mind back onto the job at hand, back into the uniform cast of soldiering, and concentrated on hating Isaac for the evil he had done, in detail, victim by victim, piece by piece of German gold. And in a moment he remembered vividly the little room above Reiner's where Felix had nursed him, and realised that this had also been the hiding place of trusting Viennese Jews, waiting vainly to be smuggled to freedom. Perhaps they, too, had peered into that cupboard room, had pondered the meaning of the gleaming purity hidden there, and wondered, too late, whether they were truly safe. Or maybe Isaac had put a lock on that door, maybe Herbert had been the first to use the room as a refuge, maybe that was how Isaac got the idea . . .

"This is it, sir," said Holmes. "Round the corner and . . . Oh, fuck me sideways!"

They had swung off the street into a small cobbled square, and stopped abruptly, almost ploughing into the backs of a dense and jostling crowd of people. The canopies of two army lorries could be seen beyond the shifting heads. Holmes stood up, and angrily punched at the horn.

"Oy, you lot! Get the fuck out of it! Some of us have got work to do! Out of the way, you dopey fuckers!"

It was no use. They abandoned the jeep, and elbowed their way a few doors along the pavement, where another officer stood without his hat, hands on hips, rigid with silent fury.

"Major Walker, sir!"

"Holmes! What the bloody hell's going on?"

"Major Christie, sir."

"Ah, Christie. Glad to meet you. I'm afraid I've got . . . Holmes, what is all this bollocks? What are those vehicles up to?"

"Don't know, sir. Just arrived, sir."

"Well it's a bloody liberty, whatever it is. Find out what they're doing, will you? And if there's anyone in charge below the rank of Field Marshall, you can tell him from me that he's an arse. Got that?"

"Sir."

The sergeant obediently plunged into the crowd, shouting more abuse as he went, and Walker turned again to Herbert.

"Bloody incredible," he said. "This office is supposed to have a low profile, can you believe it? And then this."

"Communications cock-up, I suppose," said Herbert. "From right hand to left."

"Quite so."

A shabby-looking man was pushing his way towards them, yelling at Walker and shaking his fist in the air. Then Walker said;

"Oh, God preserve us all! I thought I'd seen the last of him for today. Fellow called Heuser, informer, daft as a brush. Leave him to me."

"Murderers! Butchers!"

"Calm down, Heuser. What's the matter with you?"

"You British! You hang people in the street!"

"Don't talk rot."

"Hitler walks free in the parks, and you hang some poor man!"

"Don't be an idiot, Heuser. Damn you, we don't hang people in public, you know that."

"Murderers!"

"Now look here. . ."

Walker took a step towards Heuser, clearly about to lose a very short temper. Then two things happened. The plane Herbert had watched earlier roared into a low pass, no more than a hundred feet up, over the square, making everyone duck, then climbed unsteadily again into a ragged circle; and from near the lorries on the other side of the crowd came the crisp, joyful sound of a brass band playing *The British Grenadiers*. Walker relaxed, and laughed cruelly in Heuser's face.

"You see? Not such bad chaps after all, are we? Just a nice bit of oom-pah to boost your morale. I don't want to see you here again until you've got something useful to say, Heuser. Now fuck off."

The mood at the back of the crowd had changed radically, all the tension dispelled. Now people were chuckling with relief at the jolly music, and with amazement at the unexpected air display, grateful for something innocent to enjoy. Herbert was looking up again, amazed himself at the apparition of a different memory, from a different country not so long ago. There was no mistaking the lozenge shape of the wings, the bulbous wheel fairings, the whole machine like some bloated moth, dizzily careering through the dying hours of an Indian summer.

"What's that flyer up to?" said Walker. "Is he one of ours?"

"Oh yes. Lysander Mark III. Special Duty Squadron."

"Bloody Brylcreem Boys. Hasn't he got anything better to do? And what the hell did he buzz this place for?"

Herbert kept his eyes on the plane.

"I had to fly one of those once," he said. "And bloody hard work it was."

"Oh . . .? Look, Christie, I was going to tell you just now . . Frightful balls-up. I've just had the Comrades on the blower. Apparently our suspect went and hanged himself this morning. Which means—Are you following me? Oh God, he's going to crash that thing if he's not careful—which means, of course, they bumped him off. Bastards. Most likely they'd got the wrong man, but they'd roughed him up so badly they had to finish the job. We'll never know for sure. I haven't got any further orders for you at present, I'm afraid."

Herbert held his breath, and felt his heart-beat pounding heavy in the pit of his throat, while the Lysander dwindled to a black twinkling in a deep indigo sky.

"Christie? Are you . . . quite all right?"

"Perfectly all right, thank you." He breathed again, and looked down at last at Walker, who stood aggressively as before, more suspicious than concerned, at his side. "I might as well go for a stroll, then. Stretch the legs."

"Absolutely. Get your bearings, eh? Got a map? We've got the Russian zone on either side of us, remember."

Herbert picked up his bag, and started to walk.

"I'll be fine," he said. "I shan't go very far."

"Oh, Christie—a word to the wise. Don't go shopping in the street. You can't smile at a woman without catching a dose of something in this place. I can find you something safe for later, if you like."

Over his shoulder, Herbert said;

"Not what I had in mind, thanks."

"Play ping-pong at all?"

He pretended not to hear, and headed slowly back towards the main street, deliberately ambling so as not to be absurdly in step with the band's rendition of *Colonel Bogey*. But soon the music faded behind him, and he turned, on impulse, into the deep cool shadows of a deserted alley. Here he sat down in the doorway of a boarded shop, ignoring the signs warning of its imminent collapse. Well, he thought, either it'll fall on my head or it won't. *Thy will be done.* God, to be hauled all the way back here, just for this . . . He reached again into the bag, and pulled the cap off the whisky bottle.

3

AN HOUR OR SO LATER, BEFORE HE PUSHED OPEN THE DOOR OF THE little church across the square from Walker's office, Herbert paused, arrested by the impulse to propriety, to drain the last of the whisky and place the bottle gently on the step, noticing for the first time as he did so the legend *Joe for NAAFI manager* pencilled thick across the label. Then, as he faltered, mock-stern and sweating from the midday sun, into the cool of the place, he wondered what was the correct form on entering a Catholic church. Did one bow, or genuflect, or what? There was a priest, tall and fair-haired and no older than himself, looking at him expectantly from behind the altar rail. He swept his hat under his arm, marched a few steps, wheeled, and sat down, too heavily, in the nearest pew.

Damn Isaac, he thought. Damn this John Green, who had denied the religion into which he was born to dissemble another, only to mock its martyrdom for evil's sake. Damn him for his callousness and his crimes, and for ducking out of the only resolution there might have been in one frayed and dangling life.

He looked about him at the gold leaf and the gaudy, pasty paint, and marvelled at the variety of taste that could exist among Christian folk. Maybe the congregation of this church believed that even such a thing as Isaac would ultimately come, through aeons of purgatory, to heavenly bliss. But no, Isaac was truly damned, must always have been, a negative man, a soul burned inside out, a life that spun everything it touched into spiralling havoc. Only such a man could hide and cherish inanimate symmetry within and feed on the chaos without, could pretend to be a Jew at such a time, in such a place, and thrive on the poison. Isaac had lived only as an agent of death, was immortal only in the ever-shifting troughs and ridges of evil in the world. Herbert shuddered at having been so close to a man like that, and yet barely glimpsed the depth of the darkness in him. And what little he had sensed he had cleverly ascribed to the twistings of a Levantine mind, like any Englishman happy to take the caricature off the shelf and comfortably fix its alien face to his rotten brother's own. That's what Isaac, John Green, had done as well, an Englishman for whom the war had been won as much as for any other. The taste of it sickened. And they weren't even sure that he was dead.

He tried to focus on the statue of crucifixion at the other end of the church, and thought, *Well, and what about the rest of us?* Himself, and Felix, and Wolf, and Mariangela, and . . . They were all anonymous now, mere numbers lost in the final tally of casualties and survivors, and none of them truly what they had seemed. But then they had always been lost in a way, each of them living alone as at the centre of some circular maze, unable to see past the nearest wall, the effects of thought and action hidden behind endless corners. *Forgive them, Father, they know not what they do.* Father . . . The very bonds inherent in human life frustrated any comfort they might have found in that metaphor. They knew not what they did, so they couldn't even be sorry, and could never run to reconciliation with the Father, like the blubbering little children they all once had been, and longed and feared to become once more.

Here it was again, the chilly calm at the bottom of despair, the desolate peace beyond the futile fight. Might as well go through with it, bring it all up into the light. He knew he had killed twenty-seven men, with gunfire, the knife, the wire, and his bare hands, and every one was a murder and a nightmare that would never fade. He could be sorry for that, not because he shouldn't have done it, but because it should not have been done, because every soldier marched and slept with the mark of Cain. But there were more, so many more, caught by a burst or grenade in the dark, so many he had ordered into death, so many lives of hatred yet to come, of orphans raised in grief and anger. There was no end to it, no way to see it all, no way to be sorry. And here before him, in this foreign place, was the only hope; Christ caught in tawdry, primitive realism, all stone-white flesh and scarlet blood, calling on the Father to forgive. God saw everything, knew every truth, but only God incarnate, bound and blinded in human life, could feel the sorrow and the shame. The hope lay only in the moment of this death, the split second when divinity unconfined was yet informed by a human heart. *Oh God, please make it true.*

The priest had moved, and was sitting at the end of the pew across the aisle, watching him. He realised he was fighting to stop the tears, the welling of drunken misery, and fixed his mind on the only prayer he still recalled, mouthing the words as they rose again from the depth of childhood memory.

Our Father, hero, counsellor, judge, for whose love we perform, whose anger we fear, *Who art in Heaven*, a fantasy of life beyond life, held by the desperate living, *Hallowed be thy name*, even by squaddies and RSMs and bitter officers, who daily debase it with a casual curse. *Thy kingdom come*, so that we can all finally give up trying, *Thy will be done*, instead of the squalid horrors of our own, *On earth as it is in Heaven. Give us this day our daily bread*, whether we're occupied, or rationed, or neutral, or collaborators on the run, *And forgive us our trespasses*, all, in the end, against you, whether in action or at home, *As we forgive those who trespass against us*-— ah, but if that's the test, then forgiveness must be a distant blessing. *And lead us not into temptation*— you've made a habit of that, will you go on until we get it right? *But deliver us from evil*, or at least from the corruption that blinds us to it. *For thine is the kingdom*, the pips on the shoulder, the Empire, *The power*, to bomb and invade, to liberate, to rebuild, *And the glory*, reputation and medals, the pride in our finest hour, *For ever and ever*—which makes all of these things meaningless. *Oh God, please let it be true.*

He caught himself sobbing aloud, and sat up straight, sniffing, to pull himself together, to restore the necessary dignity to the uniform of an occupying force. This wouldn't do. Bad form. But he knew he would not be able to leave without facing the priest, and his shoulders were shaking still, and the sweat tickled his back as it ran. He stood and squared with a deep breath, and only just kept his balance in a cramped left turn towards the aisle. The priest slowly stood to face him, and smiled, and said;

"Don't forget your hat."

Herbert wiped the tears and the sweat from his eyes, his arm automatically, comically, following the motion of salute—longest way up, shortest way down—and suddenly stiffened at the immediate shame of being caught out, drunk and weeping. He cleared his throat, and said;

"I'm sorry, Father."

The priest gave a little laugh, as though contrition were the last thing he expected; then put his hand on Herbert's arm to show kindness.

"Don't be concerned, Major," he said. "You are not the first or the last."

Herbert stood for a moment on the doorstep of the church, dazzled by the bright sunlight of the square, empty again now that the band had packed up. Then he marched awkwardly across the cobbles, and Walker, correctly dressed now, appeared from the shadows to meet him at the farther kerb.

"Ah, Christie. Saw you come out of the church. Been chatting with our local God-botherer, have you? Not Roman yourself, surely?" Again, suspicion.

"C of E," said Herbert. "Just about."

"Same here. Quite so. Well look, I hope you don't mind. I've volunteered you for a little job that's come up. Something to keep you busy, for today at least. I got on the phone to try and find out what that mad flyer was playing at, and it seems he's gone completely doolally and parked his plane in a field, up in the American zone, holding off the GIs with his revolver. Nobody told him the war's over, apparently. Our chaps were just about to despatch the heavy mob to bring him in, but I said you had special knowledge. That's right isn't it? What do you think? Feeling up to it?"

"Fit as a fiddle, Walker, thank you," said Herbert.

"Yes . . . Well, Holmes will drive you to the centre, and you'll pick up a Septic Captain, name of Brunel. He'll escort you from there. All you have to do is talk the bugger down out of his plane, and get him under arrest. Shouldn't be too hard, what? Name's Edgar—Flight Lieutenant Edgar."

"Absolute bloody piece of cake," said Herbert. "And you never know, he might even shoot me. Keep me busy for good." He laughed, too hard and a little too late, and, as the sergeant again swung his jeep round the corner to join them, Walker laughed too, though without conviction.Herbert climbed back into his seat beside Holmes, and merrily slapped the dashboard twice, signalling the off. Walker watched him, the smile quickly souring on his face.

"I say, Christie," he called, "You are absolutely sure you're . . . quite all right?"

The jeep reversed and checked, and rocked forward again, back into the street and away.

4

FLIGHT LIEUTENANT EDGAR HAD LANDED HIS MACHINE IN THE Nineteenth District, right at the north-western edge of the city, a few hundred yards from Russian-occupied Austria. It was a longish drive from the centre by Viennese standards, and further out than Herbert had been before, where suburban regularity gave way to the older patterns of village streets, winding into the vineyards and the fields and woods beyond. He turned to the young American officer who sat stiffly beside him in the back of the jeep, and said;

"Rather pretty up here, isn't it?"

"Yes, sir."

Herbert was sweating heavily, and knew he must stink of whisky in the heat, but Brunel, the Yank, the Septic Tank as they said in London, was his junior as well as his guide and host in the American zone, and made no comment.

"Make a right here, Sergeant," he said. "Couple of hundred yards, right around that farmhouse. Better go easy."

Holmes slowed down from the bullying, flat-out regulation speed at which he normally drove, and they came to rest a few yards short of a U.S. Army truck that stood blocking the way, with half a dozen soldiers crouching behind it. Further ahead, the Lysander was parked with its tail towards them, pointing north along the straight, dusty track between neglected vines. One of the men half rose from his cover, and trotted towards them, clumsily shouldering the rifle over his rounded back. He gave Brunel the American salute, somewhere between the naval form and a yokel tugging his forelock to the squire, and crouched again beside the jeep. Brunel acknowledged, and said;

"Situation, Foster?"

"Stand-off, sir. He won't budge, and we can't get a clear sight on him."

"How many rounds has he fired?"

"Seven, sir."

"Which means he must have reloaded. Damn it." He turned to look at Herbert, leaning back from the smell. He was managing to keep the contempt out of his face, but there was no hope or confidence in it, either. "I guess it's your call, Major," he said.

Herbert peered past the truck and through the struts of the high wing at the front of the plane. The sliding door on the port side was up, but the pilot was hidden by the fuel tank between the front and back seats, nearly fifteen feet off the ground.

"Righty-ho," he said, and clambered unsteadily over the back wheel of the jeep. Then he marched around the front of the truck, approaching the rudder of the plane from the starboard side, and halted at its edge, ready to duck behind it if the revolver appeared.

"Flight Lieutenant Edgar!"He waited, but there was no answer. He cleared his throat, and again called up at the open cockpit door. "Flight Lieutenant Edgar! Major Herbert Christie, B.T.A. Intelligence. War's over, Edgar. Time to go home. Come down, please."

A hand appeared on the sill of the cockpit door, and then a face, distorted and bleary with fatigue. He was a grim, big-eyed boy, held loose in the battle-dress of Airforce blue so dull in the brilliant sun. Then the other hand followed with the gun, just trailing it, a useless deformity at the end of the arm.

"What about those fellows?" said Edgar.

"They're our allies, Flight Lieutenant. Yanks. Come on. Jump to it."

Edgar nodded, and pulled himself from the cockpit, leaving his parachute behind in the pilot's seat, swung and fell and staggered to the ground, and walked, head bobbing, to the rear of the plane. Herbert held out his hand and took the revolver, and at once two soldiers rushed and grabbed the airman by the arms, and led him to the British jeep. Herbert stayed where he was.

"Major? Major Christie?"

"Just a minute, Brunel."

He had known he was going to do this from the start, from the moment Walker gave him the job, maybe even before that, when he first realised that it was a Lysander he had spotted gadding madly in the haze of the sky. All the way there he had been carefully recalling the take-off drill, crammed one desperate night in France, three years before, from a crippled pilot as he drifted back and forth between the morphine and the pain. Slowly he moved forward, around the tail and under the wing, and stopped to admire the three-bladed propeller and huge radial engine in the nose.

Again Brunel called to him from behind the truck;

"Major! This man's in your custody! We ought to be heading back."

"Hold your bloody horses, Brunel, and stop panicking. There's . . . There's something inside."He put his right foot into the notch near the base of the wheel-fairing, and swung his left onto the plate on top, grabbing the wing-strut above like a chimpanzee. Then he stuck his right foot into the angle where the strut joined the fuselage, his left into the foot-hold below the door, straddled and ducked and lunged, and he was in—painfully, awkwardly in, but safely inside the cockpit, sitting on the parachute with the spade-handled stick between his knees.

Now what? The first job was on his left; throttle knob open half an inch, mixture knob set to 'normal', then airscrew pitch, to the left of the stick, pulled out. Fuel cock on, gills fully open, the priming cock, to the right, set to 'prime carb'. Unscrew the priming pump and feel for the rush of pressure. Done. Turn the priming cock to 'prime engine', and turn the engine over with the electric starter.

The propeller turned. Now Brunel would really start panicking. So far, so good. Close the priming cock and screw down the priming pump. Switch on the main ignition switches and the starting magneto. Press the starter button, tiny and easy to miss, to the right of the stick. Turn off the starting magneto, sit back and let the engine run while it warms up.

He had forgotten about the noise, shockingly loud, all-consuming, thrilling. Brunel could be screaming at him from the ground, Brunel could be firing Howitzers all around him, and he wouldn't even know. Then he wondered what Brunel was really doing. If he knew nothing about aeroplanes, he would be expecting the thing to move at once, so he wouldn't risk climbing up to the cockpit; and as long as it didn't move, he wouldn't risk calling in to say there was another loony on the loose, for fear of making a fool of himself. He would just have to stand there staring like an idiot, until it was too late. Herbert tipped his head back and laughed, unable to hear himself, drinking in the joy of the noise and the smell, and the sheer insensible power of the engine ahead of him.

That was long enough. Time for the final drill; TMP, fuel and gills. T—set the tail actuating wheel to 'take-off'. M—mixture set normal. P—propellor pitch adjusted from coarse to fine. Fuel on, engine gills open.

Amen. He took the spade grip in his right hand, settled his feet into the straps on the rudder plates, and slowly adjusted the throttle control on his left. He was moving. He was going to need three hundred yards before he cleared fifty feet, and he was fairly sure he had it, though he couldn't see ahead. He pulled the stick back firmly, steadily, and the ground vibration abruptly ceased as the plane struggled into a steep climb. God, Brunel must be going crazy.

He would be on the carpet for this, of course, a big black mark on the record, maybe even a court martial. On the other hand, he had arguably acted with considerable bravery in disarming Edgar; maybe it would cancel out. And he could always say he had misunderstood his orders, and blame Walker for that, or say that he had acted on his own initiative, doubtful of American competence, to save the plane from looters. He could probably find his way to RAF Zeltweg, across the Russian zone to the south, if the fuel held out; if not, he would have to put down somewhere and claim temporary insanity, and get carted off to the bin along with Edgar, poor devil. Meanwhile, there was something he wanted to do.

He was still climbing, getting to five hundred feet, heading north. Carefully he pulled the stick to the right, banking east, but the controls were badly balanced, heavy on the wing, light on the rudder, and he slid sickeningly round and found himself diving sideways, the detail of the roofs below becoming alarmingly distinct. Gritting his teeth, he levelled out and climbed again, and gently turned a little, this way and that, to get the feel of it. Better.

More confident now, he climbed and banked east again, finding the smooth, wide curve he wanted. The landmarks of this city were so easy to spot, standing obvious in its tiny breadth; maybe that was why it looked so badly bombed. Out of the starboard window he could clearly see the Heiligenstadt Station, and the Karl-Marx-Hof. Gently downward a minute more, and the circle he described was intersecting with the Ring itself, and winding on to embrace St Stephen's Cathedral, smashed and open to the sky; then on again, the length of Kärntnerstrasse, to the Opera, a pile of burnt-out matches, utterly destroyed.

The sun was high to the south-west, and he forced the plane into a tighter circle, following the Ring from the Opera, north towards the University, straining to hold the angle and dangerously low; but at last he found the effect he wanted, saw the Lysander's shadow, rippling thick and black over the streets as he flew. Drunk and reckless and risking death, he would honour the dead with a gesture grander than the quiet ritual flickering of a hand across the breast. He would noisily mark the sign of the cross over this whole bloodied victim of a city, and make the people shudder with the roaring terror of it as he passed.

At the northern edge of the Ring he levelled out and climbed a little, then banked the other way, south, and swept his shadow, wider and lighter now, across the tight suburban blocks of Alsergrund and Josefstadt and Neubau, where Wolf had lived and died, and where, somewhere, he had held the gaze of a little girl dependent on his love, and thought his heart had burst, and shouted her name with all his strength.

CODA: April 1984

1

THE AUDIENCE WAS STARTING TO SETTLE DOWN, THE CHATTER BECOMING quieter, briefer, as everyone found their eyes drawn reverently to the stage and the gloomy set beyond the gauze curtain. A few stragglers still trickled in to take their seats in the stalls, some of the Austrian men in grey suits with green trim at the pocket-flaps and collar, others in evening dress, and the women, all of them, dressed gorgeously as for a ball. To the composer and many of his admirers, a performance of *Parsifal* might have been an act of religious observance, but to these people it was also a social event, a long haul, to be sure, but well worth it for the thrilling sense of occasion it inspired.

High above them, three English tourists, in the smartest clothes they had packed, shuffled nervously into their box and found their places in the second row.

"Oh, Dad, what have you let us in for?"

"It's Easter next week, Margaret. Parsifal in the State Opera House is a real treat. I was lucky to get tickets."

"But everyone's all dressed up."

"You don't look so bad, does she, Mother?"

"You look very nice, Margaret."

"I wish we were at the front. Do you think those people are going to come?"

"Hush, dear."

Mickey had been leaning on the edge of the box, staring absently into the stalls below. He turned to look at the new arrivals, the father in late middle age, excited, eager, his wife dowdy and quiescent, the daughter about twenty, sceptical and tarty in a fuchsia summer dress. He smiled weakly and said;

"These seats are free. You can move forward if you like."

"Are you sure?" said Margaret.

"Quite sure. I've got the tickets here."

The family rose and rearranged themselves, Margaret pushing past her mother to be sure of sitting next to Mickey. It was not especially flattering; she was travelling with her parents, and he was English and on his own, and had better seats. She wiggled in her tight dress into the space beside him, flapping waves of duty-free scent, and grinned into his face, too close.

"It's ever so nice of you. Are you sure it's all right?"

"Oh yes. My . . . My family's not coming," he said, and then added, needlessly, "My father died this morning."

Her face fell and her mouth opened, but before she could speak the house lights dimmed, covering her embarrassment, and his, in merciful darkness. And then the strings began their delicate opening task, setting a scene of spiritual distress in a dark antiquity, rising to the resignation of a whispered *Amen*. By the time the martial grandeur of the trumpets had rung through the air, and long before the entry of the first heroic voice, Mickey had stopped listening.

2

HE HAD BEEN DREAMING ONE OF THOSE DREAMS THAT ARE NOTHING more than the perfect recollection of an event in the past, of the bright day twenty-three years earlier when his parents had taken him for the first time to the Devon coast in high summer. He had built a sandcastle, clumsily but with immense satisfaction, then stood and breathed the ozone, and watched the sunlight sparkling in the foam. He took a few steps towards the sea as it roared and hissed, daring him to come closer. He looked back to his parents, then advanced a little more, then looked back again . . .

"Miles! Don't go too close, now. Be careful, Miles . . . " And then a shout.

And at once he was back in a grown man's body, sick from the dislocation, with his wife shaking his arm.

"Wake up, Mickey! Come on!"

"What? Is it time to go? The tickets . . . "

"Tickets? *The Magic Flute*? We went last night, dummy. Come on, honey, wake up. It's your mother."

That's not right, he thought, *it's not my mother, it's my father, I heard his voice. . .* But there was knocking and a moaning outside their door, and Elspeth got up to let his mother in. When he saw the two women embrace in their nightclothes, in the clean dawn light, he knew at once what had happened, and closed his eyes again, groggily yearning only to wake up in a different world. Then Elspeth shook him again, angrily, and he got up and hugged his mother, fully awake now, bitter and ashamed.

Elspeth called the porters' desk to fetch the ambulance, while he slumped miserably in the shower, fighting off the urge to drag up other happy days, and wallow in their loss. He tried to pin down the sound he had heard in his sleep, vainly chasing it around his head. His father never raised his voice, except sometimes to hail a London cab, and yet it had shot through the wall and into Mickey's dream, like an order barked under fire. Perhaps that was what it had been, just part of a different dream. But he felt he should know, that he did know and that the knowledge was special and belonged to him. He wasn't going to ask his mother.

But later in a grim bright morning of weary muddling through, of lists and family phone calls, of cab rides and form-filling on alien desks and murmured talk, he finally discovered what it was his father had shouted as he died.

"He must have been dreaming," said his mother, sitting with the fourth cup of coffee going cold in her lap. "I wasn't really asleep. I always wake up early, always have. And he sat up in bed and shouted 'Sophie!', really loudly, like that. That was all. I don't know anyone called Sophie, do you?"

"It was only a dream, Frances," said Elspeth, and took her hand for the hundredth time that day, but her face turned to Mickey with a look that said '*Your call.*'

Mickey stalled, and fixed his eyes on his mother. So he had been right, in a way, but should he tell her? He couldn't keep the secret forever, but when and how to begin?

Then the hotel manager arrived to offer his condolences, his sympathy, his services, whatever could be of use or comfort at such an unhappy time. He did it well, the charm and dignity of his manner so very Viennese, nodding and bowing to receive their thanks. At last he turned to go, and said;

"Oh, forgive me. Mr Christie, this letter arrived for your father this morning, delivered by hand. Shall I put it down here? So . . . Perhaps I could select for you a simple luncheon, and have it sent up . . . If there is anything else we can do we are all at your disposal . . . It has been an honour . . . "

Mickey picked up the letter and opened it at once. Inside were four tickets for *Parsifal* at the Staatsoper, with the elaborate compliments of Herr Weiss, who looked forward to entertaining them at a supper party after the performance. He read the note several times, groaning. He would have to write to the fat giant, thank him and explain, and do his best to match the overblown formality of style without mocking it. He would have to call Gruber, too, he realised, and the embassy, and Sophie. He wasn't good at this sort of thing. Well, at least he had something to do to get him through the afternoon.

But as he was dully making his third attempt to produce in English the verbal protocols that such a man as Weiss might expect in a letter, the telephone rang at his side. He picked it up, and hesitated. There was muffled noise at the other end, of glass and steel, of distant laughter and the clatter of plates.

"Hello? Who's there? This is Miles Christie. Who's that?"

"Oh hello! Mickey? It's Sophie . . . Sophie Miller?"

"Sophie?" The voice seemed slower, perhaps thicker, than he remenbered. But even as he noticed he caught the sound of his mother gasping, quickly glanced up at her face, and found it staring back at him, livid with the shock of betrayal, while Sophie prattled on down the line.

"Mickey, I'm at a place called the Bar Nimitz, it's in the centre, on the Ring, near my apartment, they look after me here. Mickey I really need to see your father, it's really nice here, can you come over with your father?"

"Sophie I can't talk now. I'm sorry, I'll explain later. I'll call you later, I promise. I'm sorry." He hung up before she could protest, and waited. Still, his mother stared. "I only met her yesterday," he said, "By chance, pure chance. She knew Dad when he was here in 1934. It was such a coincidence. Mother don't look at me like that."

She was breathing harder, and starting to shake, building up for a storm. Elspeth slowly rose from her chair, ready to hold her again.

"It's true, Frances," she said. "I couldn't believe it when Mickey told me. It's just the weirdest thing."

Frances stared at her son, horribly still. Then she said;

"And had he been seeing her all this time? Writing to her?"

"Mother, no! Christ, you mustn't think that. They didn't even meet again after the uprising, and then she went to live in the States. I know it's bizarre, but she didn't even know he was here. I was just sitting in this café, and there was this woman looking at me. She recognised the face, that's all. It was just a coincidence. Really. Mother?"

She was nodding as though she believed him, with her eyes on the floor, but there was no relief in her face, just a dangerous tremor in the downward set of the mouth. He saw her clench her fists at her sides and take a deep breath, and he braced himself as she raised her head to confront him again.

"Do you know what you did, you stupid boy? You told him about this woman, and it was such a shock after all this time . . . "

"No!"

"It killed him, damn you!"

"No! I didn't tell him. He didn't know."

"You must have told him. Don't lie to me."

"Mother, I'm telling you, he didn't know."

"Liar!"

"Mother . . . "

"Liar!" His temper snapped. He grabbed her by the shoulders and shook her brutally as she began to sob and howl.

"Are you telling me I killed my own father? I didn't tell him! Get it through your head, you stupid old bitch!"

She slapped him across the face, hard, and again, and again, until Elspeth pulled her away. He stood trembling, the tears in his eyes. Elspeth said;

"Take a walk, Mickey. You need to calm down, we all do. Take a walk. Get some air."

"I'll take a walk," he said. "One of us ought to turn up and thank Weiss in person. I'm going to the bloody opera. Don't wait up."

So he marched out of the room and out of the hotel with the tickets in his hand, heading for the Staatsoper on foot, blind to the sights around him. He could see nothing but his father's face over jugs of Viennese beer, or lying still in the morning on the hotel pillow, looking as if he had died in the night—because that was how he had always looked when he was asleep. The shock would hit him later, he knew, maybe weeks after the funeral, when some little thing would trigger the grief. Now there was only anger. Why? Why? He lost his way and doubled back, still almost an hour early to take his seat, grimacing with the painful tears of a thwarted child. He could hardly believe he had left his mother like that, it was wrong, it was all so wrong and unfair. The anger flared and hurt, time after time. Only fatigue with the cycle could ease the strain of it.

He found himself on the Ring again, and turned, his eye caught by a flash of sunlight on the big chrome door-handles of a bar to his right. Bar Nimitz; he knew he'd heard of it, but where, and why? It wasn't his kind of place, and he peered in to scoff at the décor before moving on. The doors and wall were all glass, and inside there was more chrome, picking out dark red skirting and leather seats against the plain white walls. Here there was none of the usual Viennese huddling of booths under grand chandeliers, no pretty gilt or plasterwork. It was, thought Mickey, more like one of those places that were always springing up in the West End—and at once it united all the warring strains inside him in the single desire to go home. But now the vanity of the idea hurt him even more. Home was gone, it was where his father lived, it was the place before Vienna, and there was no way of getting there now. Soon, London in May would have to do instead, but for now this place was all he had.

He went in and sat down near the middle of the line of stools, and winced at the sight of his own reflection in the tinted glass behind the bar. That face, that bloody, bloodied face, remembered from childhood, merged with older photographs that he had first seen as a child—that was the face he saluted grimly in the bathroom mirror every day, and carried with him now and for good, posed in the frame, immobile, dead. He sat and stared, and might have stayed there indefinitely if the barman had not slid across to block his view. Only this broke the spell, and he drew breath again.

"Mein Herr?"

"Gin and tonic, please, a large one. But I think I'll go and sit down, if that's all right."

"But of course, Mein Herr, please."

He started to slide from the stool, but stopped at the touch of a hand on his arm, and thought *Oh Christ, no, not now. Bar Nimitz, of course! Damn!*

"Mickey! You made it! Is your father here?"

Sitting down again and squeezing her hand, he said;

"Hello Sophie. No, he's . . . not here. Sophie, I have to tell you something. Would you like a drink?"

"I have my coffee, thank you."

"Shall we go and take a table?"

"No, no, I'm fine right here." He was about to insist, but she turned a little towards the bar, and went on; "Mickey, I want you to meet my friend Jurgen. He looks after me here. Jurgen, this is Mr Christie, the young gentleman I told you about? From England?"

"Ah ja? An honour, Mein Herr."

Jurgen looked at Mickey again, a look of surprise, his eyebrows raised as far as they would go, and bowed slightly from the waist, not presuming to offer his hand. What on earth had she told him?

"Mickey I'm really glad you're here. I must see your father. I have something to tell him, something important."

"Oh God, Sophie . . ."He hung his head, and caught the fresh citrus scent of the drink Jurgen had placed under his nose. He picked up the glass, then put it down, and reached for a cigarette. Jurgen lit it. Mickey looked up at the big barman, thanked him, and waited. He didn't move. Oh, what the hell. He was going to have to get used to this, anyway. "Sophie, I have to tell you. My father died this morning, in his sleep. That's why I couldn't talk earlier. I'm sorry."

She had been sitting straight on the stool, but now she sagged, suddenly a very small woman, not crying, but murmuring quietly as though in prayer. Then Jurgen offered her his arm across the bar, and she closed her eyes and gripped it hard.

"My deepest sympathy, Mein Herr."

"Thank you," said Mickey, and took a long gulp of gin. "Yes, thank you very much. It's quite a shock. He was only seventy, and perfectly fit. You never know, I suppose." He waited, but still the barman stood there, nodding slowly in agreement. "Jurgen . . . Sophie, what did you want to tell my father?"

She looked down, and shook her head.

"It doesn't matter now," she said.

Mickey paused. He had something to tell her, as well, but maybe not now, and maybe not ever. He would have to think about that. In the meantime Jurgen still stood, immovably on guard in front of her. No, definitely not now.

"Well," he said, "I have a lot of stuff I have to do. Maybe I'll come back. I'd like to come back. Goodbye, Sophie."

He had calmed down a little. As he stepped back into late afternoon sunshine that had lost its heat, and headed, a little more slowly, back towards the Opera House, he realised he had not even offered to pay for his drink. He didn't turn back.

3

IT WAS FITTING THAT HERBERT CHRISTIE SHOULD SLEEP THROUGH HIS last hours on earth in the ancient heart of a country he loved, even if the faded imperial splendor all around him was not his own. But now he had changed hotels, and lay in the cold sterile depths of a city morgue, as befit his new status as a man just passing through. Every Viennese hotel has its own unique character, but morgues are the same the world over, just doing their job, a chain of motels for the dead. Maybe Herbert was always destined to die away from home. He survived all the wars that made him famous, yet he was still killed in action in the end, the only casualty in a one man campaign against the forces of the past.

Elspeth looked up at her mother-in-law, still miserably asleep in the opposite chair, put down her pen and allowed herself a silent sigh. It had been a tough day for Frances, and for Mickey, too. As for herself, well, she would miss Herbert, yet for her the emptiness he left was not desolate. She noticed, as she had before among her own family, how death seemed to be attended by a blessed stillness, as though before the start of something, not after its end. She never wondered what that something was. She had always been too busy with the present sensations of life to give any thought to the nature of eternity. But as a child she had identified God with Santa Claus, and had, she realised, never quite stopped believing in either. Maybe Herbert wasn't really gone for good, maybe the secrets in his head were just waiting to be brought into the light again, like a bunch of old books in a safe. That was a neat idea. She picked up her pen again, and paused, wondering where to fit it in.

There was a scraping sound somewhere to her left, and Elspeth looked up and froze as a large man in a black leather jacket carefully let himself into the room, while another stood in the corridor with his back to the door. It was a moment before he noticed her, and he started as she yelled;

"Who the hell are you? Get out! Get out before I call the police!"

"This . . ." he said, the accent thick even in a single word, "This . . . is not necessary," and he muttered something to his companion outside, and shut the door.

Now Frances stirred in her chair, and said;

"Elspeth? What's going on? Who is this man?"

"Is the General here?"

"No," said Elspeth. "He's out with my husband. They'll be back any minute."

"I must take something," he said. "No, not money. Something from the General, an old paper, yes? Too big to carry in a coat. You have it, yes? Give it to me."

"Oh my God," said Frances, "The letter with the books. Herbert said it was important. We . . . We haven't got it. We put it back in the safe."

"You are lying, I think." He squared his shoulders, and took a step towards them, swinging his clenched fists at his sides. "Give it to me now. It is . . . a matter of national security, yes? Give it to me."

Frances stood up, ready to defy him; but Elspeth moved quickly to the table and picked up her shoulder-bag, and rifled through the sections with shaking hands.

"I have it," she said. "It's here, look. Take it and go."

"Oh, Elspeth, no, don't. . ."

"Take it!"

She pushed the old envelope at him at arm's length, and he took it from her, nodding slowly, arrogant in a bully's victory. Then he pulled out the sheets of yellowed paper, and slowly unfolded them.

"You'll never make it out of the hotel," said Elspeth, and thought *Jesus! Are you crazy? What if he has a gun?* Her heart jumped as he looked up at her again, and reached into his pocket, but then he moved to the open window, flipping a wind-proof lighter under the pages in his hand. Then they stood and watched as the pages of the letter melted into the dull liquid flame, and he crumbled the ashes onto the evening breeze.

"This is good," he said. "This is very good. No problem now."

He dusted his hands, backing to the door, then slid quickly into the corridor and prodded the guard in the back. Then they were gone.

"Oh, Elspeth! How could you? We could have put up a fight! Someone might have come . . ."

"Take it easy, Frances. It's OK. Take it easy."

Elspeth dropped her bag and took a look up and down the empty corridor. Then she shut the door, and clamped her trembling fingers around the phone, and waited for the desk to answer.

"Oh dear God," she said, "I hope I did the right thing!"

4

THE HOUSE LIGHTS CAME UP, AND MICKEY BLINKED, SURPRISED TO find himself drained and calm. Margaret and her parents had already bolted for the bar. Who could blame them? Mickey stayed where he was, idly glancing this way and that at all the red and gold, and the cleavages of women filing out of the stalls below. The bar held no appeal for him tonight. It wouldn't even help to get drunk, when all it would do was make him remember the last time . . . He would just sit and wait for the next act to begin.

"Mr Christie. Mr Christie?"

He recognised the voice, from its depth alone, and turned and stood reluctantly, not ready, yet, to do his duty for the evening. But there was Weiss, groomed and beaming, vast in his dinner jacket. Mickey smiled, and took the monstrous right hand of his host.

"Good evening, Herr Weiss. It was very kind of you . . . "

"Not at all, not at all. It is my pleasure. I'm only sorry we could not have had a box to ourselves, but sadly there was not enough time. I hope you are enjoying the performance? Your family, they have already gone to the bar, yes?"

"No. No, actually I'm here alone. I came to thank you . . . "

"Alone?" The giant's eyebrows rose, and he turned to indicate the three empty seats to Mickey's right. "But, surely, I saw . . . "

"Ah, no," said Mickey, "They're just three other people who were sitting behind me. I invited them to move forward. The thing is, Herr Weiss . . . " He paused. The sentence was becoming a cliché. "My father died this morning, very suddenly. My wife and mother are back at the hotel. I only came because, well, I don't really know why, actually. To thank you for your invitation, of course, and . . . "

Weiss's huge face had flopped in shock, the lips slowly parting.

"Mr Christie I'm extremely sorry. Please accept my . . . Forgive me, I must use the telephone. My sympathy . . . Excuse me . . . "

Mickey let him go. It was a relief to be rid of him, but he was surprised to see the man so agitated, so anxious, it seemed, to detach himself. Rudely he pushed his width past two other people who were trying to leave, at the back of the little aisle, but at the door to the box he stopped short, his way blocked by green uniforms, and an argument began. Mickey stood and watched. After a moment the group shuffled out of view, but Weiss could still be heard, protesting in the corridor outside. Then another man, only about Mickey's age and build, came into the box, and offered his hand with a gentle smile.

"Mickey Christie? Peter Thorne. We met yesterday morning. May I say how sorry I was to hear about your father."

"Oh . . . You're from the embassy, aren't you?"

"That's right."

"Yes, thank you. It was quite a shock. Look . . . What's going on, exactly? Has Weiss been arrested?"

Thorne nodded, and looked about him uncomfortably.

"There's been what you might call a bit of an incident," he said. "All turned out fine, though. Your wife and your mother are quite all right, and perfectly safe, so don't worry. But we've moved you out of your hotel, to a place we keep, a bit out of the centre. You'll be staying there until you fly home. It's very comfortable."

"But we've got train tickets . . . "

"No, you'll be flying. All arranged."

Mickey sat down again, turning his back on Thorne, who moved forward to lean on the rail at his side. Together they stared into the auditorium, until Mickey said;

"There was a man following me yesterday, and the day before."

"Yes," said Thorne, "That was part of it."

"But why? I don't understand."

"Long story. Look, do you particularly want to stay to the end? I've got a driver outside. I can explain on the way to the house."

He led the way out of the box and down to the street, through corridors and a foyer empty except for uniformed attendants bemused by the early departures. At the kerb of the broad pavement outside the Staatsoper a small car with CD plates stood waiting for them, its engine starting as they approached. They got into the back, and Thorne said;

"All set, Bob. Head for the hills." Mickey stared out of the window as they swung into the rush and sweep of the Ring and nudged into the traffic, wondering what he should ask first, what he could say at all without sounding stupid. Then, on a moment's impulse, he said;

"I had a row with my mother this afternoon."

"I know. She's a bit upset about that. I'm sure it'll be all right. Anyway, about this evening." Awkwardly he pulled a packet of British cigarettes out of his pocket and gave one to Mickey, then wound down the window at his side. "Weiss has been arrested for conspiring to commit a burglary, but there's more to it than that, of course. Broadly speaking, it's espionage. It'll all come out soon enough, but I must ask for your discretion for a while."

"Of course," said Mickey. "So what happened?"

"Well... The point of it, from your end, is the packet your father found yesterday, among those books of memoirs. Ancient history, of course, but one way and another it incriminates Weiss. It's the missing piece, the proof nobody could find. And when he falls, a lot of others go with him."

"The letter? But for heavens' sake, that was fifty years ago."

"Oh, I know. Weiss was a survivor, all right, ran his operation like a natural, right from the start. He was only twenty-two. Amazing. But look, you don't need to know the details. It's all over, that's the main thing."

"But are you talking about a . . . a spy ring? For all that time?"

Thorne smiled, then raised a forefinger to his lips in a pantomimic 'shush'.

"My father gave that envelope to my wife," said Mickey.

"That's right. Don't worry, she's in no danger now. We've got it. But she behaved magnificently this evening. Terrific presence of mind. You see, the point of those opera tickets was to get you out of the hotel for the evening, so that Weiss's boys could break in and recover that packet. Corny old trick. He must have panicked. But of course, when they turned up and found Elspeth and your mother sitting there they had to think on their feet, and just demand what they wanted, with menaces. They didn't get violent, though. That's when Elspeth came up trumps. Apparently she had another letter from Wolf Winkler, the one inviting your father to stay with him in February '34, and she dug it out and handed it over. The boys didn't want to hang about, so they just took a quick look at the date and the signature, and burnt the thing on the spot. As soon as they'd gone, Elspeth called the police, and the police called us, and here we are."

"That's unbelievable," said Mickey, and slowly shook his head. "To me, anyway."

"Not exactly all in a day's work for me, either," said Thorne.

"I didn't think this sort of thing happened any more."

"Oh, it does, from time to time. Always will, probably. Especially in a place like this. Vienna's always been a crossroads, you know, even before the Cold War."

"Yes, I can see that, but . . ." Mickey paused, groping for a way to express the point he was trying to make. It would sound naive, he knew, but so what? It didn't matter what he said, not now. "It's just not part of our world, somehow."

Thorne nodded, and threw his cigarette end out of the window.

"You work in the City," he said. "Venture capital, isn't it?"

"That's not what I meant," said Mickey. Try again. "I suppose what I'm driving at is that it was my father's world, all this cloak-and-dagger stuff, it's all stories and myths and history now. It's a different time."

"Or a different place. Same thing, in a way. 'Like stepping back in time', that's what it says in the holiday brochures. I've been here a year, and I know what they mean. Do you feel that?"

"That isn't what I meant, either. I thought it was over, that's all, for people of our generation. I thought we'd missed it. And of course," he added, "I did. I even missed it this evening."

"And now you're missing *Parsifal*," said Thorne. "Life's like that, Mickey, especially in my business. You're usually left with the feeling that the big stuff's been going on somewhere else, when you weren't looking. You never see the whole story. But Elspeth didn't miss anything this evening. She's the hero of the hour. And that book of hers is going to be dynamite."

"My father's life," said Mickey. "God, she'll end up knowing more about him than I do."

Thorne said nothing, and the idea hung in the air, like a threat. No, thought Mickey, suddenly angry again, no they can't do that. He wouldn't let Vienna and the Foreign Office, and the spies, and his own wife take his father away from him. Herbert Christie had died, and at once, perversely, his story had come to life again, no longer buried in the morbid reticence of an isolated soul. It was the birthright of his son, and with a thrill at the pride and the hope it carried, Mickey remembered that he still had Sophie's card. "Of course," he said, "I'll be working with her on that."

"Really?" said Thorne, "You collaborate, do you?"

"We never have before. This is different. We should make a good team."

"Well yes, I can see that. She's a super girl. I hope you don't mind my saying that?"

"My father's words exactly. No, not at all," said Mickey, and then added, for no reason he could think of, "I love her very much."

Thorne looked at him quickly, surprised, almost amused, but friendly too, then turned again to peer over the driver's back.

"Here we are," he said.

They pulled round into a gravel driveway, and stopped in front of a large white house with the usual Viennese decorative sills at every window. Mickey got out of the car and took a long, deep breath. They seemed to be quite high, on the edge of the city, and the spring air was turning cold, the light fading fast.

"Nice view, isn't it?" said Thorne. "You can see St Stephen's from here, look, over there."

Mickey nodded and leaned on the roof of the car, feeling the tiredness of a long day in his limbs. He looked at the house and thought of Elspeth, and of his mother, certainly calmer now, waiting to forgive and be sorry, to be reconciled and start again. Then he turned to Thorne and said;

"What's going to happen to Wolf's stuff?"

"Oh, that's your mother's property. We'll have to get someone to go through the memoirs, just in case there's anything. Shouldn't take long. Then we'll just stuff it all in the London bag. Simple. Are you ready to go in?"

"I think I'd like a moment alone, out here, first," said Mickey. "Is that OK?"

"Of course. Don't go into the garden, though, or you'll set the alarm off. Just ring the bell when you're ready. I'll tell the ladies you're here, shall I?"

Mickey smiled his thanks, and stood up straight and still against the car while Thorne went inside. For a moment he watched the lights go on at the front of the house, an invitation, a promise of warmth. Then he turned again to the view of the city below him, as it started to glitter against the falling dark, a million windows lighting at the beginning of new things.

The End

Printed in Great Britain
by Amazon